To d[...] [...] [...] [...]

past, present and future......

enjoy the adventure.

(G. W. JONES).

XII. 2010.

# THE CLAY PEOPLE

By

# G W Jones

Being the first book for the
young at heart, relating
the lives and times of
*Here* and *There*.

With illustrations by
Rosy Stott

φ

PHOSPHORUS BOOKS

Phosphorus Books
4 Lusty Gardens
Bruton
Somerset
BA10 0BR

www.phosphorusbooks.co.uk


ISBN 978-1908088-000

Published by Phosphorus Books  2010

# The Clay People

## G W Jones

Printed in Great Britain by the MPG Books Group, Bodmin and King's Lynn

To all my family; and to my friends;
and to those who made this book possible.
You know who you are …

Little children have known always
What Plotinus taught the wise,
That the world we see, we are:
Soul's country beyond time and place
Her bright self-image in a glass,
Tree, leaf and flower,
Sun, moon and farthest star.

*Kathleen Raine*

CAI

# Chapter One
# A Misty Morning

"What are we going to do today, Dad?" a bored Sebastian asked his tired-looking father.

But his war-torn father was not tired, he was being overwhelmed by a violent panic attack that was making his heart pound wildly, his mind terrified by fears and visions of death, and freezing his whole body in a kind of invisible terror that stopped him from speaking, or moving, as he tried desperately to silence the voice inside him that shouted he was about to die in front of his only son.

Looking out of the window Sebastian could see that it was still raining, but not as hard as it had been for most of that dull Sunday.

"Rain, every weekend, Seb," his father groaned, as he struggled to think clearly and sound normal, "but we could still go for a walk, and try a bit of archaeology in the field behind the Tor, if you want?"

Seb felt disappointed. For quite a while he had become more and more fed up with Glastonbury, the town, the Tor, the walks, and the peculiar folk that always seemed to be hanging around wherever he went. But he remembered the interesting rusty cogs and locks and other objects that they had found last time, while digging in the clay bank by Little River Pond, and thought that it would be better than staying at home watching television or playing music or his many computer games. His childhood interest in archaeology had been waning for some months now, but he decided to give it one last try, as he knew it would please his father very much.

Pushing back the stinging tears that were forming in his eyes, his father stood up slowly and said, "Come on, Seb, let's go while we still can."

Within minutes they had packed a rucksack, with a trowel, some plastic bags, a toothbrush, a magnifying glass, a knife, a fork, a cloth, some biscuits and bread, and a bottle of water – all the essentials for a proper dig, Seb thought.

After saying goodbye to his mother, who was baking some lovely-smelling cakes as she so often did, Seb and his quiet father tramped off into the wind-blown drizzle. They took their usual route over the Hump, down to and over Big-view Stile, past the Owl Tree, across Wilf's Field, through the Mud Crossing, finally coming to the Little River Pond, nestled beneath a pair of ancient ash trees in the corner of what Seb called the Massive Meadow.

As they got out the tools for the dig, and nibbled at the biscuits and bread, the drizzle became harder, and a dense heavy mist rolled around Glastonbury Tor and all the fields surrounding it. The air became cold, very cold.

Seb rammed the trowel down into the heavy wet clay and broke off a big lump, hoping to see some artefact or hidden object behind. Nothing. The mist developed into a thick dark fog, cutting them off from the nearby path and hedges and even from the little pond not twenty feet away. As he was about to slam the trowel once more into the clay he heard a noise, and stopped, and listened.

"Dad, what's that sound?" he asked. His father listened, but he could not hear anything except the gentle dripping of the wet breeze, and the odd birdsong somewhere in the grey-covered trees beyond.

Seb listened intently; it was a hum he could hear, or more than one hum – and it was a tune that was being hummed.

The damp, milky fog swirled all around him, and the beautiful humming seemed to revolve with the air itself, round and around, slowly then quickly, it was hypnotic, enchanting and in some way very familiar. The melody became so wonderful, with voices so clear and high and low in perfect harmony that tears came into Seb's eyes, and he felt like he was going to cry. He shook his head, and thought he could hear as if

2

from far off, his father calling to him, but he could not move or speak – he was bound within a spell of air, mist and song.

At first Seb was frightened because he could not move, and then he could not hear or see his father or anything else; but the beautiful humming calmed him. Within the drifting harmonic airs other sounds were passing through: voices speaking in a language he did not know, horses running and thundering hooves, animals calling, the beating of vast wings, the massive rustling of giant trees, roaring seas rolling upon unknown shores; and yet, within them all, he thought he could faintly hear the sound of his own name being called – as if he was being drawn towards somewhere else, and to a place that he could not see. But it was not his name that was being called; it was his self alone, like the deep callings of a loving mother to her dearest lost child: "*Seb*", it softly sighed.

All this happened in just a few seconds, then the wind departed, the mist cleared, and Seb stood there on the clay bank wide-eyed and speechless, full of fantastic confusions.

His exhausted father stared at him for some time, and then threw four or five large lumps of clay into a plastic bag, put his arm around him and said, "Come on, lad, let's go home."

He could see that his son was very disturbed, but he had not the slightest idea why.

☆　☆　☆

Over tea, his parents agreed that the strange mist and songs must have been some freak of the weather, and also that Seb was very tired, having stayed up extremely late the night before. But Seb was not so sure – in fact, not at all sure that these were the reasons for his experiences. He had heard what he had heard, and he had felt what he had felt, and of this he was totally sure.

After the tea things had been cleared away, Seb and his father sat at the kitchen table looking at the still falling rain. Seb put his hands into the bag of damp clay and began to feel it.

"Dad, is this real clay, or is it just some form of mud?" he asked.

"Very real," his father replied, "and there are so many things that you can make with it."

He knew that his father had been a potter many years ago, as he had been a number of other things as well; but he had never seen him make anything at home.

"Like what?" said Seb.

"What would you like to make?"

"Mmm, a pot maybe, or a bowl," Seb replied, hoping his father would join in and help him.

So with his father's help, he tried out the clay and made a couple of little bowls; but the clay dried quickly from the heat of their hands, and the bowls soon cracked and began to crumble.

"We need to make it thicker and quicker," his father said, "and then it will keep its form and shape."

At that moment, Seb's mother, Elaine, called out for assistance with a difficult light-bulb she was trying to change upstairs.

"Make what you want, Sebby," his father said enthusiastically. "That's the miracle of clay – just a lump of earth, but ready to be moulded into the stuff of your imagination."

Seb was left alone in the kitchen, his bag of clay staring at him from the newspaper it was on, his dog making little whuffling sounds as she dreamed, and the rain now pouring down hard.

He picked off a hand-sized lump and began to make a figure – just a simple person, with a round head, a plump body, two arms and two legs, with pinched hands and tiny pinched feet. Seb was pleased by what he saw, and smiled. The little figure stood steady on its damp feet, and already seemed to have a character of its own. He quickly worked on another one – a friend for his first clay person, made from the ground in Massive Meadow.

When the second figure was finished, he stood them together on the kitchen table, sat back in his chair, and looked at them both carefully. Never before had he dug up clay from the ground and made something out of it, and he began to understand what his father had meant about *"the miracle of clay"*. He felt a deep sense of satisfaction, and smiled even more as he examined his creations, and thought that although they looked similar, they were different – as similar and as different as two friends can be. Seb liked them straight away; two little figures, two little friends, two little people made from clay in a bag. "How wonderful!" he thought.

He took the two figures upstairs to his bedroom, and stood them on the chest of drawers next to his bed, alongside his other special things. After finishing his homework, he lay down on his bed and thought about the events of the day. He could hear his parents having a "chat" (as they called it) downstairs, and tried not to listen.

Before too long, his mother came up, calling, "Bath-time, Sebby!" He thought about taking his clay people into the bathroom, but knew better than to risk them getting wet and falling apart. So he left them in his bedroom, and had a hot and healthy bath.

While he was getting ready for bed, his nervous father, dressed in his full Army uniform, came up and said that he was going now, but would see him again in six weeks or so, if all went well. As usual, this started to upset Seb; he loved his father very much and hated to see him go back into the heart of war. He picked up the first clay figure he had made, cupped it in his hands, and looked at it for a few painful moments. He heard his father's car drive quickly away. He put his face into his hands and sighed, a deep and real sigh from the depth of his soul. He laid the little figure down next to its friend, both of them horizontal as if in sleep. Seb was asleep within minutes.

Deep into the night, when all was quiet, when all was peaceful and still, one of the clay figures sat up. It took in the darkness, raised its head to the luminous stars and planets and comets on Seb's bedroom ceiling, felt the moving air of his sleeping breath, and stood up. With tiny gentle steps it walked to the edge of the chest of drawers, and stared at Seb, not with eyes, for as yet it had none, but with its own little light twinkling across the gap between the chest and the sleeping boy. With a delicate leap, it landed like a butterfly upon Seb's pillow, and walked towards him, mini-stars and sparkles lighting the way. It stood very close to his ear, and began to whisper – and then Seb began to dream.

And what a dream it was – as if through the eyes of a soaring bird, he looked down upon a sea that he had never seen, and as he swept across it an island appeared covered with giant trees and with a great hill at its middle, shining and dazzling like a fallen sun. On and up the flight took him, across a wide channel to a vast land of mountains, downs, forests, plains, rivers, valleys and other sights so many and so wonderful that they could make only a world, not a single image in a dream. Suddenly, all around him were thousands of birds, flying and singing, swooping, rising and playing, and from some inner space within them all he heard a soft melodic voice.

"*Remember this,*" it said, "*remember this well; it is still there and waiting for you…*"

The clay figure walked silently across the pillow back towards the chest of drawers, jumped, landed, took one little step forward, and stopped, one foot still above the top of the chest, frozen in its night time walk.

✫   ✬   ✩

When Seb awoke he was extremely tired. He knew that he had been dreaming for most of the night, a huge flying dream over a land so very real and beautiful, so unknown yet at the same time so strangely familiar. Then he remembered his clay figures. Smiling to himself, he rubbed his eyes, yawned, and sat up. But … one figure was lying down, as it had been left, but … but the other one was standing up with one leg raised, as if it was about to walk. He knew that he had not made the figure so; he knew he had made them both to lie down, as if like himself in sleep. He shivered, and stared, and a tingling came into his eyes.

"How?" he thought, "How has this happened? I know I didn't make them like this!"

Very gently, he picked up the walking figure and examined it closely. He felt the bent leg, and was about to try and straighten it when, "No, no!" he thought, "it's dry, it will break off, and then he won't be able to walk again – or look like he is walking!"

He was deeply confused, and finally decided that it must have been his mother during the night that had made the clay figure to look as if it was walking.

"But why?" he pondered as he got up. "Why would she do that?"

Even though it was the usual breakfast rush before school, Seb asked his mother if she had moved the clay figures, or changed them in any way. Time and again she said no, she had not. She was so surprised by the seriousness of his questioning, that finally she went upstairs to look for herself at what he was complaining about.

"That's marvellous," she said, "You've made it look like it really is walking. What an artistic lad you are."

Seb groaned and held his head.

"But Mum," he said impatiently, "I didn't make him like that; he was lying down with the other one when I went to sleep." He desperately wanted some easy explanation.

His mother went to pick up the walking figure.

"No!" he cried out, "No, don't – you might break him – please, Mum, leave him like that."

She left him like that, and so did Seb; it was time to get ready for school.

✩  ✩  ✩

The day moved on from strange to bad. As his mother drove him to school, Star, their young Welsh Springer spaniel, was sick in a very ugly way all over the neck and front of his formal uniform, which he had to wear today because it was the year photograph that morning, and he was supposed to look his very best. Seb screamed and was almost sick himself, as his mother swung the car around muttering some equally ugly words.

There was no time to clean his blazer, and the smell was truly hideous, so his mother rooted in his wardrobe and found an old one. Seb washed his hair and neck, and grabbed the first shirt, tie, and trousers he could find. As he was changing, Star came into his bedroom and lay down as if in shame and deep sorrow.

"You're a bad girl, Starry, very bad!" he growled at her.

She slunk towards the bed and looked up at him. He said nothing more to her, and finished changing.

"Come on, Star, it's outside for you!" he snapped, as he was about to leave his bedroom. But Star did not move; she just sat in her best attention pose and stared at the top of his chest of drawers.

"Star! Come on!" he ordered; but again she would not move a muscle. She sat still and to attention and stared.

"Star!" he shouted.

Star began to whimper, pulled in one direction by her training and her desire to please, but in another by something very different.

He watched her; and then realised with a shock that she was staring straight at, and as if obedient to, his little clay figure, which still stood in mid-stride, just as he had left it.

✫ ✬ ✩

Seb was late for school, very late. His so-called formal uniform was a poor mixture of odd socks, summer shirt, winter trousers, a blazer two years old and too small by far, which pushed his arms out and made him look as if he was trying to fly, and an equally old, small and raggedy tie to match.

Mrs Thompson, the Head of the senior department, did not know whether to laugh or to tell him off, as he rushed into the school office, apologising for being late. But there was no time for either; so, along with his giggling friends, Tim, Ricky, Peter, Giles, Mort and Drakey, he was rushed into the school assembly hall, bundled to the back of his year, stood upon a bench, and forced to smile his way through the second ordeal of the day – much to the amusement of his class, his year and his teachers. Yet, because he was such a bright, golden-haired, blue-eyed, charming, cheeky and harmless boy, no serious punishment was handed his way – *except*, Mrs Thompson insisted, that *all* the girls of his class would have to try to tidy him up during break-time, which to Seb was an ordeal far worse than a vomiting dog or an embarrassing photograph; it was an awful hell, he thought!

Once the humour prompted by his appearance had run its course, the lessons of the day took over. Even though he was still confused by some of the recent events, he settled into the routine, and had a fine time during the lunch-break playing football, cricket, silly-stuff, and all the usual games the boys played.

Over lunch, he told Ricky, Mort and Peter, along with anyone else on their table who was listening, the story of the clay figures, and then of Star. They all had a good laugh about it, and tried to convince him that he had been dreaming, or forgetful or imagining it; and he did not argue the point, but he knew that something truly odd had happened, yet quite what, he still did not know.

All went well until the last period of the day, when Seb left the class to join a few others in the cello group. He was tired, and daydreamed, as Mr Ransom ran through the canon they had been practising.

Seb often became hypnotised (as he described it), or in a trance, by careful and methodical hand movements, such as when his mother embroidered, or iced a cake, or when his father fiddled with the car engine, or at other times when watching hands in action. Today it happened while he was watching Mr Ransom play the canon around and around.

A mist seemed to blur Seb's vision, his head began to swim and he became dizzy. He heard strange sounds like the rushing of water upon pebbles and rocks, and windblown trees, and the callings of beasts and birds, together with thunder and deep rumblings – and within it all, that beautiful melody he had heard only once before, but which was so very familiar as to be like the air of his deepest memories.

"*Seb,*" a sweet voice whispered, "*Seb, where are you?*"

The words were sung more than spoken. They called to him from so, so far, and yet were as near as his own living breath.

"*Seb, please, please come back.*"

The melody wound its delightful course through the mighty sounds of the crashing sea, when suddenly: "Seb!" a hard voice broke into his peace. "Seb," it said, "what on earth are you doing?"

He opened his eyes, and saw Mr Ransom staring at him.

"Seb, are you OK?" asked Peter, one of his closest friends.

"Y– yes, I'm fine. I'm sorry, sir, I must have dozed off – I'm so sorry, I don't..."

"What was that piece you were just playing?" Mr Ransom interrupted, stroking his large red beard, with a very puzzled look on his face.

Seb looked at Peter, who stared back at him as if to say: go on, answer him!

"It was the canon, sir," he replied, not knowing what the question meant, or how else to answer it.

"That was no canon that I've ever heard. Where on earth did you learn that piece?"

"It was brilliant, Sebby," Peter piped up, "Awesome!"

"Be quiet, Peter!" Mr Ransom ordered. "Well?" he asked Seb.

"Sir, I don't know. I felt tired and dizzy and could hear music coming from somewhere – but I wasn't playing it."

"You most certainly were, my lad, and I've heard none better. Play it again, please!" Mr Ransom urged.

Seb froze. As is the case with so many dreams, the moment he tried to remember the melody it quickly dissolved before him, like smoke into air, and was gone in the space between breaths.

"I cannot, sir," he replied quietly. "I don't know how or why it even happened."

Mr Ransom could see that the experience was unsettling him, and his other pupils; so he called an end to the class, and let them all go – Seb to meet his mother, and Peter to return to his foster-home.

As they parted, Seb turned to Peter and asked, "What the hell happened in there?"

"I don't know," Peter answered, "but it was good, really good. Don't worry, Sebby, you're tired, but wow, man, that was really weird – not you yeah, just the amazing sound you made on that cello. Ace! Have a good sleep, Sebby boy; see you tomorrow."

"See you tomorrow," he replied, and went to the steps to meet his mother, and to go home and consider it all.

## Chapter Two
# Rainbows in Moonlight

The summer term rolled on. A warm cricketing June turned into a hot swimming July, and Seb, together with his friends, looked forward to the holidays and to a long break from the efforts of their year.

The memories of the mist, music, dreams, voices and strange sounds, and the very oddness of the time before spring, began to fade. There were no more peculiar events, or unexplained movements, to disturb Seb or his family or his friends and teachers. Yet, even now, Star would often be found in his bedroom, asleep on the floor in front of the chest of drawers, upon which the clay people still rested. They now lived on an ancient ammonite fossil that he had found on another dig years before, and he would not move them or lose them – they were very special to him, and to be cherished.

On the eve of the last day of term, Seb went to bed excited, and talked to his mother about the week away that his father had arranged for them both, camping and fishing in nearby Devon. In the middle of their chat the telephone rang, and his mother happily popped downstairs to take the call, leaving him alone in his room. He looked about, at the luminous stars on his ceiling, at his books, his models, his railway set, his computer, his still-loved soft toy friends, his posters and pictures, his special bits and pieces, and lastly at his little clay figures – one still in mid-stride, the other still lying down. He picked them up and examined them, and smiled. They were so attractive and so friendly, so something from nothing.

As he lay there holding the figures, his mother returned. She did not look happy, and her face was flushed; a *bad news* face, he thought.

"That was your father," she said coldly.

"What time is he getting back on Saturday?" he asked urgently.

"I'm sorry, darling," his mother replied quietly, "I'm so sorry, he can't make it on Saturday. He says his leave has been cancelled, and he must stay in the forward base. But he promises that he will take you away later in the holidays, when he's back from his tour." She hated what she was saying.

Seb was utterly disappointed; so much so that he would not speak, except to ask, "Will Dad be all right?" – Not being sure if his father was at all safe.

"Of course he will," his mother said, equally unsure of the truth.

There was little else to say. His mother kissed him goodnight, and went downstairs, shaking her head with sadness for her son.

He lay back with tears trying to enter his eyes. He rested the clay figures next to him on the pillow, covered them, and his stinging eyes, with his young shaking hand, and sighed himself to sleep, feeling empty, worried, and badly let down.

☆　✩　☆

Through a thin opening between the curtains, a silver bright full-moon beam slowly ranged across Seb's bedroom, marking the minutes and hours of the ongoing night.

The time was deeply silent, the atmosphere charged with a powerful waiting, the whole room ready for something marvellous and moving.

He sighed in his sleep, and began to turn over, and the two clay figures stood up straight – and looked towards each other. As if in silent agreement, they jumped lightly off the pillow, on to the chest of drawers, walked down to the bed-settee, across to the radiator, and on to the windowsill – there to stand bathed in the sharp bright moonlight, and there to begin the great adventure.

13

The clay people turned around to face Seb's bedroom, and as they did so the curtains drew back to let the beautiful silver night light wash throughout the room. The walls and ceiling appeared to dissolve into space; grass and trees sprang into view; a vast landscape of rolling downs and snow-capped mountains lined the middle and far distance; massive silhouettes of castle walls and great buildings formed in the west; and in the east, the sun arose with a dazzling splendour, to the sound of birds singing and a whooshing, roaring sea.

Seb opened his eyes, and for just a middle space in time he glimpsed two radiant figures, standing tall and upright, smiling at the rising sun, and haloed by the spray of sea water that rainbowed around their heads. Then the vision was gone in a blink…

14

He rubbed his eyes and blinked again hard – only to see his two clay people standing on his windowsill, all aglow with moonlight.

The silence in the bedroom was overpowering. He could hear his heart beating as if its sound was filling the whole space. He stared at the figures; and they stood there motionless in their silvery brilliant sheen.

"How?" he thought. "How?" he said out loud, and rushed to his window, picked up the clay people and looked at them.

Though they were dry, hard, stiff, dusty and still – they were also warm to his touch.

✩ ✩ ✩

When Seb's mother came into his bedroom at 7.30am, she was shocked and puzzled by what she saw. He was asleep on the floor by the radiator, under the windowsill. In each hand he held a clay figure, and he was smiling.

Confused as she was, she could not help but look at him carefully, with a mother's love swelling in her heart. There he was, long and thin, his olive skin and blond hair, smiling face and gentle hands, asleep with the peace of the innocent, and of the happy. How she loved him; yet how she wondered – why, why was he lying there like that?

There was no time to ponder any further, school was waiting, and the usual mad dash took over.

Though the time was getting on, Seb's mother decided to take the longer route, and drove slowly through the lanes around the slopes of Glastonbury Tor. It was a glorious morning. A gently drifting mist filled the hollows and coombes, hugging the fields and meadows, the trees seemed as if they were floating upon a sea of cotton wool, and all around birds were singing, insects were buzzing, and life was enjoying the day.

As they drove on, he considered telling his mother about what had happened during the night. But "How can I?" he thought. He had no idea himself what had happened, except that a loud rushing noise had woken him up, and that he was sure he had seen two tall bright figures standing in the arc of a rainbow, and then … and then his two little clay figures standing on the windowsill, upright and facing him, the curtains wide open, the bedroom full of dazzling moonlight. He knew at once that his mother would never play such a cruel trick on him, as she thought the clay figures were as special as he did. So how could all this have happened?

"Are you OK, Seb?" his mother asked, wondering why he was being so quiet. Yet she too was quiet, and not sure whether it would be wise to ask him why he had been asleep on the floor, holding his little clay people.

"Yes, fine, thanks," he replied, hoping she would not ask him anything at all about the night before.

He thought very hard about the night's events, and came to two conclusions. Either he had been sleepwalking, and moved the figures, and opened the curtains, or … he shivered at the thought, or – the figures had moved themselves.

He quickly decided that he must have been sleepwalking or something like that; but he knew this explanation did not answer all of his questions – especially two of them. As if it had nothing to do with anything, Seb questioned his mother.

"Mum, can moonlight make things warm?"

"What do you mean?" she replied.

"Well, you know, like if you leave something in the sun it gets warm, is it the same if you leave something in the moonlight?"

"I don't think so, Seb; not in the same way as sunlight. But moonlight does help things to grow, so maybe there is a tiny bit of warmth in it. Why do you ask?"

"Mmm, just thinking, Mum, no reason," he replied, as if the question was of no importance.

He thought about his second question. If he had moved the figures, how had he straightened the leg of the one that was frozen in its walk without breaking it, as it was so dry and fragile? He knew that water added to clay could help to make it soft again, if it had not been fired in a kiln; but then he would

16

have had clay on his hands, and there would have been clay in the bathroom sink – both of which he must have cleaned up before placing the figures on his windowsill.

"No!" he thought. He knew that he would not have tidied up even if he had been awake, far less if he had been sleepwalking.

He looked at his fingernails carefully – no, there was not a trace of clay in them at all.

Seb stared unblinking through the windscreen as the car swung into the driveway of his school, and he knew then, so very shocking as it was to realise it, that the figures must have moved themselves.

He also knew somehow, deep, deep within himself that from that moment on nothing would ever be quite the same.

Something wonderfully strange had happened, and would most surely happen again.

☆　☆　☆

With some time left before the first period, Seb quickly found his best friend, Peter, and took him to a quiet corridor between the Year 5 block and the Music Hall. Peter, though the same age as him, was broader, taller, and much harder and tougher than he was. To many, teachers, pupils and parents alike, he was a cold Russian boy, a foster-child from the age of seven, with few feelings and a difficult attitude. But Seb knew him better; he knew him as a deep-thinking, emotional and very loyal friend, and he trusted him completely.

He told Peter about what had happened during the night; about the clay people, about the bright rainbowed figures, about waking up on the floor, and about his thoughts as to what could have happened.

For a moment, Peter stared hard at Seb, and he stared back, waiting for some intelligent reaction. Then, to his great surprise, Peter burst into a big uncontrollable laugh, and started jumping up and down, clapping his hands with obvious joy. Seb was speechless.

"Magic, Sebby boy, magic! Brilliant!" Peter said, in a voice gushing over with happiness.

As Seb was about to speak, amazed by Peter's reaction, he stopped dead, and listened.

"What is it?" asked Peter, "What's the matter?"

"Sssh! Sssh, Peter, listen!"

Within the silence of the narrow corridor, the sound of soft music was moving through the air like a warm breeze. They both stood still and listened. Then Seb gasped and jumped back with shock.

"What is it, Sebby?" Peter asked, concerned now by the worried look on his friend's face.

"That music!" Seb whispered, "That's the same as..." Again, he was speechless, overcome by what he was hearing.

Then Peter gasped too, as he recognised the music as the same strange and beautiful piece that Seb had played on the cello long months ago – the piece he had played in his misty trance, and had not been able to play again since.

Seb was so surprised that he thought the music was coming from the air itself, and he could not move or speak at all. But Peter could hear exactly where it was coming from. He grabbed Seb's hand and pulled him.

"Come on! It's coming from the hall!" Peter urged.

He dragged the dazed Seb along the corridor. As they got to the large double doors of the Music Hall, Seb was stumbling and could hardly keep his balance. They looked through the two glass panels in one door, but the inside curtains were drawn and closed.

Peter put his finger to his rounded lips, as if to say 'sssh', and gently opened one door, just enough for them to slip in behind the heavy velvet curtains. The music became louder, and held them both with its beauty and power.

"Get a grip!" Peter whispered, "Let's look."

Very slowly and nervously, he drew aside one curtain, barely enough for them both to peep through. Seb's eyes widened, until he felt they were about to pop out – Peter blinked rapidly

18

– as they both saw at the same time where the music was coming from.

There, in the vast emptiness of the old hall, surrounded by hundreds of empty seats, and sitting alone on a chair in the middle of the huge empty stage, sat Mr Ransom, the big red-bearded music teacher, eyes closed, playing at his cello, with tears running down his cheeks, through his beard, and on to the bow, the cello, and the floor.

As the stunned boys were about to turn around and slip away, the double doors burst open inwards, and knocked them through the curtains on to the stacks of chairs piled behind them. The echoing noise was deafening as the chairs tumbled and fell, crashing into the music stands, which in turn dominoed into the instruments of the orchestra, set out neatly in readiness for the speech-day lunchtime concert. Total chaos. Total trouble, the boys thought as they lay there in embarrassed silence.

Seb and Peter groaned as they got up off the floor, only to see the towering figure of Mr Gordon, the Headmaster, standing over them, glaring and red with anger.

"What!" he shouted, "What the devil are you two doing here, skulking behind curtains and doors? Well?"

Mr Ransom stood up immediately and answered for the boys, who were speechless, "It's all right, Headmaster, they have an appointment with me. I must have been so lost in my practising, I didn't hear them arrive. They weren't skulking, I hope, just being polite, is that not so, boys?" The boys began nodding to him, to each other, and to the Headmaster.

"I am not surprised, not at all surprised!" Mr Gordon growled, repeating himself, as he always did.

"Right, you two – you two clear up this mess. You have ten minutes, ten minutes, do you hear, to clean up this mess and get to your classes!" Mr Gordon stormed out through the double doors, the echoing noise of his clicking leather heels fading away down the corridor.

"OK, boys," said Mr Ransom kindly, "Come on, let's get this chaos back into order."

When it was done, Mr Ransom told Peter to get back to his form room, and asked Seb to wait behind. Peter stood by the curtains, reluctant to leave his friend.

"Go on, Peter, don't worry, he is not in any trouble, and neither are you; I just want five minutes with young Seb here."

Peter left eventually, the double doors snapping closed behind him.

☆  ☆  ☆

"Please sit down, Seb," Mr Ransom requested, carefully unstacking two chairs.

They looked at each other – Seb unsure as to why he was here – Mr Ransom unsure of what to say next. Seb was not too nervous as he liked Mr Ransom very much, and knew that the big gentle teacher liked him; not because he was particularly good at the cello, which he was not, though he did enjoy learning and practising, but because they had very often made each other laugh during music lessons.

"How much of what I was playing did you hear, Seb?" Mr Ransom began.

"I, I'm not sure," he stuttered in reply.

"But enough, I think?" asked the teacher.

"Yes, sir." Seb looked down.

"Enough to know that it was my attempt at playing the piece *you* played, back in April. Do you remember?"

"Yes, I do," Seb answered slowly and quietly, not wanting to remember.

"And what do you think; was it the same?"

"I'm not sure, sir, I, I can only remember a few bars."

"I'm not surprised, Seb. But it was not the same. For try as I may, and believe me I have tried very hard and very often, something is still missing. The notes *are* the same, I'm sure of that, but the *something* that is missing is what made it so perfect and powerful." Mr Ransom paused.

20

Seb did not comment or reply, he just fiddled with his short scruffy tie.

"Do you know what it is that is missing?" Mr Ransom enquired gently.

Seb felt goose pimples prickling his skin, and the soft hairs on his neck tingled with electricity.

"No, sir." he replied, almost whispering.

The silence that followed seemed to go on for long minutes, but in truth it was only for a few stretched seconds.

"Magic, my boy, magic! That is what is missing," Mr Ransom said, without a smile or a movement.

Seb did not respond or offer any sort of reply; he knew that he did not need to, as Mr Ransom was completely right.

"Do you know what magic is, Seb?" Mr Ransom asked kindly, gently, but with deep seriousness in his voice.

Seb quickly thought about all the stories, myths, books, films and versions in which he had come across what was called magic – but none of them gave him any answer that felt right. He thought of wizards and witches, wands and flying broomsticks, rings, mirrors, staffs, toys coming to life, and even Peter jumping up and down, shouting "Magic!" But again, these did not seem to be real or truly powerful.

"No, sir, I don't," he replied.

"Then remember, and consider this well, Seb," Mr Ransom said quietly, "for I think that something special is happening to you. *Magic is the image and appearance of causes we do not know, and of powers that we do not understand.*"

A complete silence filled up the great hall, and even the air itself was still.

The moment was broken suddenly by the bell sounding for registration, and the first period of the day.

"Get on, quickly, Seb; don't be late! But if you ever want to chat, you know where I am. I will see you next term; now be off, and take care."

"See you next term, Mr Ransom." He smiled as he quickly left the Music Hall, feeling a sense of relief that, maybe, what had been happening to him could be explained and understood.

☆　☆　☆

Seb got on with the day as usual. Yet what he did not know was that since his extraordinary playing of the cello three months earlier, he had been a major talking point among the members of staff, and among a number of the parents; and that many of them had been watching him closely, to see if anything else unusual would happen. At school, nothing else unusual had happened – but still there were some that watched him with a keen and growing interest.

The short last day of term was full of fun and games and play. After lunch, Seb went to play football by the trees with Mort, Ricky, Giles, Peter, and all his other mates.

It was a gorgeous, warm, sunny day. All the playing fields were a bright healthy green, the sky a cloudless deep blue, and Glastonbury Tor looked down upon the school with its usual timeless and changeless presence, the remains of the tower at its top, like a broken finger pointing to the heavens.

It was a perfect scene, and Seb stopped to look at it all, and appreciate it, as he and the other pupils did so often. But it was the wrong moment to stop. He heard his name being called, and as he turned the football hit him smack on the side of his head, with tremendous pace and power. The impact sent him reeling backwards, and he crashed to the ground with a thump and a wheeze, as the air was knocked out of his lungs.

He struggled to his feet, holding his head, trying not to appear in too much pain, but he was very shocked and shaken. He could hear his friends calling to him, but their voices sounded faint and far off. He opened his eyes, but could not understand what he was seeing, for where the lower playing fields and tennis courts had been, there was a huge lake, shimmering and golden in the sunlight. He turned towards where the school buildings and cricket nets should have been, but instead there were two lines of very tall silver trees, forming a massive avenue and stretching as far as he could see. The road had gone, and where the junior boarding houses had been there was a gigantic stone bear, at least twice as big as the missing houses, sitting upright on its back legs, staring towards the lake, its eyes like awful jewels sending multi-coloured beams of reflected sunlight all around. He turned to look at the Tor. It was still there, but where the tower of St Michael had been on its summit there was a single magnificent tree, whose crown was almost as wide as the Tor itself, surrounded by hundreds of birds singing and flying at the same time.

"Sebby! Sebby-boy, are you all right?" He heard Mort's voice, and blinked his eyes a couple of times. All his friends had gathered around him, and he was lying on the ground, holding his head. He saw all the faces of his friends and smiled – and they all smiled and laughed back at him.

"Come on, Seb, get up, you'll be fine," said Ricky. "Sorry, mate, but you should keep your eye on the ball!" He grabbed one of Seb's hands.

"Are you OK?" asked Peter, grabbing the other, and pulling him to his feet.

"Yes, yes I am – but that really hurt," He replied, looking around and seeing the tennis courts, buildings, cricket nets, playing fields, road, and the Tor – all as they had been, and as he had known them for so long.

His friends all said "well done" to him, slapping him on the back and ruffling his hair, and carried on with the game, with Seb playing his full part. But he was wondering all the time about what he had seen, and also how he had seen it.

☆  ☆  ☆

Though it was the last day of term, and they all had on their best uniforms, Seb and his friends played in the lunchtime concert looking scruffy and bedraggled after their football game. Mr Alban, their class teacher, and their favourite teacher, tried to tell them off, but shook his head at them, and could not help smiling – they were a great bunch of boys, and he was very fond of them. But Mr Gordon glared, and frowned at them all while they played.

After the concert came the speeches and prize-giving in the marquee down by the car park. Most of the parents were there, including Seb's mother; and although he had not won a personal prize, his House had, for the best results in sport throughout the year. His friend Mort collected the cup, as they all knew he was the keenest and most successful sportsboy of his year, and even of the year above. Seb and his friends all clapped and hooted and whistled loudly, until they were told to "pipe down" by Mr Alban.

The speeches seemed to go on and on, but at last they were finished and done. Outside the marquee, Seb found his mother.

"I'm just going to find Peter, and say goodbye," he said. "He's coming back in a few weeks; he's going to visit his brother in Cornwall. Can he come and stay the night with us, or two or three, *please*?"

"Yes, that will be fine. Tell him to call us next week," his mother replied. "I'll see you in the top car park in five minutes – five minutes!" she called out as Seb ran off.

He found Peter, with Ricky, Drakey, Giles, Mort and the others. They all said their goodbyes, arranging meetings and visits to each other's houses.

"I'll see you in four weeks, yeah," Peter said in his soft Russian accent. "Then we'll have some fun – yeah."

"OK, four weeks, P." He replied, and they went off to the car park, Seb to find his mother, and Peter to find his foster-parents or the bus that would take him to their house.

After saying his final goodbyes, Seb opened the back door of their old car and threw his bags inside. As he was about to get in, he suddenly remembered his worn and trusty cricket bat. He begged his mother to wait, while he rushed back to find it.

He entered the empty classroom, and looked around. What a mess; but what a happy mess – a room full of papers and books and clothes and memories – good memories of a good year.

Even the smells of the classroom created images of friends and fine times. He turned towards his locker and remembered the peculiar events of this last day of term, and he knew that he would have to think hard, very hard, about it all, and try to make some sense of what had happened.

The room was perfectly silent as he reached towards his locker door. He paused for a moment. For some reason he was a bit spooked by the emptiness and silence, and the loneliness that gathered all around him. He shrugged it off, and then opened the locker. There was his cricket bat, along with his ball, his trainers, and his kit bag. He put them all under his arm, and was about to close the door when he looked up to the locker's top shelf, and saw a piece of card standing upon it. Seb put his stuff down. He grabbed the card and looked at it. He held his breath as he saw what was drawn and written on the brown card. For long seconds he could not move, or breathe, or even blink. For there, on the card, was a drawing of his two clay people, almost exactly as he had made them – standing side by side, with their eyeless faces looking at him. Underneath the drawing, in large grotesque letters, were the words: "*HAVE YOU SEEN THEM MOVE?*" And underneath the words was a sign or symbol: *C·ll* He panicked, rammed the card into his kit bag, grabbed his things and ran out of the classroom – as frightened as if the hounds of hell were chasing him.

He ran for his life!

☆   ☆   ☆

When Seb got home from school he was very quiet. He did not greet Star who was, once again, in his bedroom, or talk to his mother about the day. She thought it was his usual "chill-out" time at the end of the day, and went to the kitchen to get him an apple and a sandwich.

After managing to send Star out, he stood alone in his bedroom, and stared at the little clay figures.  They stood together on his window sill and stared at him in return, their eyeless faces full of feeling, full of silent confusing mystery.

"How did you move?" he whispered at them. "How? And why? What's happening? Is it all because of you?" He did not expect a reply, and did not get one, as they both remained still and silent.

He rummaged frantically in his kit bag, and found the card that had been placed in his locker. He looked intensely at the words, *"Have you seen them move?"* and then looked at the drawing of his clay people. The drawing was excellent, as if it had been made from close observation; but the writing – the writing was horrible – big, untidy, messy, dirty and horrible. The two did not go together, did not fit. Whoever could draw so well, yet write so nastily, must be like two people, two people that did not like each other.  He then looked at the symbol, which had a certain beauty, but meant nothing to his tired and troubled mind.

Hours later, sitting lonely on his bed, he thought hard about all the strange events of the year, since he had been lost in the mist and songs back in Massive Meadow. He knew that this was the time when things began to change for him. Even thinking of the music he had heard made him shiver – not in fear, or with worry, but simply in awe of its loveliness.

"But when did they move?" he asked himself, "When and how?"

As with most young people, Seb found it hard to remember every date and time and order, of all the events that had been happening. Again he looked at his clay people, and sighed, and stared. Then, as if a light had exploded into his thoughts, he realized when these awesome changes had begun. He had made the clay figures; he had taken them upstairs; he had held one of them. He had breathed his long sigh on it when his father had left. It had changed. Once again, when he was worried and thought that his father had let him down, he had held the clay figures – and he had breathed on them as he sank into sleep.

"Was this it?" he thought.

26

"My breath – I," words failed him as he began to realize what could have happened.

"My breath? No! This isn't possible, is it? My breath?" His thoughts became a confusing whirlpool, sucking him into a world that he did not understand.

He went over to the window sill, picked up the little clay people, and held them in his hands and in his gaze. Slowly his thoughts began to focus; he knew what he wanted to do, but he was much too frightened to do it.

Still he held them, and still they looked back at him, until, with a deep, sharp intake of breath, he knew what he must do, and knew somehow that they were waiting for him to do it.

"Is it this?" he whispered, "Must I breathe on you?"

As the whispered words left his nervous mouth he knew that this was the truth; but he could not do it: it was too much; too much to test and too much to see.

He wanted to ask his mother what he should do, or even try to call his father; but already she was asleep, and the evening was growing old, and his father was thousands of miles away, surrounded by the heat and the horrors of war. Twelve-o-clock – he saw on his Harry Potter clock in large lights. The click of the clock seemed so very loud in the silence of the deepening dark.

A heavy hush came over the house as the lonesome night wore on. With all his nerves tingling from his toes to his face, Seb took in a deep breath. He held it there for many moments as the night sounds grew more intense – a little owl calling outside, the drip of the bathroom tap, the little groans and whines from his dreaming dog, and somewhere in amongst them all – the sound of a rolling sea.

Breathing in deeply again, as if he could do nothing else, he raised the clay figures in his trembling cupped hands, and held them close to his mouth. He closed his eyes, and then breathed out, slowly, calmly, and carefully. His warm breath rolled around his hands and over the tiny clay people lying inside them, until he could breathe out no more.

He opened his eyes just a fraction, to see if there was any change in his clay people – frightened in case there was, and frightened in case there was not.

For many, many minutes he looked upon his figures, but there was no change at all, and he began to wonder what he was doing so late into the night, dreaming of moving clay people and the power of breath and so many strange events. "Am I going mad?" he whispered.

At that thought he became scared, put the figures onto his chest of drawers, jumped into bed and pulled the duvet over his head, determined to get to sleep and to forget everything he had been thinking about the clay people.

✫    ✧    ☆

Seb woke up to what sounded like birdsong. Daylight was just breaking through his curtains, and he sat up, forgetful of his nightime frets and worries. Slipping his legs out of the bed, he rubbed his eyes and yawned. The birdsong seemed very loud and close, as he looked around the room. Out of the corner of his eye he sensed a movement, and turned to stare at his chest of drawers – he choked on his own breath as he saw his two clay people gently waving their arms with the songs of birds surrounding them. They were moving with such grace and delicate balance, that the sounds seemed to be coming from the air sparkling around them, as they turned and bowed in the morning light – it was simply beautiful to hear and to behold.

As he stood up slowly, the bird song stopped, and the clay people lifted their little round heads as if they were watching an approaching giant. But they did not look at him with their eyes, for as yet they still had none; yet their heads were tilted backwards, and he knew that they were staring straight at him.

Seb could not move; the clay people did not move. He could not speak, but as if out of the air itself he heard from somewhere or from nowhere a soft voice say, "Hello Seb." And then another, similar, but slightly higher, saying, "Yes, hello Seb. We all meet at last."

The young boy sank to his knees, desperately trying to work out whether he was dreaming or simply losing his grip on reality. But behind it all his polite upbringing kicked in, and, before he could form any conscious thoughts, he replied, "Hello."

A smile is nearly always something that is seen, but to Seb, this moment, his room, and the whole atmosphere felt like a huge and happy invisible smile, as he said again, now full of gladness, "Hello."

The little clay figures stretched out their arms to him, and walked to the edge of the chest of drawers; he turned up his palms and touched its edge, and the clay people walked on to them, one on each, and again the most wonderful happy smile seemed to fill the complete vastness of space. He held them close to his face as they exchanged their inner warmth, and he knew somehow that he knew them, and that somehow they also knew him.

Despite this deep sense of recognition, he asked the most obvious question that had risen into his confused mind, "Who are you?"

The clay people turned to each other and paused for a few moments, and then they turned their faceless heads back towards him. The silence continued for a few more moments, as if the clay people were considering how to answer.

"We are.....people of the earth." One of them replied – and then it struck Seb like an electric shock that he did not hear the reply as sound in the air, but as a sound within his head. He blinked nervously a few times, and then asked, "Please, which one of you said that?"

The first clay figure he had made bowed its head, and answered, "I did, Seb."

The boy smiled as he looked at them both, "Do you have a name; do you both have names?" he asked.

The second figure raised its round hand, as if to signal to him which one of them was replying, "I believe we do – yes, we do, and we will remember them very soon."

This prompted Seb to ask another very obvious question, but it sounded strange to him even as he voiced it, "How have you forgotten your names? I mean, everyone knows their own name….. don't they?" He tried not to let his question sound rude.

He waited for a reply, and then his first clay person raised its hand. At that moment a number of things happened very quickly, but to Seb as if in slow motion. His Harry Potter alarm clock sounded off, smashing the stillness and magic in his room; his mother's alarm clock in the next room went off as well; both of them had forgotten to turn them off for the first day of the holidays. As he silenced the deafening alarm his bedroom door flew open, and Star rushed in wagging her tail. He turned back to look at his clay people, just in time to see a faint glow of tiny sparkling lights disappearing inside them. Star saw it too, and sat bolt upright to attention, staring at the motionless clay figures.

"Hello?" he whispered, "Hello, can you hear me? Please?" But he knew somehow that the clay people would not reply, or even move, and that their brief time together was over….. until another time.

☆   ☆   ☆

Seb tried to be his normal self over breakfast with his mother. As a naturally honest boy, his first impulse was to tell her about what had happened during the night, and how he had seen the clay people move, and had spoken with them. Yet some real doubts held him back, some uncertainty as to whether this would be the first and only time that they would move, or whether he could prove that they had moved and spoken at all, or even whether they would ever move in front of anyone else. Until these doubts were settled he felt that he should keep very quiet about the clay people; but he was tremendously excited and impatient to find the time to be alone with them again, and to see if the magic would continue.

Unknown to Seb, his mother, who knew him much better than he understood, was aware that something serious was on her son's mind. She asked him if the business of his father was troubling him, and he answered honestly, no, it was not. Of course he was worried and missed him, a very great deal, but he knew that his father was there behind him all the time, and that he loved his son deeply.

Seb's mother was also aware of the behaviour changes in Star, who could be found so often in his bedroom, sitting or sleeping close to his chest of drawers, and would move only with great reluctance. She decided to observe them both closely, not because she was worried, but because her experienced intuition told her that something real was occurring in her family; yet it did not tell her what that something real was. Time would surely tell.

✫  ✩  ☆

The day had been arranged so that Seb would go to his friend Mort's house, in nearby Pilton, to unwind after a very busy term, and to spend some time riding their bikes around the yarrow and honeysuckled lanes of that sleepy village. His mother was taking a break, and going off to meet with a close friend for the day.

Although he knew that the day would be fun, he would rather have been at home, trying to speak with his clay people again. He thought about telling Mort about them, or even taking them with him, but realized instantly that he should not do either, and that he should wait and see what was to happen next.

He did manage to have fun that sunny day, and even to forget for hours at a time what was pressing in the back of his mind. But he was glad to get home finally, have his bath, watch a bit of television in comfort with his mother, and then be left alone in his bedroom – feeling tired, but ready for anything.

His clay figures were standing just as he had left them; one looking at the other, and the other with its pinched round hand raised, about to speak. As he picked them up, he felt the same sense of confusion he had experienced the previous night; the same deep question - was it really possible that his breath could bring these simple clay figures – made from stuff he had dug up in a field – back to life? But this time he knew he was not dreaming, and that he was not overtired or sleepy, and was not imagining what he was certain he had seen and heard and felt.

There was also the same sense of excitement and wonder as he stared at his clay people; but this time he was focussed, concentrated, and definite about what he was going to do.

The clay figures were warm in his hands, not cold and dusty as ordinary clay would be, and this did not surprise him. He smiled as he took in another long deep deliberate breath. He then breathed out slowly for what seemed like many minutes, and held the little figures in the warm currents of his young and purposeful breath. Putting them down, he sat down on his bed with his back against the wall, this time to wait until he saw something happen from the beginning, no matter how long it took.

Minutes passed by slowly as twilight turned into evening dark, and Seb sat peacefully patient in the stillness of his expectant room. He looked up for a moment, to stare at the luminous stars on his ceiling which he knew so well; but – but they were gone, as was the ceiling, and in their place was a huge, curved, deep blue night sky full of bright white stars he had never seen before, and a shower of multi-coloured flashing lights that dazzled his surprised eyes. He looked away for a second to rub his eyes, then looked back to see the familiar ceiling and the familiar plastic stars as they had been for so long. He laughed; happy if it was his imagination, but even happier because he felt convinced that this vision of a different heaven was all part of these amazing events, and part of his adventure with the clay people.

As he pondered upon what might happen next, he became aware of many small twinkling sparks gently lighting up the room. He turned to the clay figures, and saw that they were surrounded by tiny flickering micro-lights, like millions of minute stars packed into a deep red nebula. As they faded, the clay people began to walk to the edge of the chest of drawers, and then stopped and looked towards him.

Even though he had been expecting something like this to happen, he was speechless, awestruck, and unable to move a muscle. A patient waiting flowed throughout the room until, finally, he whispered, "Hello. Hello again."

"And hello again to you, Seb." His first figure said as it raised its simple hand.

"Yes, and hello again from me, Seb." The second figure said bowing its featureless head.

Already he could tell the difference in their voices; one was lower than the other, and one was gentler or more round than the other – like the voices of any two different people would be.

Seb was not sure what to say next, but then he remembered that the night before he had asked them about their names, and how had they forgotten them.

"Please, have you remembered your names yet?" he asked politely. There was a small silence as the clay people turned to each other, and then slowly back towards him.

"Yes, we have." The first figure answered, this time not raising its hand, and Seb not needing it to, as he knew which of them was talking now.

"And we have remembered much more, Seb." The second figure said, turning up its hands, as if to express itself more clearly.

"What are they then, please? Your names, I mean." Seb asked.

"I am Serren." The second figure replied, holding its hand to its chest.

"And I am – " There was a brief pause, which seemed to grow in importance as the second figure turned towards the first; "I am called - Lynn." the first figure said, as a deep hush filled the room. Seb did not miss this magic moment, as the words, "*I am*," and," *I am called*", echoed through his deeply puzzled mind.

In fact he was very deeply puzzled, and quite a bit disturbed, as a number of questions began to form rapidly, and which needed some kind of real answers; the whole business was so extremely difficult to grasp.

"I know that I asked you your names," he began, "but, but how can you have any names? I mean, I dug up the clay, I brought it home, and I made you just for fun. Then ... then I breathed on you a couple of times, and you came to life. If I made you – how can you have names already? And ..." he hesitated, "and, I do not understand how you know my name. You called me Seb, and said that at last we were all meeting – but how can this be? I mean ..." he was becoming lost for words, and even nervous, as he realised that he was not sure if he really wanted to know the answers to his questions, preferring to think that he had made these figures, and that by just a little magic they had somehow come to life – like something brand new. "I mean, how can you know me? And *who* are you, please?" He added the please in order not to sound too demanding; but his questions were urgent, and he could not disguise that.

The clay people looked at each other, and even though Seb could not hear any words, he knew that they were talking to each other in some silent manner. He waited patiently, and was about to ask more questions, when they both turned back towards him.

"These are good questions, Seb, very good." Lynn began to reply, "But I am not sure at this moment how to answer them. We have given you our names as we remember them; and we have begun to remember many things about the earth from which you took us."

"Yes." Serren spoke, as Lynn seemed unsure of what to say next, "Yes, Seb, we are now sure of the earth in which you found us, and of all that is moving within and upon it. And we know your name because we have heard it said so many times since you made these bodies of ours. But, at this time, we do not know very much more. It is as if Lynn and I have been in a deep, long, silent dream, surrounded by darkness; and such a darkness that has made us forget who we are, what we are, and why we are here. Yet, even though we knew your name from having heard it, we were certain that we knew *you* as soon as we became aware of you."

As Serren finished, Seb realised that he had the same feeling now, the same certainty that he had heard these voices before, these names, this deep sense of recognition, and this same feeling of closeness.

"Seb," Lynn spoke gently, "Seb, at this point we are as puzzled as you are. But as the days have unfolded, images and fleeting memories are happening more and more often – but as yet we cannot form them together and understand them. Serren and I both believe that you have found and rescued us, and released us from somewhere hidden and very dark where we could not move or find each other. We also believe that as you get to know us, we shall continue to get to know ourselves and to know you, and that we will finally understand the truth of all of this."

"What Lynn says, Seb, I can only agree with; and I thank you with all that I am, for delivering us from a timeless and dark existence, which seemed to have no meaning, or purpose or end. But it does appear that we are in this together, bound in this strange adventure – you Seb, Lynn, and me, Serren – and we will all discover the truth of this as we spend much good time together, and share our growing lives. And you should know, Seb, that although our bodies are made of dry clay, we have now put something of ourselves into them, and they cannot be broken, or damaged by force, or changed by water or by fire. We are ready to learn as you learn, and to share with you whatever is to come. In any way we can we will protect you, for this is our debt to you, and we shall never forget it."

Seb was astonished by these answers and amazed by what was now happening. In some way the whole situation was even more incredible than he had first thought – the magic was deeper and more serious than just cute little clay figures coming to life – it was real and it was powerful.  He smiled and shivered at the same time, and then remembered suddenly the words of Mr Ransom, as they sat in the music hall back in the summer term: *"Magic is the image and appearance of causes we do not know, and of powers that we do not understand."*

They talked together for another hour or so, until Lynn said, "We should stop now, Seb, I feel the strange darkness that comes upon us when we are about to be unable to move or speak. I do not know how it happens, but it is happening now."

"I feel it too." said Serren, "But enough is enough for one night, Seb. There is much more to come, and I believe that as the days go by our time when we can move and speak will get longer, until it is permanent at last."

"I do hope so," said Seb yawning, "I really do. But you are right, it is getting late, and I have the yawns.  Goodnight Lynn; goodnight Serren, and thank you."

"Goodnight Seb." The clay people said together, as a pale luminous mist seemed to disappear inside them.

# Chapter Three
# Shadows among the Trees

Today was to be a big day for Seb, as he jumped out of bed, pulled on his jeans and t-shirt, and thought about being allowed to take Star out *on his own* for the very first time. As he sat at breakfast with his mother, who was explaining to him everything he knew already about crossing roads, not talking to strangers, avoiding the gang on the corner, and being careful of the bull-terriers and other hippy dogs and owners that wandered around the Tor, the telephone rang out loudly.

After a lot of "O dears," and "reallys" and "yes I understands" came the final "Of course she can; no, it's no trouble at all." Seb's heart sank as his vision of the day vaporised before his eyes.

"That was Inga." His mother said in her *"I'm preparing you"* voice.

"I know." He replied sullenly, anticipating the inevitable.

"Hannah is coming over, just for the morning, or maybe a little longer – is that OK?"

He pondered upon the radical change to his day – Hannah, Inga's tall, tomboy and independent daughter, whom he secretly liked quite a lot, was coming over to his house for half a day or more. "Great," he thought, *"Great!"* He had planned to walk off with Star, and take his clay people with him, and see what new things would happen. But he knew that he had no choice in the matter, either in seeing Hannah or taking his clay people with him – he knew he had to do both.

It was a beautiful, warm, sunny morning, and as he brushed his teeth and watered his hair, he thought about being out and about without grown-ups leading and directing him; about Star and games and sticks to throw: about his clay people, and about Hannah – and all of these thoughts made him smile. He looked in the mirror, tweaked his hair, rubbed his nose, and made a silly grin, and knew that he was ready for anything.

When his mother opened the door, and Hannah walked in, Seb was in the kitchen, determined to play the reluctant host, and ready to make Hannah very aware that she was just tagging along with *his* pre-planned day. But as soon as Hannah said, "Hi Seb, you've grown again!" he became lost for words, and just smirked as he said, "Oh, hi, uh, um Hannah."

Again, his mother warned them of things to avoid and to be careful of, as he slipped upstairs, picked up his clay people, and zipped them into his fleece pocket, shouting "Yes Mum, OK!" all the way up and down the stairs. Hannah giggled at him, while taking in politely all the instructions from his mother.

Seb and Hannah were almost the same height, almost the same age, with almost the same darkening blond hair and blue eyes. She was good at football and cricket and running and climbing, and did not care a jot about getting wet or dirty or scratched and bruised; she loved to be outdoors in the fields and woods, very much the same as Seb. His only reservation was that she was a *girl*; but as he glanced at her, and she smiled at him, he knew in his heart that he admired her, and that girl or not she was good and fun company, a friend always ready to do anything for the sheer thrill and adventure of it all.

As they walked away from the estate, the heightening sun became much warmer and a light breeze carried the sweet scent of honeysuckle and cow-parsley in all directions, and Hannah tried to chat with Seb. But he was shy at first, and gave only one or two word answers, until she asked,

"What's the matter, Seb? You seem sad or, I don't know, quiet or something. Are you OK?"

He put his right hand onto his fleece pocket and could feel the small shapes of the clay people inside, and knew that he wanted desperately to tell Hannah about them, but he could not, there were still too many uncertainties and too many confusions surrounding them.

"I'm alright." He sighed, "Sorry, I don't know, I just feel a bit odd today."

"You're always *odd*, Sebby." She replied with a mischievous grin.

He looked at her, as she tapped him on the arm and ran off over the Big Stile. He let Star off her lead, and they both ran after Hannah, Seb laughing and Star whining and barking with excitement.

After a while they found themselves approaching Little River Pond, which Hannah had never seen before. In the height of the summer it was dry, and cracked and uninteresting, but Seb stood by the hollowed bank where he had dug up the clay for the clay people, and began to remember what had happened since that dreary morning so long ago now. Hannah watched him closely, as his hand rested on his fleece pocket in which his figures were concealed. He was so still and silent, and lost within his own thoughts. Star sat by his side as if waiting at attention. He looked towards the Tor, the tower on its summit dotted around with people playing and picnicking. His pocket began to get warmer and warmer, and his eyes started to smart and go out of focus. He blinked, and for just a millisecond the tower had gone, and in its place was the gigantic tree that he had seen once before – all the people had disappeared, except one, who stood beneath the tree shining a bright light, which beamed straight into his eyes. He blinked again, and it was gone; the tower and the people there just as they had been.

"Seb," Hannah said quietly, "what are you looking at?"

"I don't know." he replied slowly, "I don't know what to say."

"What's the matter, please..." she asked, "You look so worried."

Truly, he wanted to tell her about all that had happened, and was still happening; but something stopped him, like a quiet voice in his head saying – no, not yet.

"I'm fine." he replied, "Honest. Sorry, I was just daydreaming."

"Look, if you've got a problem or something, you know you can tell me. I won't laugh or tell anyone else – I, I do care." She said kindly.

"I know." He said, turning to her. "I know, sorry. Come on, let's go and have our food down by the stream."

"What stream is that?" she asked.

"It's not far, and it hasn't got a name – yet. When we get there you can name it, if you like; and then we'll put it on my map."

"OK." Said Hannah, and they ambled on, down Paradise Lane, past Maidencroft Farm, and into the fields beyond. As they walked and talked, slowly the conversation turned to more unusual things, with Hannah asking him what he thought about fairies, and nature spirits, and even angels. He answered from his heart as well as he could, for he had talked about these same things a number of times with his father.

"But do you think they are *real*?" Hannah asked.

Seb pondered the question, as they walked up to Gog and Magog, two huge oak trees rumoured to be of the oldest in England. Tall, wide, hollow and alive, with numerous broad arms, and branches like old fingers, they stood like two wrinkled watchmen towering over the winding path.

"Yes," he paused, "Yes, I suppose I do; but I'm not sure why – and even if they aren't actually real and true, they should be!"

"That's what I think as well." Hannah said. "And I would love to see just one and prove it.

Seb stopped beneath the two great trees, looked at Hannah and said, "So would I. There's got to be some truth to it all; there must be."

While he spoke these words, two massive shadows moved smoothly across the ground, joined themselves to the bases of the oak trees, and passed over Seb and Hannah. They both shivered and stared at each other, as the deep shadows passed and disappeared through the lane side hedge.

Hannah spoke first. "What was *that*?"

Seb tried to be brave and reassuring. "Oh… just, just some shadows from the trees."

"But the shadows were moving." She urged.

"It must have been clouds or something." He said, with little conviction, as they both looked up at the cloudless creamy-blue sky.

"It's the *or something* I think, Seb, and I don't like it."

"Mmm." He replied, as he felt a small movement inside his fleece pocket. "I don't know – where's Star?"

"Seb," Hannah was concerned, "What *were* those shadows – they were cold, weren't they?"

He did not know what to say, and answered abruptly, "Yes, but they're just shadows, they don't mean anything, and it doesn't matter! Come on, let's find Star."

41

He trotted off calling his dog's name, with Hannah following on closely, but looking back at the two trees, which she now thought looked hideous and ugly rather than ancient and amazing.

They found Star down by the footbridge that led over the shallow stream, and into the surrounding wood. She was lying down, panting, and looking up at the trees. As they passed her, they both urged Star to come on; but she just lay there staring in a peculiar kind of way.

"She'll be alright." Seb said, "She'll catch us up in a minute – she looks tired." Yet even as he said this he did not believe it, for Star could run for miles and miles and still she would *never* look tired.

"I'm hungry, and thirsty." Said Hannah.

"So am I." Seb agreed, "We'll stop down there by the little dam, and then we can have our stuff."

They walked into the woods to the left of the bridge, and instantly the air became hotter, thinner and damper. Pushing their way through the coppiced alders, horsetail ferns and nettles, they found a broad flat spot beside the dam, overlooking the stream and the bank beyond, the sunlight dripping through in roundish patches of moving light.

"Phew!" Seb exhaled, "It's stupidly hot in here. I'm going to wash my face." He threw off his fleece and shoulder bag, slid down the bank to the edge of the stream, crouched, and started splashing water all over his head and face.

Hannah watched him carefully, feeling equally hot and in need of refreshing water, but then she looked at his fleece, and at the pocket, and wondered. She put out her hand slowly, and was about to touch it, when she stopped, her heart frozen for a second. She did not want to deceive Seb, or to betray his trust, so she pulled her hand back and watched him again.

"Come on Hannah!" he beckoned, "It's cool."

Hannah took off her tracksuit top, but still she sat there watching and thinking.

"No, no thanks." She replied, "I'm thirsty." Then she opened his bag to get out the water bottles.

"Ha!" He laughed, as he slid up the bank to sit beside her, "OK, it's a bit dirty in there anyway."

"Right!" he said, gulping down his water, and letting out his usual 'aaahh' sound as he finished. "Right, what do you want to call it?"

"Call what?" Hannah answered.

"The stream, Hannah, the stream; come on, wake up!" He replied giggling, and she started laughing as well, and for just that moment everything was splendid and delightful.

As they sat up again, Star ran out from behind them, jumped into the stream, and started snarling, the hair on her back rising like the fin of a well-hooked perch. They stopped laughing as Star's fierce snarling turned into a low deep growl, the type of growl that Seb had never heard her make before, or had even believed that she could make.

"What's the matter with her?" Hannah demanded.

"I, I don't know, she looks frightened." Seb answered.

Star began to back off low to the water, staring wild-eyed and sniffing, and as she reached the middle of the stream, now whelping and growling in a bizarre and frantic manner, Hannah screamed. Seb fell backwards with shock, and started to roll down the nettle-covered bank. Star covered up her eyes as a shadow darkened across the stream and went over her, and on to Seb and Hannah, and was gone.

Seb looked up the bank towards Hannah, but she had her face in her hands and was calling out, "Seb, Seb, I'm cold!" Plumes of steamy breath came from behind her hands, as if she was gasping in the depths of winter. He struggled to his feet and made to get to her, but then Star howled crazily behind him. Looking over his shoulder he saw another shadow, a deep black hole of a shadow in the distorted shape of a huge man, moving down the opposite bank  and over the stream, and over Star, and slowly up towards him.

"Seb!" Hannah screamed, and thrust out her hand to pull him away. He grabbed it and pulled with all his might, and forced them both into the bubbling stream, the deep shadow crossing quickly and disappearing into the trees.

As they looked into each other's frightened eyes they gasped at the same time, "What's happening" and "What was that?" But no sooner had they sat up, when another great formless shadow slid its way down the bank, and then another, and another.

"Seb!" Hannah shouted as she grabbed his arm, "Come on!" She pulled him around and they scrambled up the slippery bank. In no time the shadows were upon them, and passed like frost-heavy breaths in the darkness of an icy night – and silence moved closely behind them, far beyond hearing and beyond sight.

For just a moment, there was only the sound of their hearts beating hard, but then they both took in their breath sharply and at the same time, and looked at each other, raising their eyebrows and grinning.

"What the hell was all *that* about?" Seb whispered, and he was shivering and shaking.

Hannah just closed her eyes, and shivered in reply, "H, heaven knows! But, but it's shadow."

"What's shadow?" he asked after a few moments.

"The stream"

"The stream?"

"Yes, the stream. I'm calling it the Shadow Stream." Hannah finished.

He shook his head and laughed, and fell backwards onto his fleece.

"But Seb, what on earth do you think those shadows were? They looked like shadows of people, but there were no people here, were there?"

Seb did not answer. He had a worried look on his face as he sat up quickly and gasped "Oh no!" His head had been resting upon his fleece pocket, the pocket with the clay people inside, and it had become as cold as ice. He unzipped it quickly and put in his hand.

"What now, Seb? Have you lost or forgotten something?" Hannah asked.

He could feel the little clay figures, and they were indeed icy to his touch, almost painfully cold. For a few seconds he did not know what to do, but eventually he took the cold figures out and looked at them, and frowned. As he did so, two things happened immediately – a great all-encompassing shadow enveloped the wood, making it almost completely dark, and making it bitterly cold like in a freezing deep mid-winter; and an instant later a brilliant flash of lightning tore through the quivering trees, and hit the opposite bank with a sizzling tearing *crack*, followed by the most horrendous clap of thunder that either of them, or the dog, had ever heard. They grabbed each other in terror, but being embarrassed quickly let go, and stared at the far side, where steam was rising from the bank, and great lumps of clay and mud were tumbling into the rushing Shadow Stream. Before either of them had time speak, they heard the rain hit the leaves above their heads, like gravel being thrown at a window.

Seb thrust the clay people back into his pocket, zipped it up hard, and said, "Come on, Hannah, I've had enough of this, let's go back!"

"OK, OK, but what were those little figures you had in your hands?"

"Oh, oh, nothing really, just, I don't know, I'll tell you later maybe."

The rain began to fall very much harder, and they left the wood just as great drips and drops of water came pouring through the sheltering leaves. Emerging into the open fields, the change in the day was almost unbelievable. The bright clear skies had been replaced by a miserable grey-black scene, with rain fit to punish anything that was abroad. It was now falling so hard that they could only hear each other by shouting, and could hardly see each other at all through the mighty sheet-like

45

torrent. It was as if they were running under a constant and relentless waterfall.

After only a few minutes they could not run any further, as their clothes were so heavily wet, their trainers caked in thick sticky mud, and they were exhausted. Although it seemed barely possible the rain beat down even harder, and as they passed Paddington Farm they saw a dark brown river pouring down the steep hill road, bubbling and splashing its way over the old cattle grid, and racing away over their feet and beyond. A great lightning fork ripped its way above the Tor, and the ground itself was shaken by the booming thunder-burst that followed it.

Seb grabbed Hannah's hand again, and shouted, "Come on! Over here!"

He pulled her forwards as fast as he could, and they trudged through the rushing water into one of the open barns that stood by the broken pathway. It was dry inside, to their relief. Two tan mountain goats cowered in the far corner, in fear of the noise of the hammering rain on the old tin roof, of the thunder and lightning, and of the water that was threatening to wash them away.

"I'm cold and hungry." Hannah said.

Seb smiled and replied, "You're always a hungry Hannah!"

"I know, but all this excitement makes me even hungrier. What a weirdly weird day."

"And it's not over yet." he said very quietly.

"But it is fun. I mean, I could have been at home helping mum with.....whatever, but instead I'm...." she looked at her soaked and mud-splashed body, and then at Seb, who looked like he had been pulled through a muddy river by his feet, and she laughed, "Instead, I'm here with you being chased by hideous shadows, terrified by storms, and whatever else is going to happen! No contest, Seb, it's been a great day to remember."

46

"Look," he started to apologise, "I'm sorry, OK? But I didn't know *any* of this was going to happen, I'm, I'm just as confused as you are."

"I'm not confused!" Hannah responded, "Things like this don't happen by accident. Something else is happening, isn't it? You've been spooky all day, holding your pocket, not talking, not being surprised at anything that's happened. So what is *really* going on?"

Thankfully for Seb the rain suddenly stopped, and as he went to get up to look at the sky, a magnificent rainbow appeared, and its end was at the top of the lane.

"Hannah, I don't know." He replied, "I want to tell you something but I ……. I'm not sure of anything myself. Do you really want to know, and you won't think that I'm mad?"

"Look Seb, I've always thought you were mad ….. no, not like that, I mean, *boy* as you are, you actually seem to think."

"Thanks." He replied.

"You know what I mean, Seb. You've always been the clown, the, I don't know, the *I'm just here to have fun* sort."

"What?" he questioned.

"Don't be like that, you know what I'm saying; it's like you are always watching yourself, and I don't mean in mirrors, and you always seem to know exactly what you are doing."

After a long silence, Seb responded, "Yes, but….. but this year has been so strange." Hannah did not say anything, she just looked at him and willed him to speak.

Seconds later, they heard crunching footsteps pacing over the broken driveway, and Ralph, the caretaker of Paddington Farm appeared.

"You all right?" he asked, in his soft Somerset Levels accent.

Seb and Hannah got up, and as they moved, their shadows stretched across the straw covered barn floor and onto the goats in the corner, who panicked and started snorting and kicking at the barn walls as they tried to back away.

"C'mon you two, don't know what's up with them goats, but t'is the second time in the last hour that they've been and gone

47

mad. Now where's their food to?" Ralph said in his friendly manner.

The two friends climbed over the gate and onto the rough farm drive, the water still sloshing about their feet from the flooding hillside road. Slowly, the goats began to calm down, as Seb told Ralph that they were OK, they were just very wet and a bit cold.

"You'd better get on then." He replied, "Look over there, there's more of that on the way, a lot more." Ralph pointed over to the Mendip Hills, and the sky looked slate-grey and heavy. "D'you want a lift?"

Seb and Hannah looked at each other, and Hannah shook her head saying, "I'm all right, and we haven't got far to go."

"Thanks," said Seb, "but if we get off now, we should make it before that lot comes over." He nodded at the dark doomy clouds, looked around for Star, and whistled.

"I saw her go runnin up the lane not a minute before you two turned up. Lord, she can move!" Ralph said with a grin.

"Ok, that's alright, she does this sometimes, but she'll find us along the way. Thanks, bye!" Seb replied as he turned to set off.

"Yes, thanks." Said Hannah, shaking her wet hair, and looking West, to where some awesome clouds were gathering. "Come on, Seb, we'd better be quick!"

They jogged up the road together as fast as they could, heavy in their soaked clothes, and, unknown to each other, both hoping that nothing else would happen before they got home. At the best of times it was a steep hill, but with water running at them, and with very tired legs, it began to feel like a mountain. Seb became concerned for Hannah.

"Are you alright?" he said, stopping to catch his breath.

"Yes, yes, I'm ok, just a bit puffed, and my ears are still ringing from that lightning blast by the stream. I thought I was going to, *you know*, in shock!"

"Same here! I don't know what's going on. This has always been such a peaceful walk, I've been coming here for years – but today – a giant tree, shadows, lightning, thunder, more

48

shadows, a weird dog, even weirder goats, monsoon rain, and
……..and nothing, I hope."

"What giant tree, Seb?" Hannah asked.

He was getting confused with the events and the seeming
events of the day. He could also feel that his clay people were
still very, very cold, and he was worried about them.

"Oh, I'm not sure, Gog and Magog I think." He stuttered,
"But come on, it's getting dark again!"

"Seb," Hannah said, holding his arm as he turned to look at
her, "don't worry about me, I'm alright, really. In fact it's been
one of the most amazing days I can remember, and I won't
forget it. Do you have many days like this?" She finished with a
giggle.

"No, not if I can help it, but …." He paused, as he considered
telling her about the clay people and everything else. He
needed to tell someone, and he wanted to tell Hannah, but even
now he was holding it back. Many moments passed.

"But what?" urged Hannah.

He opened his mouth to reply, but before he could utter a
sound a deep rumbling boom rolled across the valley, followed
by another, sending the nearby sheep scattering across the
hillside fields.

"Let's go!" They both said at the same time, and laughed as
they turned to run.

As they trotted up to the brow the hill, the rain came; not a
few spots at a time, but all at once, with a weight and power
that startled them. Without thinking, Seb grabbed Hannah's
hand, and they began to sprint as fast as they could. The day
turned dark, and darker, as if vast cosmic curtains were being
drawn against the light, and then *flash, flash, flash* as blinding
lightning bolts forked over the nearby hills. There was nowhere
to take shelter. To the left was a thick blackthorn hedge, and to
the right was a mass of tall nettles and vicious old barbed wire.
So they ran on, the rain battering them, and the thunder and
lightning strobing against their every step, until they came to
the stile in the corner of Massive Meadow. They stopped, and

could run no more. Puffing and panting they looked at each other.

"Is this fun?" Seb shouted, lifting his arms in the air.

"I think so!" Hannah shouted back, and she was barely audible over the hammering rain.

Seb looked across the short distance to Little River Pond. He could just make out the clay bank behind the ash tree, and wondered if any or all of this was to do with the clay people, when a streak of brilliant light smashed into the bank, sending up great sparks and lumps of clay in all directions. They instantly put their hands over their ears, just before the deep shuddering bang of thunder that seemed to tear and tear through the very makeup of the air itself.

They climbed over the slimy stile, and made their way towards the pond; but on the path side it was now a raging river of mud, and on the other side was the steaming hole left by the lightning strike.

"This way!" Seb shouted, moving quickly to the clay bank.

"No! This way!" shouted Hannah, as she ran towards what was the path.

Within moments they had lost sight of each other, on either side of the broad ash tree and the thick sheets of rain which now obscured their vision.

As Seb scrambled up behind the bank, he called out, "Hannah! Hannah!" But he could not see her or hear her. He got to the top and stood up, looking all around him, almost unable to see anything because of the rain driving into his eyes.

He turned towards the Tor; but it was hidden inside the storm clouds, and great folds of mist or steam seemed to be rolling towards him out of the relentless deafening rain. But then he heard another sound, like the beating of approaching drums, and he could feel rapid vibrations coming up through the ground. Instinctively, he took a step backwards, and was on the very edge of the streaming clay bank, which still hissed and steamed like a dread dark hole. He shielded his eyes and tried to look into the vapours, as the drumming sound became louder and louder, until, to his wonder and astonishment, a huge scarlet horse came thundering into the clear with its rider standing up in the stirrups. But his wonder disappeared as suddenly as it had come, as the horse pounded straight towards him, parting the mist like a jet-wind through smoke.

Seb had no time to get out of the way, and the immense horse bore down on him, its hooves thumping and tearing at the ground. All in one instant the rider leapt down off the horse; it stopped and reared wildly on its hind legs, snorting and whinnying loudly, as the rider strode towards Seb, pulling from its belt a great shining sword. He looked at the approaching rider, but could not tell if it was a man or a woman, as its long mass of hair was billowing across its face. Yet he could see a pair of eyes, and the eyes looked straight through him to a point away in the distance. He turned his head to look in the same direction, and lost his balance, slipping backwards and down into the clay bank. He grabbed at the slimy clay with all his might, and just managed to halt his slide. Then he looked up, there to see the windswept rider lift up the sword with both hands, point downwards, and he shouted "NO!" At the same moment, the rider plunged the shining sword down into the steaming bank, deep, deep down, and it made a loud and dreadful *clang* as it sank into the dark soft clay.

Seb let go for a split second; there was a blinding flash of light, and he thrust out his right hand and grabbed onto something solid. He began to panic as his eyes refocused after the flash; he looked down the bank and saw the Little River Pond, boiling and bubbling like a cauldron, and he held on with every measure of strength he possessed.

"Seb." A voice said from above him, "Sebastian!"

He squinted up through the rain, and saw a beautiful woman stretching out her hand to him. His right hand was burning painfully, so he slung his left arm over and up to her. The woman grabbed it and began to pull, and as he let go of the solid object he saw a small reddy-gold light shining through the mess of clay. But in a few more struggling seconds he was up and over the bank, lying down as the rainstorm ceased, and staring up at his smiling mother.

"Seb." She said; but his eyes closed, and for just a moment everything was dark and peaceful.

"I, I'm ok." He said, opening his eyes again and getting to his feet.

Elaine held him close, and comforted him.

"Thanks, mum, thanks." He looked down to the pond and it was flat calm as usual. There was no horse, no rider, no sword, no rain, no thunder and lightning, or steaming mist. It was just a normal day.

"What are you doing here?" he asked, "And where's Hannah?"

"I'm here!" Hannah answered.

He looked at her, and she appeared as if she was made of chocolate, covered with mud from her head to her feet, with just her blue eyes and pink lips smiling at him. He burst out laughing, and so did she and his mother.

"Star came for me." Elaine said, "I knew that something was wrong, and so did she." Star stood up and put her front paws on Seb's chest.

"Come on, we'll talk about it later. You two need a bath and some clean dry clothes. You *have* been through an ordeal, I think." She said, in a peculiarly knowing way.

"Yes." He said, smiling.

"Yes," Said Hannah, "It was amazing!"

As they walked away from the clay bank, Seb looked back, and he knew exactly what he had to do next.

✫    ✬    ✩

After baths and wholesome food, they all sat around the kitchen table and reflected upon the events of the day; not *all* the events, as Seb and Hannah had agreed to not mention the stranger things that had happened, not to deceive, but to make sure that they would be allowed out again, and because even they did not know how to explain some of the things that had occurred that day. For, it was not as if any thing that they had been warned about had happened, just some things that they did not understand.

They had hoped to have some time together to find out what each other had thought of the day, but Hannah's mother turned up early to pick her up. Yet she did ask Elaine if it would be alright if Hannah came back tomorrow, for most of the day if possible.

"Are you sure you want to, after today's *adventures*?" Seb's mother asked.

"Yes, I'd like to, and tomorrow will be different." Hannah replied.

"I hope so." Seb said under his breath.

When Hannah had gone, and Seb was ready for bed, he and his mother chatted some more.

"You don't seem yourself these days, Seb. Is something bothering you?" his mother asked.

After a few thoughtful moments, he replied, "No, not really, but its been a hard year at school, with lots of changes, and ……." He paused, and became silent.

"And what?" his mother prompted.

"And, oh, look, I don't know, I've just been feeling a bit odd lately, a bit tired, no, not tired, just sort of daydreamy, like I'm not fully awake a lot of the time."

"I've heard the same from your school. Some of your teachers are a bit concerned, not with your work, just about *you*. Mr. Baines especially; I kept bumping into him after school or at odd times during the day in town. Does he work full-time?"

"I think so, but we don't see him at all at breaks or lunch, just during maths. Anyway, he's a bit weird."

"Mr. Ransom has also been asking after you. He thinks you're very talented, and says that he keeps an eye on you whenever he can."

"I know, he's a nice man, and he's kind to all of us, but he often stares at me, and makes me feel as if I'm being spied on."

"I'm sure he's not spying on you, it's just that he cares."

53

"I know, but, no, I know he does." Seb thought of his cold clay people, and then remembered the horrible note and drawing in his locker, saying 'Have you seen them move?' He shivered, and realised that at the back of his mind he was suspicious of nearly every teacher at school, and a lot of the pupils as well, because he still had no idea who had written it, and drawn the picture, and had left *that* symbol.

His mother changed the subject, and said, "Steven Ade popped round this morning, he was asking after you as well."

Steven was the father of Julian, a boy he knew from the year above him, and a boy he did not trust or like. This struck him as odd.

"Why did *he* come round?" he asked.

"We've talked a lot over the summer term while I am waiting for you, and he has been round before, as you know, to drop off spare sport's equipment he picks up during his travels for work."

"Did he drop off anything today?"

"No, nothing today, he just wanted to know what size feet you've got, as he is going to a trainer factory next week."

"What size did you say?"

"I couldn't remember, so we went to your room to find your school shoes. He loved your bedroom, and looked at everything, saying what a great boy's room it was."

Seb thought, "He looked at *everything* ....." and was glad that he had taken the clay people with him. Then quickly, and without thinking, he said, "I don't want *him* in my room, ever, or anyone else for that matter, unless *I* invite them. I'm not a baby any more, and it's private!"

After a few seconds his mother replied, "You're right, I'm sorry, it just happened and he didn't touch anything, he just looked around. But it is your room, and I'm sorry."

"That's ok, mum. Sorry to snap, but he is a bit odd, like Julian. They're a strange pair, and they always seem to be smirking or sneering, or maybe it's just their faces."

54

"I understand what you mean, but he's harmless, and Julian just wants a friend."

"I know, it's just me," He said as he yawned, "I know. I'm going to bed now, I feel whacked."

He looked down at his hands, and the right one was throbbing in the centre of his palm. Something had burned him when he grabbed the rock by Little River Pond; but there was no blister to be seen, and in fact there was the opposite – a small circular hollow, throbbing but not quite hurting. Something about it made him shiver. It was all too much for one day, but there was still something he had to do.

When his mother had gone back downstairs, Seb got up quietly and found his fleece on the chair. He removed the clay people out of its pocket, and looked at them. They were still very, very cold, and seemed heavier and more solid than before. He also noticed that where their round blank faces had been, he could just make out some outlines of eyes, and mouths, and tiny lumps as if the beginnings of noses and ears, and even their round bodies had changed slightly to more oval and subtle ones. He stared at them for what seemed like ages, and wondered at these developments, and how they could have happened. Yet, like so often of late, he did not find any answers.

Hoping, and yet knowing, he took in a deep breath, and gently let it out over and around the clay people, its warmth and life an attempt to revive the little figures. Many, many minutes went by, but, as Seb expected yet did not wish, there was no movement or warmth or life to be seen.

He let out a deep sigh. He was tired, confused, shocked, pained and amazed by all that had happened that day; and in his heart he was sad, miserably sad, as he had no idea what to do next to bring back to life his little clay people, or even how to try. Seb went to sleep with tears in his eyes, and tears on his favourite pillow.

# Chapter Four
# Odd Meetings and Diggings

Thankfully, the new day dawned bright and warm, and Seb awoke feeling focussed, and ready for what he had to do. The clay people remained cold and heavy, but, charging his will power, he got up, determined that he could change things, sure that the adventure was not over, certain that this was only the beginning.

Hannah and her mother arrived at 9.00am on the dot. Though her thoughts were still confused from the day before, she looked very happy and was excited by her expectations of the coming day.

Elaine had made them packed lunches, and insisted this time that he took his mobile phone with him, "*just in case*". He persuaded her that because they were going digging for fossils and things, it would be best if Star stayed at home. After a few minutes the companions set off, chatting as they ambled, their mothers glowing with pride as they watched them and waved goodbye.

"Where are we going today, Seb?" Hannah asked, as they walked down Sandy Lane.

"I want to go back to Little River Pond and see what it looks like now, after all that rain and the weird storm."

"Ok, but can we go up the Tor first, I haven't been to the top for years, and it's *such* a beautiful day? Please...."

"I don't mind, as long as there aren't too many tourists and.....and other people up there." He replied.

They turned right, and walked through the scented woods and along the high root covered path that overlooked the road. Then they climbed over a small broken gate and headed straight towards the Tor, which, at this time of the day, was apparently deserted. Skirting the Massive Meadow, they rambled around the flower bedecked lanes at the foot of the famous Tor, discussing all that had happened the previous day.

Nervously, Hannah asked, "What do you think those *shadows* were? What made them, I mean, how did they happen, and why were they so cold?"

"I don't know." Seb answered, "I really don't know. At first I thought I was imagining them, down by Gog and Magog; but how could we both imagine the same things and feelings? Maybe it was something in the sky, crossing the sun…."

"And maybe it wasn't, Seb. When those shadows went over me, or whatever they did, they made me feel *really* cold, like, ugh, like they had walked right in and through my body. It was horrible."

Seb did not want to admit it, but he knew that he felt the same, and then he said so.

"And when we were at the Shadow Stream, there were so many of them, and they were icy and felt like they were touching me, and, and, they were foul." Hannah continued, not enjoying the memories at all.

"Hold on!" he said as he stopped, "Let's think about this; let's try and work it out. Now, shadows are caused by something, what's the word, not thicker, but….?"

"Denser?" Hannah put in.

"Yes, by something denser than light, passing in front of a light source."

"Ok, I agree with that."

"Try to remember, Hannah, when we first saw the shadows by Gog and Magog, where exactly was the sun?"

"It was straight behind us, back towards the Tor."

"Yes, it was, and where were those hideous shadows? I mean, were they pointing away from us or towards us?

They both thought for some moments, trying to recall exactly what they had seen.

"They were pointing towards us." Hannah said very quietly, but definitely, unsure whether she really wanted to get to the conclusion of this.

"Towards us, Hannah, towards us; yet the sun was behind us, so normal shadows would have been pointing *away* from us. Well, normal if something was passing in front of the sun, that at the time we didn't see."

"Yes……. So what does that mean?" She quizzed, trying not to answer the question herself.

"What it means is, it means….." he stopped speaking as he realised what he was about say, and he began to stutter,

"I, it, means, one o-of two things." He slapped his own face in a jokey manner, trying hard to collect himself.

"It means, that either there was another light source ahead of us, that we didn't see, or……"

"Or that the shadows were things in themselves, and weren't caused by something dense passing in front of a light, at least not a light that you and I could see." Hannah spoke quickly.

"Yes, that's it, that they were *shadow things*, not shadows *of* things!" he blurted out.

"But which, Seb? I didn't see any other light! It would have been so bright that we couldn't have missed it."

"And there aren't such things as shadow things, I mean, shadow beings or shadow creatures – are there?" He added.

An intense silence surrounded them, and they were unaware of everything around them; they were locked together in deep thought.

"And what about down by the stream, in the woods, there was hardly any sunlight in there, you know, *direct* light, but those shadows were dark and deep and cold? And they were pointing away from us, when the sun was in front of us!" Hannah said.

After another long pause, Seb spoke, "Well, if it can't be any of those reasons, there's only one thing left."

"And that is?"

"It must have been some freak of nature, or light, or something else which we don't understand. And if it doesn't happen again, then that is what it was."

58

Though it did not sound correct to either of them, it was the most desirable of the three causes, and they both began to convince themselves of its truth.

"Yes, you're probably right, Seb, just a natural phenomena or something. And although they were horrible and cold, they didn't hurt us did they?"

He held his head, and muttered, "But they did hurt them."

"Hurt them? Hurt who?" Hannah asked.

After a few moments, Seb answered, "Come on. Let's go, let's go to the top of the Tor and I'll tell you. I'll tell you everything, but you must promise me, on your soul, that you won't tell anyone else, *anyone*, not even one other person."

"I promise, Seb, honestly, I do. And will you tell me about the giant tree, and about that hole in your hand?"

"What h....." he stopped, and realised that he had been pressing his thumb into the round dent in his right palm; it was a perfect circle, like a tiny bowl or crater. He closed his hand hard and tight.

"I, I'm not sure about that, I don't know how it happened, but we'll see if we can find out later."

"Does it hurt?"

"It's strange, but no, it doesn't hurt at all."

✫　✫　✫

Without another word, they both turned and walked up the road towards the gate that led to the Tor. There was an opaque shimmering mist around its base, which made it appear as if it was floating above the lush green and flower peppered fields that surrounded it.

When they got to the top, they found that it was one of those rare summer days when no one else at all was up there; and they were both very relieved. The view was staggering for miles around, and from above, the thick mist beneath them looked like an enormous white ring, separating them from all that was hidden below it.

They sat down with their backs to the warm tower, and Seb began to tell his story, starting from the grey wet day when he had dug up the clay down at the Little River Pond, and found himself in the middle of swirling air, mist and beautiful songs. Hannah did not speak while the story unfolded. She was entranced by all that she heard, and was captivated by his vivid and gentle descriptions, caught up as much by his voice as by what he was actually saying.

"Well, that's it. That's all of it, Hannah." As he said these last words, he heard the sound of the wind coursing through lively leaves, and he turned. Hannah turned as well.

"Did you hear that?" He asked quietly.

"I heard something." She replied.

"What did it sound like to you?"

"Like, like, a fast whooshing, or someone saying shoosh."

"What?"

"It was, it was a long shoosh. What did you hear?"

"The wind in trees."

"I think it might have been an aeroplane, high up."

"Mmm, I doubt that. Think about what I just told you."

"The tree?"

"Yes, the tree. I know what I saw, twice. But, but what do you think of all that I've told you? Does it sound completely crazy?"

Hannah did not reply immediately, she just stared across at the flatlands beyond the town of Glastonbury, and considered carefully all that she had heard.

"No, Seb, it doesn't sound crazy; but I've never heard anything like this in my whole life. You say that these clay people actually talked to you?"

"Yes. Well, not talked like you and me are, but I could hear them somehow and they could hear me."

"And they moved, and walked about?"

"Yes, they did."

She looked deeply into his blue eyes. He closed them. She thought for a moment, and then said,

"No, it is not crazy. You would never, *never*, make up something like this. You don't need to, and you don't want to fool anybody. I, I really do believe you. But where are the clay people now?"

"At home, by my bed, cold and heavy as I said."

For a long time they were silent, staring through the midsummer view, pondering upon what he had said.

Seb looked across the fields to Little River Pond away in the distance, and thought he could make out two shapes by one of the ash trees. Quickly, he opened his rucksack and took out his binoculars. Focussing as fast as he could, he saw two fuzzy people, almost shadowlike, looking around the pond. He took in a sharp deep breath.

"What can you see, Seb?" Hannah insisted.

"I'm not sure, look, down over there, there are two people by the pond, I think."

Hannah took the binoculars, and just as she focussed them the small shapes moved off to the North.

"Do you see them?"

"Yes. But no, they've gone now."

Seb lay back on the grass, staring up at the cloudless blue vault of the sky, and tried to work out, once again, the truth of all that had happened.

"Seb." Hannah said gently. "I *do* believe you; I believe every word you've said. Yet I feel sad that I didn't see the clay people move, and that I didn't hear them speak. Do you think they will ever do it again, or are they….. are they dead?"

"They *cannot* be dead, Hannah, they can't be. The clay itself may be dead and cold, but whatever made the clay move is not; but it's gone, or is stopped from making them warm and alive – but *they* are not dead, I know it, and somehow I *will* bring them back."

Hannah lay down next to him, and they both thought about what to do next, and about how they could bring the clay people back to life. Long minutes passed slowly by, as the sun rose higher above the Tor. The light mist had risen up its sides, hiding the tower and its narrow flat top from everything below. The mist billowed as delicate clouds, mingling with the sunshine in tiny bursts and rays, and like a silent spray it moistened and warmed the Tor's soft summit. The peace was perfect, and the moment was alive.

From everywhere and nowhere a quiet pipe began to play; like a tiny flute or whistle almost birdlike in its song. Seb heard it, but thought it was in his imagination, so confused and relaxed as he was. Hannah heard it too, and sat up, enchanted by the beauty of its melody. She turned and looked into the mist, and gasped.

A shadow stretched towards them out of the mist, though their own shadows pointed back towards it. But it was not the shadow alone which made Hannah, and then Seb, stare back in amazement. Through the swirling mist came six or seven rabbits, dancing and jumping like pets do when their owner has returned from some long time away. They were followed by three foxes, spinning round and around with happy excitement, as they came into the full light of day. Small birds of different kinds flew into the clearing, finches, sparrows, long-tailed tits and wrens among them, singing their hearts out and beating their tiny wings; quickly followed by assorted butterflies and bees, all fluttering in circles in front of the approaching shadow. As the pipe playing became louder, two deer emerged from the mist, shaking their heads and snorting, and tapping their hooves as in a proud and joyful strut.

Seb and Hannah turned around, sitting on their knees, intensely watching and waiting. All the animals turned around and stopped, and looked into the parting mist. Very slowly, a shape began to come through. First a bare foot and leg appeared a few inches above the ground, and then, gradually, as if landing in slow motion, a whole person became clear, holding a long shiny whistle in its left hand, still playing the haunting tune; but not by blowing into it – simply by the graceful arcing of the flute through the air, and the movements of its graceful fingers.

The figure smiled and held out its right hand, and all the animals began to stir. Seb and Hannah could not be sure if this person was a male or a female, for as the moments passed, sometimes it appeared to be one, then the other, then both and then neither. In its short loose clothing of a dark silk, its form was a unique sight to behold, and whatever it was it was young, handsome, beautiful, attractive and powerful all at the same time, and in equal measure.

It moved towards them slowly, smiling, as if in recognition of them. The animals scampered around and past Seb and Hannah, and the figure, accompanied by the music he had heard so long ago, laughed and walked straight by them. A delicious scent surrounded them, as they turned to watch the delightful figure stop at the summit's edge, turn, and raise its long right hand. A bright light seemed to beam out from its palm, its smiling eyes sparkled like polished precious stones; and then it bowed gracefully, the mist rushed in from all directions, and it was gone, save for the distant sound of dreamy pipe music.

The sun burst through the departing mist. Seb and Hannah stood up and looked at each other, and then around at the deserted Tor. What had happened, what on earth had happened, was the look they gave each other. Eventually, Hannah spoke first.

"I've always thought that Glastonbury was an odd place, but he, or she was the oddest thing I have *ever* seen in my life. How did it do it? I mean, all those animals, and that music and… do you think its something to do with drugs?"

Seb snorted with laughter, "Drugs!" he chuckled, "Drugs – what us, or that…… person?"

"Not us, fool, him or her. That wasn't anything normal!"

"No, you're right, it certainly wasn't normal, and I'm not sure if it was even real." He replied, as he tried very hard to stop smiling.

As he finished, again they heard the sound of rustling leaves moving in a gentle breeze; and this time there was a scent with the sound, a spicy, earthy, hot sort of scent. They breathed in through their noses, looked at each other, and laughed.

"What's happening again today?" Hannah asked, "Seeing things which may or may not be real, hearing music, and leaves, smelling….. who knows what? This *is* becoming normal, all this abnormal stuff!"

"Hello Seb." A deep voice said from behind them.

They spun around to see a tall, thin, well-dressed and silver haired man standing there, and he was smiling at them.

"Mr. Baines!" Seb blurted out, "H, hello Mr. Baines."

"Yes, hello Seb, and who is your lovely friend?"

"Sorry, sir, this is Hannah. Hannah, this is Mr. Baines, a teacher from my school." Hannah and the teacher shook hands.

"So, first day of the holidays eh, Seb?" Mr. Baines said, and after a smiling pause he continued, "I hope you remembered to clear out your *locker.*"

Seb stared hard at his teacher, and was speechless, struck dumb by the last memory of his locker. The palm of his right hand began to itch quite badly, and he tried to scratch it on the backside of his jeans. Hannah looked at him, and then at his hand rubbing his bottom, and nudged him hard.

He snapped out of it, and said, "Yes, sir, yes, I did."

"Good. Good lad. Don't want anything frightening its next occupant, *do we*?" He pierced Seb with his sharp green eyes.

"What do you mean by that?" he replied sharply, a surge of anger rising inside him. Hannah looked at him, surprised at the change in his voice and tone.

Mr. Baines leaned forward, all the while staring directly into Seb's eyes, and said quietly, "Listen to me, *boy.* In or out of school I am your master, and you will speak to me with respect, and not, I repeat *not* with that demanding tone in your voice. Do you understand?"

"Yes, yes sir; but what did you mean, about my locker, sir?"

"It is a sunny day, Seb, and I do not wish to think about the variety of unwholesome objects that teenage boys leave in their lockers. Is that not so, Hannah?"

Hannah did not reply, she just offered a false giggle instead, as her face began to blush.

"Anyway, enough of that! Tell me, was that one of you playing the pipes or flute a few minutes ago?" Mr. Baines asked.

"No." They replied, almost at the same time.

"*No*? Well, you had your backs to me, and there was no one else up here, yet, I distinctly heard music coming from where you were sitting. Was it a radio, or a bipod, or whatever you call those things?"

"i-pod, sir, and no, it wasn't."

An uneasy silence followed for a few moments, until Hannah asked, "Did you see the mist then, and the animals?"

"Mist? What mist? *Scotch* mist? The air is as clear as crystal today, you were sitting in bright sunshine. And what animals are you talking about, elephants, wildebeest or migrating elk?" He laughed at his own humour, yet Seb and Hannah did not; they were feeling increasingly uncomfortable with this apparently chance meeting.

"No, not those sir. Rabbits, and deer and birds." Seb said quietly, not really wanting to hear the reply.

"Ah! *Those* sorts of animals, Seb. Why did you not say so? But no, I saw no animals and I saw no mist, as there was none of either to be seen. Yet, again I say, I *did* hear music, so where was that coming from if not from you? Unless the rabbits were playing the pipes to the deer!" Mr. Baines finished sarcastically.

Seb smirked, but now it was Hannah's turn to feel angry at this strange teacher.

"No, they were not!" she said firmly, "They were dancing, dancing to the music being played by, by.......... someone. That is what you heard!"

Mr. Baines rubbed his long chin, and stroked his nose as if thinking hard. Then he asked, "Someone? What someone? Was it a man or a woman?"

"I'm not sure." Hannah replied.

"Well?" he asked, turning to Seb.

"I don't know sir; it was sort of both, or neither."

Mr. Baines looked lost for words, but said, "At your age you should know the difference. But, ok you two, it's a hot day, and good for fun I'm sure, but as for me, dancing rabbits and deer, invisible mist, and a mixed or no gender pipe player, are all too much I am afraid. So I shall take my leave, and trust that you both......." At that moment they all heard the sound of pipes playing from the slopes of the Tor.

"Hah! Pipes again; good day to you both, and, nice try!" Mr. Baines said, as he laughed his way to the edge of the summit. Seb and Hannah followed him, and saw him stride down the

66

Tor towards a man in a kilt playing the bagpipes, surrounded by long-haired bongo players, dogs and dancing hippy women.

✩  ✩  ✩

Half an hour later, Seb and Hannah were walking down the Tor's eastern steps, having discussed what had just happened, and agreeing that it *had* actually happened, no matter what, and no matter that they did not understand how it was done. They came to the conclusion that it was some "hippy trick", which was harmless but also lovely; but no mention was made of the sound of leaves, and the hot spicy scent in the air.

The day became very warm as they ambled along the road to the Massive Meadow. Seb decided to take a short cut, and climbed over a rusty gate set into a high wild hedge. As Hannah did the same, her skirt caught on some rusty barbed wire, which spoiled her jump and cut her on the thigh.

"Are you all right?" Seb asked, "Sorry, I should have helped you."

Hannah looked at her leg, which was hurting a lot and bleeding, and she dabbed at it with her torn skirt.

"I'm ok." She said, "No, don't worry, it will stop in a minute." She rummaged in her shoulder bag, pulled out a large plaster, and put it over the jagged cut. "There, perfect!"

"Yes, perfect." Seb echoed quietly.

They walked to the middle of the meadow, which was a vivid spread of many-coloured flowers, tall grasses, and hosts of lively insects, and turned to the right. Suddenly, Seb grabbed Hannah's arm.

"Look!" He whispered.

Instinctively they knelt down, and peered across the meadow to Little River Pond, and saw two people, or two dark shapes, moving quickly to and fro between the trees and the clay bank.

"What's the matter?" Hannah asked, "They can be there if they like."

"Watch!" he whispered, "Watch, look, they're not people, they're...."

He stopped mid-sentence, as they both saw the two shapes get larger, and larger, yet less and less dark, until like powder in a swift breeze they became invisible, and disappeared into the pure summer brightness.

Seb stood up quickly and ran towards the Little River Pond, almost in panic, with Hannah following behind him calling out his name. As he got to the clay bank he leapt down into it, and turned, and stared at its dry dusty surface, holding his head as if in great pain. There were many large holes in the bank, with deep ridges scored all around them, like the claw marks of some raging beast that had been ripping and tearing at the hard earth.

"Oh no!" he cried out, "No!" And he began pulling at the holes and smashing up the clods of dusty clay that were scattered on the ground, kicking madly at the bank in a wild and uncontrolled frenzy.

"Seb!" Hannah shouted, "Seb! What's the matter, what is it? Stop! Please stop!"

Seb sank to his knees, his breath now fitting fast and shallow, as a violent asthma attack overtook him and crushed at his pounding chest.

Hannah grabbed him as he fell, whispering urgently, "What's happening, what's…. Oh hell! Seb, don't, please don't, what can I do, *please*?"

"My bag, in my bag, inhaler." He gasped.

She pulled the bag off him and scrabbled inside it, almost screaming with frantic fear. "There are two, two, which one?"

"Blue!" He said, choking from the effort.

She pulled out the blue one, turned her friend over and sat him up, placing the inhaler in his trembling hand.

"Go on! Use it Seb!" she cried out.

He used it, and within a minute or two he was breathing normally again, lying in Hannah's arms, and smiling up at her.

She smiled back, and said, "Better? Oh for heaven's sake, you terrified me you…."

As if from nowhere two shadows came upon them, and stopped, obscuring the light from the sun.

"Well, this *is* a pretty scene, is it not?" A thin and strange voice said.

"Yeah, it sure is." A higher pitched voice answered.

Hannah and Seb looked up, but they could only see silhouettes, with the blinding sunlight blazing behind them.

"Have you seen them move?" the man with the thin voice asked.

"What!" cried Seb, jumping up, remembering the words in hideous writing that he had found on the card in his locker.

"Seb, don't, please; don't make it happen again." Hannah said, trying to calm him down.

He shielded his eyes, and could then see Steven Ade and his skinny son Julian, standing there and staring down at them.

"What do you mean, *have you seen them move*, what do you mean by that?" He asked, in a calm but forceful tone.

"Nothing, I *meant* nothing at all, Seb. I was just asking Julian here if he had seen either of you move, as you looked like statues from here, all covered with clay dust and dirt." Ade replied slowly.

"Yeah, yeah, right Dad." Julian agreed, with a similar half sneer to his father.

"Oh, sorry, hello, sorry, but you surprised us and I was….."

"I can see exactly what you were doing, Seb, very plainly." Ade interrupted, "But what a mess it is here, and that you're both in. Are you looking for something?" He finished.

"No, not really, we just came out for a picnic and a walk." Hannah replied getting up.

Seb looked long and thoughtfully at Steven Ade. He did not like him, and he did not trust him since his mother had shown him his room; but there was something else about him that disturbed Seb – the half sneer, the sunken eyes with eyebrows meeting over the bridge of his sharp broken nose, the thin all-knowing voice, all too animal like for Seb's liking.

69

"Yeah, huh, *picnic* eh, Seb? Yeah, we know what you mean." said Julian.

"Back off, Ade! Keep your nasty thoughts to your nasty self." Seb retorted.

"Now boys, ease off, save it for the rugby pitch. Come on you, we've got work to do." Ade said, as he clipped the back of his son's head, and marched away towards the main road; with Julian scuttling behind him, while making rude gestures at Seb.

☆  ☆  ☆

The two friends sat in the glorious sunshine and ate their welcome packed-lunch, chatting about what had happened that day, relaxing, and allowing Seb to recover from his asthma attack.

"Why did you run off like that, and go so crazy when you got here? I've never seen you behave so weirdly before. What's up?" Hannah asked.

He finished his drink, scratched his head and said, "I was looking for something, but, but I think it's gone or been taken."

"What was it?" she questioned.

"I'm not sure, but...... but look at this." He answered, holding out his right hand, and showing her the concave circular dent in its palm. "Look at it. Yesterday, during that freak storm, and, and whatever else was going on, I saw something here, in this clay bank, something shining and bright. As I slipped I tried to grab it, but I couldn't hold on to it, and it felt hot, no, not hot, but warm or sort of electric, or something like that. That's why I wanted to come back here today. I wanted to find it, and, and I'm not sure what else, I just felt that I had to try to find it, whatever it was."

"Right, where was it you grabbed this thing?"

"Just here somewhere; but look at all those holes and scrapings, someone or some thing has been digging here, and it's gone."

"Not necessarily, Seb." Hannah said, trying to be optimistic, "Let's dig around a bit, come on!"

70

They threw their bags to the top of the bank, found a couple of broken branches, and started digging and turning over the dry clumps of clay, breaking some while examining others. After about twenty minutes they sat down again, very hot, tired, and disappointed.

"It's gone. Whatever it was it's gone, or lost, or it's been taken." Seb said, as he put his head in his hands, closed his eyes, and tried to shut out the empty feeling he had inside himself.

Hannah sighed, got up, and edged her way down the bank to Little River Pond, which was still half full from the freak storm the day before. There was no wind, and the air was still, the trees and grasses were still, the insects and birds and animals were still, the earth and the day seemed to be totally still as she stared at the glassy smooth surface of the pond. In its reflection she saw a bright full moon appear, from out of a dense moving cloud. She gasped, and looked up, only to see the midday sun dazzling in a clear azure sky. Shocked and confused, she looked back at the pond, which now appeared to be black, as if reflecting a pitch dark night. A twinkle of light began to appear in the darkness, like a tiny star in the reflected night sky; but as she looked deeper and deeper into the pond, she saw that the light was not a reflection *on* it, but a sparkling glow *in* the pond itself.

"Seb, Seb, come here, quickly!" she ordered.

He jumped up and stumbled to her side, "What?" he asked.

"Look, look down there at the bottom, no there, what is it?"

He focussed his eyes, and then he saw the shining light too, in the darkness of the silent little pool. Hannah bent down and picked up a long broken branch from the ash tree, and went to poke it into the pond.

"No, don't do that!" Seb said urgently, "You'll stir up the mud, and bury it. I'm going in. Keep your eyes on it, Hannah!"

He took off his trainers and socks as quickly as he could, rolled up his jeans, and stepped carefully into the pond. Although the water was only a few inches deep, he sank up to his knees in the dark soft mud, which oozed great bubbles and created a most foul smell.

"Here, hold on to the branch!" Hannah ordered, as she leaned over and stretched it out to him. He grabbed the branch with his left hand, and lowered his face to the surface of the pond, trying hard to ignore the awful smell.

"I can see it, it's just, just, oh damn it's just out of reach!" He said.

Putting his right hand under the water, he stretched down as far as he could go. At that moment his other hand slipped off the branch, Hannah shouted, and he splashed down into the filthy muddy pool. As he sank he grabbed through the water, and held on to a solid heavy object. He tried to get up, but he was stuck in the bubbling blackness of the vile mud, which seemed to be sucking him deeper and down. He felt his jeans being pulled as he ran out of breath, and held onto them as they started to come off. Seconds later he was yanked backwards as Hannah wrestled with his jeans, trying desperately to pull him out of the pool. He twisted, lunged out his hand, and dug his fingers into the solid bank. Hannah slipped in the mud and fell face down on top of him, and then into the foul stinking pond. Holding each other's hands, they struggled and strained and finally emerged out of the black water, covered by dark mud which had the most disgusting smell. Coughing and spluttering they cleared their eyes and looked at each other, and then burst out laughing at what they each could see – a totally filthy smelly mess!

When they finally stopped giggling, Seb held up what he had taken from the pond, a mud-covered lump of stone, not much bigger than a cricket ball; but it was heavy, very heavy for its size. He tried to wipe off the mud, but only added to it with the slime from his hands.

"Come on, let's get the water." He said, and again they looked at each other, and at their wet and filthy state, and had to laugh.

They slipped and stumbled their way up the bank, sat at the top, and found their bottles of drinking water. They poured some onto the stone, and looked; but it was only a stone – grey, marbled, solid and heavy, but still only a stone. Seb sighed, but Hannah turned the stone over, and they were dazzled by the light that sprang out of it; a searing piercing red light, as brilliant as a miniature star.

Seb put his rucksack behind the stone to shade it from the afternoon sun, and they looked at it long and hard. There, half sunk in or half emerged from the encasing stone, was the top of a shiny reddy-gold or golden red ball, so smooth and clean and perfect in its shape and vibrant colour, that it astonished them and held them speechless by its most peculiar beauty.

"*Wow!*" exclaimed Hannah, "What on earth is it? It's incredible!"

Seb did not reply, but gently touched the surface of the ball with his index finger. Hannah did the same.

"It's warm!" she said after a few moments, "Warm, and…. What is it? Glass? Or metal? Or…"

They bent over and took a closer look at it, then at the same time looked at each other, with ever widening eyes.

"What are you thinking, Seb?"

"I, there are no….. I mean, it doesn't, I mean…"

"You mean there are no reflections." She whispered, "No reflections of anything at all, even though it is so shiny and smooth and clear."

"Yes." He whispered back, "It's like….. it looks…. it feels…. like it's alive!"

They both looked at it carefully again, and indeed on its red-gold surface and within its gold-red form tiny movements could almost be seen – almost, but not quite, so subtle were the minute changes upon and within it, like golden clouds evolving above a living red planet.

After what seemed like a long silent hour, Hannah said again, "Wow! That is really, I mean *really* awesome. What are we going to do with it?"

"We're going to take it home, now. But, but Hannah, please, we must keep this to ourselves until we know what it is. Tomorrow I'm going to try and get it out of this stone, and then maybe we'll see what it really is."

"Ok, I agree, sounds good. This is *so* exciting, but I want to be with you when you try to release it, if that's ok with you."

He looked at Hannah, and then smiled and said, "I think we're in this together now. I felt it, you saw it, so it's down to us both to see what happens next. Agreed?"

"Agreed; *definitely.*"

As one they shook dirty hands firmly, as if making a pact to help and stand by each other, whatsoever may come or happen next.

# Chapter Five

# Impatience

"I'm not sure, Sebastian, not at all sure about that." His mother said, in reply to his request that Hannah be allowed to come over the following day.

"Two days running you have come home filthy and worn out, after doing heaven knows what; and I'm concerned, very concerned that you two don't know how to look after each other, and that one or both of you will get hurt. While Hannah's here it's *my* responsibility to see that nothing happens to her."

"Look, I know, I know Mum, but today was an accident, we were just mucking about, I slipped, Hannah helped me and then she slipped. We're fine, and I promise we won't go near water again tomorrow."

"*Mucking* about is right; but what are you both doing all day? Come on, are you hiding something?"

"No, I'm not, we're just, just exploring, and it's great that we're allowed to do it. We *will* be safe, please, we *will* look after each other better, we've already agreed to that, and we'll stay away from anything even the slightest bit dangerous."

"Mmm. I'll call Inga and see what she says."

Elaine went into the garden to make the telephone call, and after a long ten minutes came back in and said, "Inga feels the same as me, but we have agreed to give you both another chance, even though Hannah's leg is hurting a great deal from that barbed-wire cut. So, no water, no climbing trees, no barbed-wire and no digging; just *safe* exploring, do you understand?"

"Yes, I do; and thanks Mum"

"And you must take Star with you. She needs the exercise, and *you* need her dog-sense about doing silly and dangerous things."

"Ok, Mum, that'll be great. Thanks." Seb gave his mother a kiss on the cheek as he went upstairs to have a long hot soak, and an early night for once.

✫ ✩ ☆

Before getting into bed, Seb took the stone out of his rucksack and placed it on his table, shining his small bendy lamp light upon it. The first thing he noticed was that the protruding ball had changed colour; instead of red and gold, it now appeared to be blue or green, or bluey-green and silver. Yet still, whichever way he looked at it, or shone his light on it, no reflections could be seen of his lamp, his face, his room or anything else; it was just shiny and deep in a way he could not understand.

He rummaged in the boxes under his bed and found his magnifying glass, and a couple of old watchmaker's screwdrivers. He focussed the glass on the ball and examined it carefully, and again, in a way almost impossible to notice, there seemed to be very subtle movements of the silver within and around the bluey-green; but the most peculiar thing was that the deeper he looked into it the deeper it appeared to be, until it felt like he was looking into its centre from a great height, or even from outer space. He put the magnifying glass down and shook his head. Whatever it was, it was not made of glass, or metal, or stone, and even though it had a surface it seemed to have no obvious edge, it just phased into the space and light around it.

He picked up one of the screwdrivers, and began to chip away at the stone around the ball, trying carefully not to scratch its shiny surface; but the stone was hard, extremely hard, and he could not make even the smallest part of it break off. He dug stronger and harder, and, as could be predicted, the screwdriver slipped and dragged quickly across the blue-green ball. Seb gasped, and whispered, "Oh no!" He grabbed the magnifying glass and looked at the ball, but there was no scratch, or mark, or dent to be seen on it. Then, as any inquisitive teenage boy would do, he deliberately tried to scratch or mark the ball's surface – but try as he may he could not change it or damage it, it was like trying to cut thick air, or dense water, or heavy light, and felt as if it was made of a shiny liquid, at once both soft and yet strongly solid. No matter how hard he poked at it, he could make no impression on the little living sphere.

Seb smiled and was relieved, but also amazed at whatever it was in front of him. Finding an old t-shirt, he wrapped the stone inside it and shoved it far back under his bed. He sat on the floor and looked to the top of his chest of drawers, and at the two clay figures that stood there. Placing them in his hands, he looked long and affectionately at the clay people, and, once again, though they were cold and heavy, he could see that their features and bodies had changed. Tiny eyes and noses and mouths were fully formed; clay hair shapes had begun to appear, small well-defined hands and fingers, feet and toes, and even the beginnings of some sort of clothing were now revealed. The one, Serren, now looked definitely more like a female; and the other, Lynn, had the features and form more like a male; but still they appeared to be lifeless, unable to move, and void of any warmth.

He took in a deep breath, closed his eyes, made a profound wish, and slowly breathed onto the clay people. When all his breath was spent, he looked at them and waited; and waited, and watched and waited, but after many minutes he knew that his breath alone was not sufficient to bring them to life again. Yet he was sure that something, somehow, would.

Putting the clay people back in their place, Seb slipped into bed, impatient for the next day, impatient to find out what the shining ball was, impatient that his clay figures were still lifeless; but most of all impatient to understand everything that was happening in his life, or, as it was now appearing to him, his two lives – the one that he knew so well, and the other that was so astonishing and which brought such daily surprises.

As he drifted into the place of sleep and the hours of the night, somewhere, far off, soft familiar ethereal music was playing; and he smiled as it soothed him into dreams and deep rest.

# Chapter Six
# Hannah's Dream

That same evening, Hannah suffered a similar talking to from her mother as Seb did from his. The same warnings and cautions were issued, and after a hot bath, Hannah went to her bedroom and reflected upon the events of the day.

There was so very much that she did not understand, and her feelings were all jumbled up; but she felt clear about one thing, that what was happening was exciting, and amazing, and more enjoyable than anything else she could have been doing at the start of her long summer break. She was glad that she was a part of it, glad to know Seb, and very glad that there was definitely more to come.

As she sat on her bed, impatient for the following day, she could feel her leg throbbing from the deep barbed-wire cut. She had treated it, and covered it as best as she could, but still it was painful, and hot and pulsing hard. She was concerned that it had become infected, as she began to feel rather odd, like she had the beginnings of a temperature or a fever; but she was also very tired, and needed to rest and to stop thinking.

Within moments of getting into bed, Hannah was sinking peacefully into sleep, and walking into a familiar dream.

*It was a very hot day as she climbed her way to the top of the steep rocky hill, and when she got there the view was immense and one that she loved so well. A flat plain stretched out for many miles in front of her, and upon it, running wild, fast and free, were thousands upon thousands of horses.*

*She was wearing her short tunic and interlaced belt, with her bow and a quiver of arrows over her shoulder. She sat down and smiled, feeling at home and safe and excited, as she looked to the end of the plain and watched the mighty sea rolling in over the shining sands. A long way out from the shore was a huge towering rocky island, which looked red as it soaked in the sunshine, and darkened the sea with its shadow. A great range of snow-capped mountains stretched across the far horizon, and to her right in the distance, was a bright shimmering light, from the mountain made of crystal.*

*There was someone sitting next to her, but she did not look at him or speak to him; yet she was very glad that he was there beside her. She stood up, and walked down the grassy hill onto the plain, feeling the vibrations of innumerable hooves beating upon the fertile ground. The grasses on the plain were long and seed-topped, and the air was full of dust and scented pollen. She walked along the edge of the plain, laughing at the horses that ran and played not far from her; and she called out many names as if she knew them all from of old.*

*When she got to the sea, she took off her sandals, her belt, her quiver and bow, and walked into the long shallow waves. The water was warm and clear, and she dived into it with familiar pleasure. Swimming underwater she could see as clearly as if she was on land, and she smiled as brilliantly coloured fish shoaled all around her, and followed her, and mirrored her every movement. She could stay beneath the waves for as long as she wanted, as she did not breathe and did not need to breathe, because she was in an element she felt easy to move and to live in. So she swam and rose with the dolphins, and then dived and swam again.*

*Emerging from the sea, the heat of the day dried her as she walked along the soft sandy shore. Turning to the hill she had walked down from, she saw a small figure standing there and waving his right hand. She waved back, and smiled, and went off into the plain. Beautiful horses walked all around her, and snorted and nodded their heads as they greeted her return. She was looking at them all, but seeking one in particular, and then she saw it and it saw her; a tall deep blue-brown mare with a white star on her fine brow. She walked for miles with the friendly horse, and they both watched as vast flocks of birds scattered from the long grasses as they approached. It was a beautiful day, and she was happy, and she never wanted to leave this lovely place.*

*Putting her belt and her sandals back on, and shouldering her bow and quiver, she leapt up onto the back of the horse, held its soft white mane, and whispered a few words into its upright ears. Without a pause the horse turned, and skipped up its front legs, and began to run across the great plain. The tall grasses parted before them as the horse*

80

*increased its speed, and the hot wind blew into her face and hair as she laughed with such a wonderful feeling.*

*The horse was heading back across the plain, to some gentle downs that rolled at its distant end; and behind them, dazzling ever brighter as she rode on towards it, was the mighty crystal mountain sending rainbows through the day.*

As she lay in sleep Hannah's leg began to throb, and she turned in her bed to ease it; and the delightful dream departed swiftly into the night.

# Chapter Seven
# A Child of The Sun

It would be difficult to imagine a more beautiful day in England. By mid-morning the splendid sun had warmed the fragrant air, and delicate breezes seemed to dance over and through the lovely grasses that swayed in long rhythms to their movements; millions and millions of long seedy stems moving as one with the great graceful tempo.

Star rushed around at the hedges, as amused birds eluded her springing chase, and butterflies played flirtingly in the quickening meadowy air. Everything seemed well, and healthy and alive; the whole scene a near perfect naturally beautiful experience. Seb pointed out to Hannah the ripening orchards of Paddington Farm, the huge gothic cathedral of Wells, the long spine of the vividly green Mendip Hills, and the great cut in their march that marked the rift of the Cheddar Gorge. Then for some while they were quiet, both appreciating the gorgeous scene in their own particular manner and silence.

"I tried to bring the clay people back to life last night." Seb began.

Hannah sat down next to him on the log seat, which looked over the valley towards Wells and the far off hills.

"And?" she replied.

"And nothing, nothing at all." Then he told her of the changes he had noticed in their faces and forms.

"So they *are* still alive!" she said quickly and excitedly.

"Well….. I just don't know. Yes, they *have* changed, but…… but they are still cold and…… but you're right, something is happening to them, and that's got to be a good sign."

"Did you bring them with you?"

"No, I didn't want to risk losing them after all that's been happening over the past couple of days; but I did bring this!"

He opened his rucksack, took out the old t-shirt, and unwrapped the stone they had found in Little River Pond. He gave it to Hannah, who looked at the bluey-green ball in its centre, with growing amazement and wonder.

"I tried to get it out of the stone, but it wouldn't budge, and the stone is too hard to break…… so," but he realised that she was completely absorbed by the little sphere, and had not heard a word he had said.

"Ohhh….." she sighed, "Oh Seb, it's so, I mean it's, it's like a little world, and it's warm and soft and hard and shiny and …….. fantastic!"

"Yes," he agreed, "it's all of those and maybe more, and it can't be damaged, believe me I have tried; but what the blazes *is it*?"

He held out his right hand for Hannah to give it back to him. She looked at his palm and at the circular dent in it. Then she looked at the shiny sphere, and back to his hand, and gasped out loud.

"What is it? What's the matter?" he asked quickly.

"Keep your hand there Seb, don't move it!"

He did as he was told, and watched, as Hannah turned the stone so that the sphere was underneath. In total silence, she lowered the stone slowly with both hands, so that the sphere was just above the depression in his hand. They stared at each other with mouths open, as they realised that the sphere was *exactly* the same shape and size as the concave impression in his palm.

"Shall I, shall I put it in?" Hannah whispered.

Seb did not answer. He just stared at the sphere and at his hand, and somewhere inside him he knew that this could be another life-changing moment, whatever he decided to do next.

"Seb! Come on, it's really heavy!"

In a split second, myriads of images flooded into his imagination – seas, cliffs, islands, giant trees, horses, huge birds, shadows, clay people, stars, rainbows, suns and worlds; and finally, he whispered, "Yes."

83

Hannah carefully lowered the stone, and the sphere appeared to fit perfectly into his dented palm.

"Help me to hold it up!" he urged, and together they supported the heavy stone.

Almost immediately, they heard a quiet *crack*, and then another and another, as the stone began to split in many places. Within a minute the stone was crazed all over with an intricate web of cracks, until, with one final straining creak, it split apart, and turned into dust as it fell to the ground, and was blown away by the warm hill-top breeze.

✫  ✪  ☆

Seb and Hannah continued to stare at the bluey-green sphere, and to their deep surprise it began to turn slowly in a clockwise direction.

"It's not me, I'm not doing that," Seb whispered, "and it's not touching my hand, look!"

They looked, and could see that the little sphere certainly was not touching his hand, but there was a tiny gap in between it and his skin. It revolved very gently in its own space, and neither of them could move, such was their amazement at what they were observing. Hannah opened her mouth to speak, but before she could draw a breath, for an instant there was total darkness, and then it was daylight again. It was as if the sun itself had blinked.

"What the…….?" Seb tried to speak.

"Good god, look!" Hannah exclaimed.

The sphere was no longer bluey-green, but was red and gold and shining, and was turning quite rapidly now. They looked away as it was so blindingly bright, and then it was Seb's turn to exclaim as he stared across the valley.

"Hannah…… look……get up! For heaven's sake what's happened?"

They stood up quickly, still supporting the revolving sphere, and for a few moments Hannah could not see anything different, as she looked across to the Mendip Hills; but then she saw what Seb meant, and took in a lightning fast breath of realisation.

"My god, Seb..... oh! Wells has gone! And, and, where is Paddington Farm, and the road has gone, and, and all the houses and orchards and fences, and cars, and…."

At that moment, the sun seemed to blink again in a flash of darkness to light; and the scene was just as it had been seconds before. Wells was there, the farm was there, and everything else was there as it should be. Before either of them could speak, an icy cold shadow passed over and through them, and Star bolted out of the hedge barking and snarling at it.

"Come on!" said Seb. "Let's get away from here." And he said this not from fear, but from his awe at what they had both just experienced.

He closed his hand around the beautiful sphere; they grabbed their bags, and walked quickly down the footpath and into the big meadow which led down to Paradise Lane. Star trotted quickly behind them, yet looking back nervously in fear of being followed by shadows.

☆ ☆ ☆

Avoiding the path leading to Gog and Magog, they dropped through a gap in the hedgerow, and made their way down into the valley and the orchards behind Bearclose Farm. They followed the Shadow Stream, away from where they had been two days before, and after a tussle and struggle with deep undergrowth and briars, they came to a little clearing surrounding a small still pool. Sunlight dappled the water and grasses as they came upon a wooden bench, partly hidden behind some reeds and rushes. Sighing and sitting down at the same time, they stopped in silence for many moments, both of them unsure of what to say or do next.

Seb opened his hand, and it was no surprise to see that the sphere was bluey-green once again, and still revolving gently and slowly. He turned his hand over so that he could catch it with his left hand, but it did not drop out. He turned his palm up again, and down, but still the sphere stayed in its own position. Hannah watched in silence as he lifted his arm quickly, trying to throw the ball into the air; but no, it just remained there where it was.

"Let me try." She said, holding his wrist, as she carefully closed her thumb and middle finger around the sphere; but although it stopped turning it stayed close to the dent in his hand, no matter how hard she tried to pull it out.

Seb shook his hand roughly, flicking it backwards and forwards; yet no matter what he did the shining ball remained in its place, gently turning all the while. He was about to speak, when Hannah said,

"Try picking it out with your left hand."

Very carefully, as Hannah had done, he closed his thumb and index finger around the little sphere, and it stopped turning. With no effort at all, he lifted it away from his right hand, and held it up in the air.

"Good grief!" he said, in exasperated surprise, "What on earth *is it*?"

"May I have a look at it, Seb, just for a minute?" Hannah asked.

"Ok, but, …… ok", he replied, as he placed it in her left hand.

Instantly she realised how light it was, merely the weight of a small flower. She held it up to the light, but could not see through it. Then she put it in front of her face, but it did not mirror or reflect her image at all. Again she placed it on the palm of her left hand, and felt how warm and soft and solid it was. Moving it to her right hand, she sat back and stared as it lifted itself a finger's width above her palm, and then began to turn slowly. She closed her hand and the sphere stopped revolving, and stayed still in the grip of her fingers and palm. She opened her hand, and again it rose to a small height above it, and revolved in its own gentle yet powerful way. They looked at each other as if to say "*Weird!*"

"Well, whatever it is, it's beautiful and harmless, and ….. and I don't know what." She said with a certain puzzlement.

86

"I agree, but …. I mean, I'm not sure what I mean, but what's it for? Someone made it somewhere for some reason, so what *is* it for? I mean, what use is it?"

"Beautiful things don't have to have a use, or if they have, their use is simply to *be* beautiful." Hannah replied quietly, still looking at the little sphere.

Seb looked sideways at her, as the sphere turned above her hand, and asked, "Where did *that* come from, about beautiful things?"

"I don't know; but some things just are what they are, never mind what use people can put them to. This beautiful little *thing* is, I think, all part of what is going on, with you, me, the clay people, shadows, vanishing buildings, storms and everything else."

"You're probably right. Heavens, look at it, its staggering ….. But I think we should put it away for now, until we've thought a bit more about all these things."

Seb got out his small digital camera, and opened the black velvet draw-string bag it came in, saying, "Put in here, Hannah."

As if handling a delicate bird, she gently placed the sphere into the darkness of the bag, and Seb pulled the string closed and put it carefully into his rucksack. They both sat back and sighed, full of questions but empty of answers.

"Come on, let's eat." he said, elbowing Hannah in the ribs.

After they had eaten their sandwiches, generously sharing them with Star, they sat on the bench and chatted about all that had been happening.

"Well, at least we're safe today, in a *mum* sense; no mud or water or anything going wrong." Seb remarked.

"Except for the shadows, and my leg." Hannah replied.

"I don't want to think about shadows, but, but what's up with your leg?"

"When the shadows came it was like stepping into a freezer for a few seconds, and then the cut on my leg started to burn and burn. It's hurting now, throbbing, and I'm frightened to look at it."

"Do you want me to take a look?" He asked innocently.

"Mmm, not sure that you should, it's right up here." She answered, pointing near to her hip.

"Ok, you look at it, I'll turn away if you like."

He turned away, as Hannah lifted her skirt and examined her leg. It was badly swollen and bleeding a little, and felt like it was on fire.

"It doesn't look good." She said nervously, "It may even be poisoned or infected. You can see it, Seb; what should I do?"

He examined the swelling which had erupted all around the plaster, and he shivered a little when he saw how bad it was.

"Maybe we should go home, and call your mother, or get mine to treat it; she used to be a nurse and knows what she's doing."

"I know, I know, that's what I *should* do, but today has been so amazing that I don't want to miss whatever may happen next. I've never known a time like this, *never*, and that living ball is so ..... so magical, that ....." Hannah stopped talking, and sat still with her mouth half open, as if looking at something deep inside herself, or listening to her own growing intuition.

"Hannah? What's up?" Silence was the sole reply. "Hannah?" But again a deep thoughtful silence, as she sat there immersed in her ponderings.

She half closed her eyes and said quietly, "Get the little sphere out, Seb."

"What?"

"Please, get the little sphere and put it in your hand."

He took the black velvet bag out of his rucksack, opened it, and placed the little ball in the palm of his right hand. It was reddy-gold again and, as before, it began to revolve slowly just a fraction above his palm. Hannah twisted to her left, and removed the plaster from her leg, revealing a vivid jagged cut surrounded by thick yellow liquid, and an awful red raw swelling.

"Put the sphere near the cut, Seb." She whispered.

Without questioning he did what she requested, and the little sphere turned gently just above her painful leg. Hannah closed her eyes, and felt the burning heat of her wound change into a deep and comfortable warmth. Seb's eyes opened wider and wider as he saw the poisonous liquid appear to evaporate; the swelling changed colour from a violent red to her normal light-olive skin colour, as it got smaller and smaller until it had gone; and a delicate scab formed over the Z shaped cut, until it looked like any other small wound should look – healing, healthy and painless.

"I don't believe it! I, I just don't believe it…" He whispered to Hannah, "Look!"

He took his hand away, and she gasped as she examined the healed wound.

"I knew it; I knew it was alive and good! My god, it's ….." But she was as lost for words as he was, astonished again by what was happening. She put her skirt back in place and hugged her knees, her face beaming with an uncontrollable smile. Seb did the same, with a similar big smile, and tear-tingles in his startled eyes.

After a few moments he asked, "How did you know that was going to happen?"

"I don't know how I knew, but I knew, I just did, and it *had* to be so. Put it back in its bag, Seb, please, it's …….. it's not of this world, no one could have made it, no one, it's *so* special, and you must *never* lose it."

Without hesitation he did as she requested, placing the bag back into his rucksack.

"That's why I didn't want to go home, I just knew that something was going to happen, something good; and I saw this image in my head." Hannah said.

"What did you see?"

"Do you remember, yesterday, when we were on top of the Tor, and that mist came, and the animals, and that ……. that beautiful person?"

"I'll never forget that, no matter what else happens."

"Do you remember as he passed us, he turned and held up his right hand, and it shone like a tiny star?"

"Yes, very clearly."

"*That* is the image I saw in my head; that beautiful person, with the bright light shining in the palm of his hand!"

From out of nowhere a deep voice said, "Huh! The redolent boy!"

☆　☆　☆

"What?" Seb said, turning quickly and looking all around, "Where did *that* come from?"

"*There.*" Hannah replied quietly, pointing with a nod of her head, "Over there, across the pond."

It looked like a deep shadow in the shape of a man, half in and half out of the tangled mass of bushes and briars. They made to run off, but Star trotted around the pool, wagging her tail, and sat down calmly in front of the dark shape.

"Ohhh, typical!" Seb whispered, "That dopey dog!"

"There's no need to run." The deep voice said, as the shadow became a broad, short, limping man. "No need at all. I am no danger to you, or to your clever dog." Star followed, as the dark man began to walk around the pond towards them.

"Do not worry, you two, I mean you no harm, I really don't, and that is my word and promise." The dark man's voice was almost unimaginably deep and solid.

"Don't come any closer!" Seb ordered, "What do you want?"

The broad man stopped, and said, "I want only to talk with you."

"Why?" Seb demanded, "You don't even know us. We just want to go home, so go away and don't try to stop us! Grab the bags, Hannah."

"I am sure you do, and I will not stop you or bother you." The man said.

"You've already bothered us, so stay there and we'll leave. Come on, Hannah!"

90

"You may go if you choose to, but be careful of that dancing pipe-player, and his herd of friends; be very careful, and avoid him at all cost if you can."

"Right, that's it, let's go, Hannah. Come on Star!"

Star ran quickly to his side, and stood quietly, still wagging her tail. He grabbed Hannah's hand and turned to move away, but she resisted.

"Come on, Hannah, please, we've got to go!"

"No, wait Seb …..wait." She turned to look back at the dark man, who was in truth very dark, his face appearing as black as any skin she had ever seen; and his shock of hair, if anything, was even blacker. As she stared at him he began to cough, and he looked so strange on such a hot summer's day, wrapped up tight in a heavy black coat and a ragged thick red scarf.

"Hannah!" Seb pulled at her; but again she resisted, as she turned back to the dark man and asked,

"Why did you call that person *the redolent boy* like that?"

"Because he stinks, and gives off a bad smell wherever he goes." Was the surprising reply.

Hannah frowned at this, but Seb, for some unknown reason, began to giggle.

She dug him in the ribs, and said," Is that what *redolent* means?"

"Well, roughly." was the deep reply.

"But the smell that surrounded him was lovely; it was so, so…"

"Artificial!" The dark man finished her statement, "And far worse than anything that you or I could produce."

Again, Seb tried to suppress a giggle; but Hannah was getting annoyed, and said, "That is *your* opinion; and thankfully we're not close enough to you to find out how redolent *you* are!"

"That is a fair comment." He replied, "But at least mine would be honest, whatever your opinion of its loveliness, or lack of it."

"How can anyone have a dishonest smell?" she continued.

"Your shops are full of them; but they come and are made from the outside. *His*, as you put it, come from the inside, and are designed to trick and fool such as you two, as with everything else he does."

Seb stopped giggling, and began to consider what was being said; but Hannah was getting angry.

"What do you mean by *that*? He was beautiful, his music was beautiful, all the animals, everything about him was ......... good!" she almost shouted.

"You are confusing what appears to be pleasant, with what is good. A pleasant deceit it may be, but it is still deceit, and even more dangerous for that."

"Deceit is it – how do *you* know that?"

"When you looked at *him*, what did you actually see?"

"A boy, or, or a young man; a handsome boy, playing lovely music and dancing beautifully."

"Was that your first thought?"

Hannah considered the question, and then answered honestly, "Well, no. At first I wasn't sure if it was a boy or a girl, or even both; but then it became obvious that it was a boy."

"I won't ask how his boyness became obvious to you."

Again, Seb began to laugh a little; there was something about the man's voice that amused him and intrigued him, so deep, strong and gentle as it was.

"And you, boy, what did *you* see?"

Seb composed himself, thought, and then answered, "A bit the same, but........." He went quiet for a few moments.

"But what?" the dark man asked.

"But, then it became obvious to *me* that it was a girl."

"What kind of a girl did she appear to be?"

"Well, a, I suppose a, well, a beautiful girl or woman."

"Again, I won't ask you how her girlness became so obvious."

It was Hannah's turn to snigger now, as Seb began to blush and scratch his head.

"There you have it. To you it was a male, while to you it was a female, and to both of you it was very attractive. A lovely and charming deceit; you saw what was desirable for you to see." The man finished with a beaming smile.

Silence surrounded the clearing as the day became even hotter. Star ambled down to the pool and drank of its refreshing water.

"But what about the light in his, I mean her, heavens, in his hand, and the animals and music and mist?" Hannah asked, feeling totally confused.

"*She* is both, and *he* is neither, remember this. The rest is all deceit, apart from the music, which is what it is."

Again there was a long silence, until Seb asked, "But why is she so dangerous? She looked so, so, I don't know, so innocent I suppose, and lovely."

"Desire's disguise; she wants something from you."

"Me? Or both of us?" he asked.

"Both of you; otherwise she would have appeared only to one of you."

"But what could he want from *us*?" Hannah asked, struggling to understand.

"I am not sure, yet."

"Do you know him? "She questioned further.

For the first time, the dark man did not answer immediately, but sat looking at his pale palms. Slowly, lifting his head, he replied quietly,

"Yes. I know him."

"And where does she come from?" Seb asked.

"I cannot say."

"Why, don't you know?"

"Because you would not understand; but yes, I do know."

"Do you know her name?"

"She has very many names, but she answers to none of them."

"What about her real name? What's her *real* name?"

"That is a profound question; but I cannot say."

93

"Don't you know it, or wouldn't we understand that either?"

"I am not sure; as I said, it is a very profound question."

"And what's *your* name?"

"If you ask me more politely, boy, I may tell you; if you are really interested."

Hannah knew this would annoy Seb, so she asked, "He might not be interested, but I am. What is your name, please?"

"You may call me, Shale."

At the mention of this name all three of them became silent and even Star sat up at attention, as if waiting for what was going to happen next. After what seemed like many minutes, Seb looked at his watch and said,

"I don't want to sound rude or anything, but we've got to go soon, so, so what do you want with us?"

"I only want to help you, if I can."

"With what?" What do *we* need help with?"

"If nothing else, certainly with that redolent boy; he is trying to stop you."

"Stop us doing what?"

"Understanding."

"But, but, understanding what?"

"Understanding what is happening to you."

"But there's nothing happening to us!" Yet even as he said this, the statement sounded hollow, shallow and empty to all three of them.

"Yes, well....." he continued, "some things have been happening, but, but you say we can't trust that, what you called, redolent boy; but why should we trust *you*? We don't even know you, and you look, well, a bit odd – and I'm not being rude."

"Well said; but I have not always looked like this, and, as for trusting me, I think you are wise to be cautious, as I am of you."

"*Me*?"

"Both of you; for as you don't know me, I don't know you, yet."

"But we're not dangerous!" Hannah spoke up.

94

"Maybe not deliberately; but maybe so, when you don't know what you are doing."

"We know what we're doing."

"Do you, do you really? I am not even sure that you know what you are seeing, and even less about what you are doing?"

"We're seeing what you're seeing." She replied impatiently.

"At this moment, I doubt that."

"What do you mean?"

"Get up, and look behind you."

They did as he said, and saw the terraced hill which led to the foot of the Tor, and its shadowed scarp and tower, with many people on the flat summit.

They turned back to face Shale, and Hannah said, "We're seeing what's there, just the same as you. This is a bit silly."

"Silly is a loose word. Look again, and you may see what I mean."

They turned and looked again, but were stunned, and gasped at what they saw. On top of the Tor was a huge towering tree in full leaf and bloom; the people were gone, as were the terraced ridges, and great smooth slopes stretched all around; and the misty air above the trees was full of countless birds.

"But……." Seb began, as they turned back towards Shale, "Ah!" he cried, as they both saw that where Shale had been, was a tall broad handsome black man, wearing a shiny deep green cloak. They spun back to look at the Tor, and it was as they had always seen it; the tower, and the ridges and the people as before. Slowly turning to face Shale, they saw him again sitting on the ground, dark short and broad, wrapped in his heavy black coat and thick red scarf.

"Who are you? Come on, what's happening?" Seb demanded.

"I have told you my name; but I am not sure what is happening to you both, *except*, that I believe it can only be good."

"Good? You say we're in danger, and that's good!"

"You are only in danger from that redolent boy, and I will take care of him. Believe me, I will not let him harm you, and his influence is your only danger; but I will stop him."

"But why us?" Hannah asked, "Why is this happening to us?"

"Because you are…… different, I think."

"We're not different; we're just like anyone else."

"Not so. If you were, you would not have seen what I see, either of you. But do not worry." As he said this, Shale stood up.

"But what *are* we seeing, and why are we seeing it?"

"Listen to me, carefully. I do not know you, and I am not sure who you are, as you are not sure of whom I am; and you are wise to keep much of this to yourselves. I will deal with *that boy*, but you must deal with the rest according to your own judgement. It could be that we can help each other, odd as that probably sounds to you; but I do not know what all this means, yet. I am very old, and getting extremely tired, and I have forgotten so very much; but you are young, and maybe will remember very much, so watch and learn, and be happy. If nothing else, you are having quite an adventure, so enjoy it and trust in each other." As he finished, Shale turned as if to leave.

"But you said you wanted to help *us*, will we see you again?" Seb asked.

"Yes, you will." Shale replied.

"When?" Hannah asked.

"I will find you soon." Again, he turned to go.

"Please, Shale, my name is Hannah, and this is Seb."

Shale bowed his head silently to each of them in turn, and said, "It is a relief to meet you both."

"One last question, please." Seb said politely, "Why are you wearing those heavy clothes on such a blistering day?"

Shale looked at them, and smiled in a way that warmed them deep inside, and answered, "This place is cold to me, as I am a child of the Sun. I will see you again, so take care."

He turned, parted the tangled undergrowth with a brush of his hand, and slowly limped away. Star started to whimper a little, as if she was already missing him; but Hannah and Seb were speechless, as they watched him disappear through the bushes. They turned to each other, and smiled, and felt perfectly safe and happy.

# Chapter Eight
# Certain Doubts

As both mothers were happy that no more mishaps had occurred, and that Hannah's leg had healed so well, even though so strangely fast, the following day Seb and Hannah were allowed out again. It was a hot humid Friday, and the sun was veiled by linen looking clouds, the air loaded with moisture and intense warmth. They chatted as they walked, and both of them felt the tiring effects of the increasingly heavy air. Just half a mile from the barns of Paddington Farm, they wandered into a wooded area known as Ten Man Copse, and sat down at the log and plank picnic table that one of the farm volunteers had knocked together.

"Well, "Hannah began, "what next?"

"I don't know." Seb replied, wiping his brow, "It all seems like a bit of a strange dream at the moment."

"I know what you mean." She continued, "And as for Shale, I'm not sure of him at all. He seems sort of harmless, but how did he know what we were seeing? And why wouldn't he tell us what it was that we were *really* seeing? And, he said he would deal with that *boy*, who didn't seem at all dangerous to me, in fact the opposite; but he didn't mention the shadows."

"Neither did we." Was the factual reply.

"True, but if I was reading this, like in a story, I don't think I would trust Shale. He looks like he has been sleeping rough for too long and I'm not sure he knows what he's talking about."

"He said that much himself, as well as about trusting him; but I bet we probably won't see him again, or that boy or girl. So that leaves us with these."

Seb took the black velvet bag out of his rucksack, opened it, and placed the clay people, and the little sphere, in the middle of the picnic table. The clay figures now looked fully formed, distinct, with facial features of their own, well defined hair and hands and bare feet, delicate clothes and knee length capes.

"Heavens, they look *so* lovely now." Hannah said, "I wish and wish they would come alive again."

"So do I." agreed Seb, "These changes are incredible, but I think that may be the end of them. There is nothing left to change, except their cold lifelessness, and there's nothing I can think of to make that happen."

"I know," Hannah comforted, "I know; but I do believe you, I do believe they were alive."

"Thanks, I mean it; when all this first started it was so……. so, I don't know, so magical and, well, safe. But I'm not so sure now. I've thought a lot about telling someone about it all, my mum or dad, or grandpa, but, but they'd never believe me about the clay people. They'd probably take this little sphere away to be examined or tested or something like that; and if I told them about the shadows, or the countryside changing, or that boy or whatever he is, and then Shale – they'd lock me up and never let me out again. Most of what's been happening has been amazing, but, s, some of it is getting a bit, I don't know, *scary.*"

"I feel the same, Seb, "Hannah agreed, "and I've only been involved for a few days. Last night I thought about telling mum, but I know the thought of me talking to a scruffy old odd limping man in a wood, far from any houses, would have sent her ballistic; and, as I said, I'm not at all sure about him myself, and part of me hopes we won't see him again. But, there was something about him that made me feel sort of safe, for a while."

"Yes, he is pretty weird, but I don't think he's dangerous, at least not to us; but he does look very strong, and I wouldn't fancy mixing it with him. I suppose, what I've been thinking and worrying about is what to do next; or maybe it would be best to do nothing next, and try to forget about it all, and just keep the sphere and see if it does anything else; and if not, hide it away until we know what to do with it. Also, I don't want to get you, or me, into any more trouble with even more things we can't explain or understand."

"Thanks, Seb, but I'm in this with you, and I'm not sure that even by doing nothing next that all this would stop. I mean, every day something different *is* happening, but *not* because you or I have made it happen, or even looked for it to happen. And the only thing we want to make happen is the clay people to come back to life, and that has *not* happened. It *is* a bit scary, but, for me anyway, not in a way that really frightens me a lot, more like, like I would feel if I saw a unicorn, or a dragon, or a giant or something like that...... more awesome than frightening."

Seb turned and looked at her with a smile on his face, and said,

"Well put, hungry-Hannah, I agree. And there seems to be two sides in all of this – what you and I have been doing and seeing, and what other people have been doing."

"What do you mean?"

"Well," he paused, "well, I haven't shown you this before, but I found it in my locker on the last day of term."

From the bottom of his rucksack, he took out the brown card with the lovely drawing of the clay people on it, and the hideous scrawny writing saying – *Have you seen them move?*, and the symbol *C*ll beneath the words.

Hannah studied the card carefully, and asked, "Who did this?"

"I don't know. I don't even know how it got into my locker, which is always locked; it was just there."

"Did you tell anyone about the clay people?"

"Yes, a few of the boys at school; but they just laughed, and probably thought I was just making it up for fun."

"It's one of them then; they probably slipped it in when you weren't looking."

"No, that's not possible, Hannah. Look at the drawing, its brilliant; I do art with all of them, and *none* of them can draw like that, not even half as well, and even if they could, how did

100

they know what the clay people looked like, *exactly* how they looked as I had made them? No, it was none of them."

"So who could it be?"

"I really don't know; but it was someone who knew I had the clay people, and that they had moved, or *could* move, or even *might* move. And that sign or symbol, or whatever it is – what the hell does that mean?"

"That writing is pretty disgusting; but if it wasn't one of your friends, what about a teacher, or a parent?"

"That's what I have been wondering, especially that creep Ade's dad. Do you remember what he said, in that weird voice, *'Have you seen them move?'*

"So that's why you got so angry; but how could he have known about the clay people?"

"I don't know, I don't think he could have. He has been round to my house, but that was after I found the card, I think, I don't know, it's all so confusing." As he finished, Seb scratched his head again.

"Yes, it is. I've read loads of books, as you always remind me, like Narnia and Harry Potter, and Lord of the Rings, and lots of others where magic happens, and there are incredible adventures and amazing events; but there's always *someone* who knows what's going on, or a wise teacher or a wizard master or something like that. Even in the Wizard of Earthsea, Ged knew that he had something to do even if he wasn't sure how to do it; but all this seems so random, wonderful at times, but random, and I can't see anyone wise turning up at the moment to tell us what's going on."

"No, nor can I; unless it's Shale."

They looked at each other, and then laughed a little, as Seb continued, "I don't think so. He only seems to know about that *redolent boy*, as he called her, even though he seems to have seen something similar to us; but for that split second he did change, didn't he, into that tall handsome figure? I wonder how he did that."

"Another hippy trick, do you think?"

"Maybe, but we'll probably never find out; maybe he just stood up into the bright sunlight or something, yet...... But he didn't strike me as a wizard, or a time lord or mystical teacher, or anything like that."

"Nor me, but he was, different, in a strange sort of way. By the way, I looked up *redolent* in the dictionary last night, and it means, *fragrant, or smelling of,* from the Latin redolentis, to emit smell."

"Well, he had that right then, even though he used the word stink instead of fragrant." Seb chuckled.

"I carried on reading the dictionary for a while, before I went to sleep."

Seb pretended to yawn.

"No, don't be like that, it's not a habit of mine; but just near the end of the Rs, I came across the word *rutilant*, which means shining or glowing ruddily, or redly, from the Latin rutilare, to be reddish."

"Marvellous; did you fall asleep then?"

"Please don't, that's not what I meant. Look at the little sphere, shining and glowing ruddily."

She was right, the word described it near perfectly, and they both knew it.

"So;" he summed up, "we have a *redolent* boy, and a *rutilant* sphere. At least we're making progress."

"Don't be sarcastic, Seb. The boy is one thing, but this rutilant sphere is something else; and we do know *something* about it, or, at least about what it can do. But we know nothing about that boy, except that he's...or she's, you know."

Seb picked up the rutilant sphere, and gently placed it in the palm of his right hand; and, just as before, it began to turn slowly as if on its own axis, a fraction above the dent in his hand. For a few minutes they were enchanted by its pure form and motion, until he said,

"But what is it? It seemed to heal your leg, or help heal it; but where on earth does it come from?"

"It's incredible," Hannah replied, "really beautiful, and I can't imagine anyone making it, it's like nothing else I have ever seen before, even what it is made out of is…….. I don't know, I just don't know. It is unique."

"Well, at least we're certain of some things." Seb said quietly, still observing the incessant revolutions of the rutilant sphere.

"Really? And what are they?"

"Our doubts; our doubts are certain, and that's a start, and that this little sphere is unique. My dad has often said that, the better the question the nearer it is to its own answer. *So*, I think we should start asking ourselves better questions, and maybe then we'll get closer to the answers."

"You are getting profound, Sebastian; be careful, you may be in danger of really thinking."

"That's not fair. I've been thinking about all this for months now, it's just that……. It's just all too different, there's too much difference. And that reminds me of another thing my dad has said to me." He stopped, and thought about what he could remember.

"What's that?"

"Well, something like – all things, and everything is made up of sameness and difference; and that where you find the one, you will always find the other. And, what was it? Ah yes, permanency or stillness, and motion. That's it, I remember him saying it in one of his *'never forget this, son'*, moods, and somehow it's stuck. Everything is made up of sameness and difference, and motion and permanency, and, like a recipe, depending upon the amount of each in any thing, so you get different things, or types of life and existence."

"Cakes?"

"Cakes?" he replied.

"Sorry, I'm being silly. What a thing to say to you, your father, I mean. But I suppose, thinking about it, you're right; there have been a lot of different things happening, maybe we should think about if there is anything the same, or similar, in them."

"That sounds tiring."

"Yes, it does, I suppose. Or maybe it will all become obvious in time."

"Let's hope so."

Seb looked at his watch, and said, "They'll be here in a minute." meaning that their two mothers, and Star, would be joining them for a picnic lunch.

For a few more minutes they sat in silence, and looked at the clay people, and the rutilant sphere. Each of them was searching for better questions, and hoping to come up with some real answers; looking for something the same in all the differences, and something stable behind all the change.

Seb put away the little figures and the sphere, and said,

"Wow, that's too much, whatever next, Hannah?"

# Chapter Nine
# A Child of The Moon

Two hours later, Seb and Hannah were walking beside the Shadow Stream, slowly making their way down to the levels north of Glastonbury Tor. The day was still very muggy and humid, but the veiling cloud cover had moved away, leaving the air clear and bright once again. They continued to discuss carefully all that they had been experiencing, but still could not see anything that linked the various happenings together.

"Do you remember what Shale said about the redolent boy, when you asked him where the boy came from?" Hannah asked.

"Yes," Seb replied, "something like, I do know but I cannot tell you because you wouldn't understand."

"That's right; what do you think he meant by that?"

"Well, the more I think about it, the more I think he was just trying to sound knowing or wise, like one of those characters in the books you read. I'm not sure he knows anything really, about that boy, or us, or what's actually going on. He admitted his memory is bad, and everything he said was grumpy and negative; I think he's just old and confused, and as he said, we should be cautious of him. I don't really want to see him again, and I wish you hadn't told him our names."

"I'm sorry, I don't know why I did it. But, just for a moment, I felt I had to, as if he was sort of demanding it or wanting me to. He also said that it was a relief for him to meet us, do you think that was just an act as well?"

"Probably; he didn't say why it was a relief, in fact he didn't say much at all, though he said it in a way that sounded as if he was trying to be mystical or knowing. Maybe he's read too many of those books as well."

"But you've read most of them too."

"I know; but my views on magic and all that stuff have changed, since what Mr. Ransom said to me, and also after all that's been happening."

"What do you mean? You haven't mentioned this before; what did he say?"

"He said, let me try and get his exact words, he said, *Magic is the image and appearance of causes we do not know, and of powers that we do not understand.* "

They stopped, each of them considering these words in their own way. Moving on a little distance, they sat down in the shady avenue that vaulted the babbling stream, and did not say anything for two or three minutes.

"And that, to me, sounds wiser than anything that Shale had to say about all this." Seb said quietly.

Hannah took in a deep breath, and sighed; but as she breathed in again, she became aware of the most delightful scent in the air. She closed her eyes, lay back and let the intoxicating fragrance infuse her sense of smell, and it made her smile.

"Can you smell that, Seb?" she whispered.

"Yes, I can smell something." And he too was captivated by the scent that drifted all around them.

Almost immediately, they heard the gently tripping notes of soft pipe-playing, and opening their eyes they saw not far away down the stream, a beautiful female figure resting on a rock in the middle of the water. It was the redolent boy, or girl as it appeared now to Seb and Hannah. She was lightly dressed in a short shimmering one-piece garment, which reflected the rippling currents of the sparkling stream and the roundels of sunlight that filtered through the leafy canopy. Her long red and gold hair rose and fell in the breeze, as her right foot stirred the water in delicate circles. Her left arm moved as in a graceful dance, and in her hand there was a silver pipe, from which came the most enchanting music, through the mere movement of the air itself and her long slender fingers that moulded the

106

flowing notes. It was a most beautiful sight and sound to behold, until finally the music ended.

She turned to look at them and smiled; and it seemed as if her eyes were like rainbow coloured jewels, emitting a twinkling light which held their gaze for many moments. Putting the pipe under her belt, she stood up on the rock, revealing how very tall and slender she was; and both Seb and Hannah were captured by her most stunningly lovely appearance. She stepped into the stream and began to walk towards them, the water parting like a river of mercury around her long graceful legs. Her face appeared to shine or glow as she stopped a little distance away from them, and said,

"Hello. What brings you here today?"

Her voice was indescribable. It seemed to surround them and charm them, and penetrate into their very hearts; it was young and old, near and far, gentle and strong, lively and calm, and flowed naturally like the stream itself.

Hannah spoke first, and said, "Nothing, nothing at all, we're just out for a walk. Can we help you?"

"I am just out for a walk too. It is so hot, but this stream is always cool and refreshing. I do not wish to disturb you, but I have seen you somewhere before today, if my memory is correct; is this not so?" The redolent girl replied.

"Yes, on top of the Tor the other day; and you had lots of animals with you." Hannah said.

"They do that sometimes, but most of them do not like the water; look at them." She said, laughing and pointing into the trees.

Hannah and Seb turned and saw numerous little faces in the ferns and undergrowth; a few rabbits, a weasel, two badgers, and a number of tiny birds among them.

"Why do they follow you?" Seb asked.

"I think it is because they like me, or feel that they can trust me."

"And can they, trust you, I mean?"

"Seb!" Hannah exclaimed, "What sort of a question is that?"

"It is a good question." The redolent girl replied, "And yes, they can trust me, because I understand them."

"Do you live in the town?" he continued.

"No, I do not. I live here." She replied, crouching down close to Seb, and drinking a handful of water.

"What, in this wood?"

"Sometimes; but really I live wherever I am."

"So you sleep rough?"

"Do I look as if I *sleep rough*, as you put it?" She smiled as she poured water onto her face and neck.

"Well, n, no, not at all; so where is it that you sleep?"

"There are many places for sleep near here, maybe I will show *you* them one day if you like."

He blushed, and became silent; but Hannah changed the subject,

"What's your name, if you don't mind me asking?"

"Of course I do not mind. My name is Lemma."

"Do you know a man called Shale?"

"Yes, I do." Lemma replied; her tone of voice becoming a little more serious, as she stepped out of the water and sat on a fallen tree to their right.

"He said he knew you. He also said we shouldn't trust you."

"Hannah!" It was Seb's turn to object to what he thought was a rude statement.

"What reason did he give for saying that?"

"He said you wanted something from us."

"What would I want from you?"

"I, I'm not sure, he didn't say."

"I do not want anything from you, apart from a little of your time."

"What for?"

"To warn you. You must be careful, Shale is not what he appears to be, and he cannot be believed."

"Are you? I mean, are you what you appear to be? You seem to pop up from nowhere."

"Well, I know I look unusual, and I do not mix with many in this place; but yes, what you see is me, and I never just pop up."

"But, can we trust you?" Seb interrupted.

"Yes, of course you can, both of you. I always mean what I say."

"Shale said that he wouldn't tell us where you come from, because we wouldn't understand; and now you tell us that you live out here somewhere. And he was right, I don't understand. Where exactly do you come from?" Hannah asked, as she became increasingly suspicious of this woman.

109

"I come from exactly here. There is nowhere else but here, howsoever far you may travel."

"What does *that* mean?" Hannah questioned her further.

"You are young, both of you, and are becoming confused. Things are happening to you that you do not understand, or even believe at times. Shale pretends much but remembers little. He is old, weak, angry and foolish, and his time is quickly running out; he knows this. So do not look to him for guidance."

"Do *you* know what has been happening to us?" Seb asked quietly.

"I do." Lemma replied, her lustrous eyes looking deep into his.

"Then tell us, please."

"You are beginning to see more of *here* than most have ever done, and this is what is confusing you."

"But what does *that* mean?" Hannah asked, getting more and more agitated, "How can we see more of here?"

"Here is like there." Lemma replied with a smile.

"And where is *there*?"

"It is here."

"That doesn't make any sense. How can there be here? Here is here, and there is there."

"Not so, Hannah; there is here and here is there, and this is what you have been seeing."

"How do you know my name?"

"A little bird told me; that one above you to be precise."

Hannah looked up, and saw a lively robin sitting on a branch a few feet above her head.

"And did it tell you my name as well?" Seb asked.

Lemma turned to look at him, and stretched out her long legs; she touched her knees slowly and smiled into his attentive eyes.

"Yes, *Seb*, it most surely did."

She said these words in such a way that it made him shiver and feel very peculiar. Hannah could see what effect she was having on him, and started to become quite angry.

"So, why us? Why are *we* seeing these things, if most people don't, and why everything else that's been happening?"

Lemma turned now to Hannah, and looked at her in a way that made her feel small, unimportant, immature, ugly and very childish; but still she smiled, as she said,

"Why, what other things have been happening to you? Have you met anyone else?"

"Well…." Seb began, "Mm, where do we…"

"No; no we haven't." Hannah interrupted, being sure that Seb would tell this person anything she wanted to know.

"You were saying, Seb?" Lemma said, so very affectionately and directly, and totally ignoring Hannah.

"I, I, I'm not sure…" he stammered, "But, no, we haven't met anyone else, only you, and that Shale."

Lemma stared hard at him, as if trying to read his thoughts; but he was so nervous of her, and distracted, that at that moment his thoughts were too scrambled even for him to read them.

"You didn't answer my question about, why us?" Hannah spoke up, trying to be as mature and un-childish as possible.

"Because someone has shown you these things, there is no other way."

"No one has shown us anything, and neither, to be honest, have you."

"I will show you something, if you both so wish."

Hannah looked at Seb for some sort of guidance. She was not the least bit sure that she wanted to be shown anything else; but he just sat there, with a glazed look on his face, staring at Lemma as if hypnotised.

"What will you show us?" Hannah finally asked.

"I can show you one of my resting places."

"Is it far?"

"No, it is just over there." Lemma replied, pointing her finger downstream.

"I'm not sure. What do you think, Seb? Seb, wake up!" she nudged him hard with her elbow.

"Well, I, I suppose so……. but we can't be long, we have to go home soon."

"I understand; but you may find it interesting, and it is on the way to where you are going."

Although Hannah was suspicious, for no obvious reason, she was also curious to know where Lemma came from, and of what kind of life she led. Seb shook his head, as if coming out of a dream, rubbed his eyes, and said,

"Do you want to?"

With some hesitation, Hannah replied, "Ok; but like you said, we must not be too long. Are you sure?"

"As sure as you are." He answered.

"Huh! Typical; come on then. Yes, please, let's have a look at your place." She said, turning to Lemma.

Lemma stood up, saying, "Follow me." And she began to walk away slowly.

Picking up their bags, they followed her; whispering to each other and agreeing that although this was pretty weird, it did not seem at all dangerous. They also agreed to have only a quick look, and then to get off home.

As they walked, Lemma kept stepping into the stream and playing. She laughed as she splashed water over herself, and over Seb and Hannah. This made them laugh too, and in the heat of the day it was fun to play in the cool clear water. Near a sharp bend in the stream, Lemma jumped out and onto the path, and then down into a hollow.

"Here we are." She called out happily.

Seb and Hannah looked down into the shingly little bay, and saw in the steep bank side what appeared to be a door; but it was so much like the earth of the bank, that it was as if someone had drawn a door shape with their finger.

"Come on." Lemma urged, as she pushed at the bank, in which a door did indeed really open.

They jumped down, and closely followed Lemma through the door, which clicked gently, but firmly, behind them.

☆    ☆    ☆

Although now underground, the light around them seemed natural, like a summer's twilight, and try as they may neither Seb nor Hannah could see where it was coming from. They descended a few steps and came into a high arched passage, seamlessly lined with some kind of golden wood, in which were embedded many small round mirrors, which sparkled and reflected as they passed.

Lemma hummed to herself as they walked on, and emerged into a huge room, the walls of which were completely covered with clothes; but these were not the type or make of clothing that Hannah had ever seen or imagined before, as she stared, astonished, at their incredible and beautiful variety.

"Oh!" she exclaimed, "They are *so* gorgeous!"

Even Seb could see what she meant, as he examined the multitude of bedazzling garments. Some seemed to be made of the most pure smooth silk, dyed in the richest of colours, which reflected light and shadows as they moved. Others felt like soft and delicate metal to the touch, cold yet strong and amazingly thin, shimmering in various golds and silvers and bronze greens and coppers, and shining hues of cobalt. Yet others, and these the most striking of all, appeared to be formed from transparent reflective liquids, the colours of which changed when looked at from different angles; and they even felt like liquid as they rippled to the touch, and moved in slow gentle waves. Last of all was an array of garments which were made of all things natural. Leaves, twigs, flowers, stalks, grasses, seeds, petals and filigree roots, and these did not look so much as if they hade been made by any skilful hand, but more as if they had simply grown organically into their wonderful and varied designs.

"Wh...... where did all these come from?" Hannah stuttered, overcome by such stunning variety.

"Some I have made, and many I have been given on my travels." Was the matter of fact reply.

Yet Seb, startled as he was by the fantastic clothing, was even more intrigued by the size and structure of this underground place, and searched for some source of light that bathed the room in such a natural splendour.

"Who built this place, Lemma?" he asked, voicing his thought as it arose.

"Some friends of mine did, a long time ago."

"It doesn't look old, it looks, well, it looks brand new, as if it has just been made; and you can't be much older than us."

"I am older than I look, Seb; and time can be measured in numerous ways."

"But, look, I don't understand, I don't understand any of this. You aren't old, anyone can see that; and this place, it must have cost so much to build; and all these clothes – where did they come from?"

Hannah turned to listen, as she had been asking herself the same questions.

"Many of them I made myself, as I have already said; the rest are gifts from many peoples and places. And as for the cost; like time, it can be measured in many different ways."

"So what, I mean, what do you *do*? Do you have a job, or does your family pay for all this, and for all your travelling?"

Lemma began to laugh gently, and in such a way that it made Hannah and Seb smile too.

"Sorry," he continued, "it's just that all this is so, I don't know, so strange."

"I am alone, Seb, and content to be so for now; and the cost to me is time, not what you call money."

"What do you mean?"

"I have no need of money." As Lemma said this, a gentle wind disturbed all the beautiful clothing, and made what she was wearing ripple like a pebble dropped in a pool.

114

"Is, is that because you have so much that you don't need to work any more?"

"I am always working, as you put it, but it may not appear so to you. And money is of no use to me, though it is to some that I know; but come, I will show you more, and maybe then you will be able to answer your own questions."

She walked to the end of the room, where a large round stone-like door opened up into another space. As Seb and Hannah stepped through the doorway, they gazed in bewilderment at what they saw next. A scene so tranquil, so naturally perfect, so vital and vivid with colour, and so deeply attractive unfolded before their eyes. It was like a large clearing in a forest, with trees and bushes and shrubs, and lovely green lawns bedecked with multi-coloured flowers; and in its centre was a long flat-calm lake fed by a waterfall that came from some hidden stream. It was bathed in bright sunlight, and as they looked up they saw the domed transparent roof rippling with water and little stones, and fish and tree roots, as if they were looking at a river from underneath. In this space no walls could be seen, and the floor was soft bright green grass; and the whole scented scene was unbelievably beautiful.

"This is where I rest, and bathe. Come, let us sit down over there by the stream, and relax." Lemma said.

Seb and Hannah followed, but they could not speak, as all that they were seeing was beyond their comprehension.

"Do you wish to swim?" Lemma asked them.

They could not reply, and felt as if they were in shock.

"I understand; but I think I shall. I will not be long."

Lemma stood up and walked into the perfect pool, and swam with ease towards its centre, gracefully dipping deep under the water.

"What the hell's all this, Hannah?" Seb whispered strongly.

"I don't know! It's, it's…… I don't believe it, I just don't believe this is real." She whispered back.

"Nor do I." he agreed, grabbing a handful of grass and smelling it. It felt like grass should, and smelt and looked like grass, but it was almost too perfect to be real – too green, too uniform, and too *grassy*.

"I think I want to go." Hannah whispered, "This is incredible, but I don't like it. It's like a dream getting out of control."

"Yes, you're right, it is. Whoever she is, I don't want to know any more. This is not for us, she's....... she's too much, like everything else here; and it's getting so stuffy, and hot."

"What is she, Seb? She's like this place, lovely, gorgeous and, yes, too much." Hannah wiped her brow, as they both began to perspire in the growing heat.

"I don't know, I don't know anything at the moment, but I agree with you; we should go as soon as we can. I'll tell her."

"Tell me what?" Lemma asked, as she rose out of the lake; her hair, clothes and body drying instantly as she emerged out of the water.

As she stood still in front of them, so very tall and beautifully formed, Seb found that he could not speak, so much in awe of her was he.

"We need to go now." Hannah said, "If you don't mind, I think it's getting late." Yet she too was almost dumbstruck, by the sheer extreme of Lemma's physical presence.

"Do you need to go too, Seb?"

But Seb felt confused; his emotions were all jumbled up as he fumbled with his bag. Squeezing it hard as he stared at Lemma, he suddenly felt the shapes of his clay people inside it, and that of the rutilant sphere, and for just a moment his head seemed to clear.

"Yes." He answered, "Yes, we should. It's been amazing, and thanks, but we do have to go now."

"That is fine. I will show you one more place on your way out. But you look hot, both of you; would you like to drink?"

"Yes, please." They replied getting up.

"Just here." Lemma said, pointing at the little running stream, "This will refresh, and relax you."

Hannah and Seb knelt down, and cupped handfuls of water into their mouths, and it was indeed very refreshing. After a few minutes, Lemma led them along the edge of the lake, which was much longer than it appeared at first. As they followed, Hannah grabbed Seb's hand, and whispered,

"I feel dizzy."

"So do I." he answered, as his body began to tremble.

But at that moment they came to what looked like the entrance to a cave, from which a dim reddish light was glowing.

"There is much more to see here." Lemma said, as she turned to them and smiled, "But you are both tired I can tell, and another time may do. When we pass through here, I will show you the way you need to go."

They followed her into the cave, where a path led them gently downhill. It was dark at first, but as they walked the dim red light began to get brighter. For just a moment it went totally black, and then they stumbled into what seemed like a vast dark space – and there, some twenty feet above the ground, was a great round reddy-gold revolving sphere of light, exactly like the rutilant sphere they had found, but a giant one, which hung in mid-space without visible support or suspension.

Seb dropped his bag and sank to his knees, his head swimming and his heart beating hard and fast. Hannah touched the top of his head, and stunned as she was by what she was seeing and feeling, she knew she had to take charge, and sensed danger.

"Do you like it?" Lemma asked quietly.

"Wh, what is it?" Hannah questioned in reply, again almost unable to speak as her dizziness increased.

"It is an image."

"Of what?"

"Of here; and it is a reminder of something I seek. Does it look familiar?"

"No, no it doesn't. It's incredible, but, but we *have* to go. He's not well; I think it's his asthma." Hannah replied, trying not to look at the silently revolving sphere or at Lemma.

"Yes, he does not look well; and I think we have all seen enough, for now. I will show you the way there; this way."

Hannah helped Seb to get up, and carried his bag for him. Both of them looked away from the sphere, as they followed Lemma towards a square black door at the far end of the gigantic cave.

"*Help!*" Seb heard a voice shouting.

"What was that?" he said out loud.

"What?" Hannah replied looking worried.

"That voice!"

"What voice, Seb?" Lemma asked softly.

"That...... oh lord, I don't know, please, I just have to get some air."

"Come on, let's go home." Hannah said reassuringly.

"This is your way." Lemma said.

As they walked up a high arched tunnel, again with mirror studded walls and soft twilight around them, it became *very* cold suddenly. Seb and Hannah shivered as they approached a door at the tunnel's end. They stopped; it was freezing, their breaths all steaming like on a bitter winter's day. Lemma went to push the door open.

"Aren't you cold?" Hannah asked, looking at Lemma, who was still dressed in her short thin silk garment.

"No, I am not." She replied, shaking her head.

"How come? It's, uhh, horrible."

"Because I am a child of the Moon." She answered, pushing the door open. Bright light rushed in and dazzled all their eyes.

"Push the thicket up there out of the way, and your path is close by." she finished, pointing to a screen a few feet in front of them.

"Thank you, and, well, thanks, it's been..... amazing." Hannah said.

"Y, yes, thank you." Seb agreed, but just wanting to get away from the place and back to something familiar.

"It has been my pleasure, and my gain. Be careful on your way home." Lemma said with a smile.

"See you later then." Hannah said out of habit.

"I do not think so. Enjoy your walk." Lemma replied, firmly closing the door as she went back into the tunnel.

For a few moments Seb and Hannah stood in silence, totally unsure of what had happened, and how swiftly it had all finished.

"Thank heavens we're out of there." he said with a sigh.

"Yes, come on, let's get away from here and back to what we know." Hannah agreed.

They pushed the thicket screen aside, and in a dazzling light ran up the little path that led away from the cave. They got to the top and unshielded their eyes, and saw where the light was coming from. Instead of brilliant daylight it was now a deepest night; and instead of a warm summer sun there was a massive full moon – and, most shocking of all, as they looked up towards the silhouetted Tor, instead of the tower on its summit, there was a great and fully crowned tree.

# Chapter Ten

# There

The moon was so large, and its light so illuminating that they could see each others faces clearly, and the shock in each others eyes. Neither of them knew what to say, and the silence around them felt vast. Something had changed, or everything had changed, and they felt it deep within themselves. Not only did the moon look much bigger than they ever imagined it could; as well as the huge tree where the tower had always stood, and the fact that it was night when it should have been day – but it was as if the atmosphere or the air itself had changed, and was infused with a smell or a tang which was so very familiar to them both.

"Quarter-past three." Seb said eventually, looking at his watch, and trying to sound as normal as possible.

"Quarter-past three!" Hannah almost shouted; then realising the stillness surrounding them, she lowered her voice to a forceful whisper, "Look, Seb, its night! Where's the tower? Where are we? What the hell do you mean quarter-past three?"

"I know, I know, I'm sorry, slow down and keep calm. Listen, we went to her *place* at quarter past two, and we can't have been in there for more than an hour; so its right, my watch I mean, it's quarter-past three, and look, its showing p.m."

"Brilliant, fantastic! That's great news about your watch; but it's *wrong*, it can't be that time, it's night!"

"Not according to my watch, it's day."

"Fine! Ok, you believe your watch and I'll believe my eyes. It's night, and we've got to get back, my mum will kill me, and you!"

"But, Hannah, look, look at the Tor, we are not where we thought we were."

"I know, I know, so where *are* we?"

Seb scratched his head roughly with both hands, and started humming to himself as he tried to think clearly, and tried desperately to understand what could have happened.

"We're *there*." He said, with some effort.

"There? Where's there?"

"Remember what she said, Lemma? She said to you, *there is here and here is there, and that is what you have been seeing.*"

"What does that mean, really mean? It sounds crazy."

"I know, Hannah, it does, but *that* is not the Tor I know; and that smell in the air, you know what it is, don't you?"

Hannah sniffed the air, and it was unmistakeable.

"The sea!"

"Yes, the sea; and judging by that smell it's very near."

"So what has happened? Where....... " Hannah stopped in mid-sentence as she realised what Seb had been trying to say.

"I know, it's unbelievable, but, but somehow *there* has become here, and where we were has now become there." And even as he said it he knew it to be true; inexplicably but certainly true.

"But, but I don't want to be here, Seb, I want to be back there, where we were and where we live!" Hannah said, feeling tears well up inside her eyes.

It was Seb's turn now to try to take charge of the situation, even though he felt too the overriding desire to be back with the things and places and people that he knew.

"Listen, listen to me, Hannah, we've got to stay cool and...... oh, listen, all this has happened since we came through *that* place." He said, nodding back down the path that they had just run up. "I think our best bet is to try and go back through it, back to where we were before we went in there."

"I don't want to. For heaven's sake, she scares me, really, she does."

"I know, same here; but we've only got two choices. Stay here and...... and I don't know what, or go back the way we came and hope we can find where we were."

Hannah looked around at the lush silver-grey landscape bathed in moonlight, saw the mighty tree, and breathed in the vibrant sea air. Confused and frightened as she was, she felt as if it was not the place itself which was causing her fear, but the change, the sudden and incomprehensible change that had

121

happened so very quickly. But a more powerful and urgent feeling made her long for what she knew.

"You're right, sorry, I'm sorry. You're right, wherever we are it's not for us, come on, let's go back."

"Well done; good!" he said, giving her a manly pat on the back, and trying his best to lighten their mood.

They made their way carefully back down the slope, until they reached the little thicket. Drawing it aside, they scrambled down slowly and fumbled their way to the mound where the heavy wooden door had been. Moonlight shone upon their efforts, but try as they did they could not find any trace of a door, or a hole, or anything to show that a door had ever been there at all. The grassy mound was as natural as any grassy mound should be.

Seb began to knock the mound with his knuckles, listening out for any hollow or wooden sounds. Hannah did the same, but after a few minutes they stopped, and realised it was futile.

"So what now? What are we going to do?" she asked.

"This!" Seb replied angrily, as he banged and kicked hard at the mound over and over again, while shouting Lemma's name and ordering her to let them in. All to no avail; his voice seemed to be trapped in the space around them, as if locked in a sound-proof room.

"Aaargh!" He screamed finally, kicking his hardest at the mound. "Right, that's it! That's it, Hannah, we can't get back *that* way! Damn it!"

"Stop, please Seb; I'm sorry, let's stop and think this out."

"Sorry, sorry Hannah, I lost it a bit there. Ok, but one of our two choices has gone."

"I know, but we can't just sit here for ever."

"No, we can't; we need to try and get home somehow."

"Listen, Seb, you don't live far from here – yes, I know about the Tor and the sea and the night, but maybe *everything* hasn't changed. Let's go and find your house, and hope it all changes back, somehow."

"I wish I'd brought my torch, I don't fancy stumbling around in the dark." He replied.

122

"Neither do I, but look, there aren't any clouds at all, and I've never seen a brighter moon. You know the way; we can at least have a go."

"Yes, you're right." He answered after a few moments, "And it's not cold, and we can't stay here; and apart from *everything*, there's nothing in particular to be scared of."

Hannah giggled at his boyish logic, as did he. Mustering all his courage, he said, "Right, here's the plan. First, stay cool and calm. Second, let's find my house. Third, well, third, whatever happens we've got to help each other, and stick together, agreed?"

"Agreed!" she replied positively, as they did a high hand shake.

"Ok, are you ready for this?" he asked, trying his very best to be, and to sound strong.

"Yes, I'm ready, I think. But will you pinch me first? Pinch me hard." She replied, holding out her bare arm.

"Why? Why should I?"

"Because I want to know if I'm dreaming this, and that might just wake me up."

"Are you sure?"

"Go on, as hard as you like."

Seb held her hand, and pinched her forearm very hard.

"Ow! Not that hard!"

"Well, have you woken up?"

"No! And that hurt. Maybe I should slap you and see if *you* wake up."

"I can do that for myself." He said, slapping his face a lot harder than he had intended.

"Right," she laughed, "that's that sorted. Either we're both in the same dream, or this is real. In any case we're stuck in this for now, and I suppose we should try and make the best of it."

"Yes, ok. If we go down here to the left, we can cut across the paddock and over the stream by the bridge. That way we'll avoid walking past Gog and Magog, and pick up the path that runs through Paddington Farm. Ready?"

"Ready."

"Right, let's go, and stick close by me."

"Don't worry, I will!"

They trotted back up to the top of the bank, turned left, and made their way across the thick meadow, down towards the paddock by the stream. After a few minutes Seb stopped, and stood still.

"Listen!" he said quietly.

Hannah listened carefully, and then said, "What? What can you hear?"

"Nothing, nothing at all." He looked up and carried on listening. "There's no wind, no owls, no night noises; but there's something there, something in the background."

They both stood very still, trying to hear anything at all; and there it was, deeply quiet around the edges of the silence – the sound of the sea waving upon some hidden shore.

Seb sighed, and said, "Well, I suppose if we can smell it, it's no surprise that we can just about hear it; and yes, I know, there shouldn't be any sea between here and the channel, but there is, somewhere."

"I know; but I'm not sure if I want to see it."

"Same here, but there *is* something that we should have seen already."

"Seb, I'm not sure if I want to hear this."

"Stars."

"Stars?" Hannah questioned as she looked up. Yet he was right; it was a cloudless night, the moon was well up and full, but there was not a single star to be seen from horizon to horizon.

They both blew out deep breaths, and shrugged their shoulders, and smiled.

"Whatever next?" Hannah said.

"Whatever comes." Seb replied strongly, "Come on, let's push on."

As they walked, they tried to make some sense of where they were; but the more they discussed it, the more they could only say what was not there, rather than what was.

"I've been night walking with my dad a few times, "Seb said, "and two things you always notice are that you can hear more clearly, and that you can smell more than usual in the daytime. I know we can hear and smell the sea, but I can't smell anything else. We're crushing grass, and weeds and who knows what, but none of it smells at all."

"I didn't notice that," Hannah replied, "but I did notice something else; which I suppose shouldn't surprise us after everything that's happened. There are no lights, anywhere. No house lights, no car lights, no street lights and no town lights – nothing."

"I know; I didn't want to mention that."

"Thanks; but do you know, I mean, it makes me feel like, well, like we're the only people here, anywhere."

"It feels the same to me; and it doesn't even seem as if there are any animals here, or insects, or anything else moving except us."

"I agree, and I feel sort of glad. I don't really want to bump into any strangers out here."

"I know what you mean. It's almost as if we have the whole place to ourselves, and *that* never happens in dreams."

They pushed their way through a few bushes, and coming to the bottom of the valley they stopped, and looked around.

"It's gone." He said seriously, walking a few steps in every direction.

"What's gone?" Hannah replied, trying to stay close to him.

"The paddock, the fences, the horse-troughs, the horses, they've all gone."

Though they should not have been surprised, considering all that they had experienced so far, they were. Seb looked around carefully, and noticed that the coppiced willows that usually lined the winding course of the stream had also disappeared, replaced by many tall broad-leafed silhouettes of mature trees.

"Right, come on; let's see if the bridge is still there." He said nervously, adding, "But I don't think it will be, and I'm sorry to have to say it."

A deep sigh was Hannah's only reply. They walked down towards the stream, which was still there, though a great deal wider than before; but the bridge was indeed gone. Poking the dark stream with sticks, they found that it was quite shallow, and waded across it with ease. Scrambling up the far bank, they got to the top, and to their amazement their legs and footwear were dry, completely dry.

"Don't say anything." Hannah said with a smile.

"Ok, but I think I know what's coming next."

They walked on over the rise in the land, and headed straight in front of them for about half a mile. What Seb had thought would happen next, happened; and they both stopped to look at the scene. Paddington Farm was not there; not a brick, a wall, a barn, an animal, an orchard, a fence, a path or a road – all of it had gone. For many long moments they were quiet, speechless, and then sure of what this really meant.

"It's not going to be there." Seb said quietly, his voice both heavy and sad.

"I know," Hannah replied, holding his arm, "I know; but we've got to go and look, just in case."

"It can't be there, Hannah, any of it! My house, the garden, my mum, Star, the car, the neighbours, the street, the, the...... everything. It will all be gone."

She took in a deep breath, and tried to hold back her tears, saying,

"I know, and, oh god! My mum and my sister, my......." She put her head in her hands and slumped to the ground by Seb's feet, crying uncontrollably and shaking with fear.

He could not stop himself from crying as well, and they were both hurting very badly and deeply. Long minutes passed, and then Hannah stood up slowly and looked at the huge white moon.

"*Tears before strength.*" She whispered, "It's what my granddad used to say. He said that many soldiers used to cry before going into battle, and somehow it left them with the courage to fight on – like rainfall before sunshine."

126

"I hope so, I really hope so, Hannah." he replied, wiping his eyes, "But however brave we feel, we've got to go and see, and then decide what to do next."

"Ok, I think I'm ready; which way?"

"Over there, there's a……. no there isn't, the road has gone, I forgot."

Where the steep hill road had been, now there was just grass and trees; but Seb knew the way, and led them up the ridge, along the line of the scarp to where Little River Pond should have been. In its place was a wide and long lake, which stretched back towards the foot of the Tor, its glassy calm black surface reflecting the brilliance of the moon.

Skirting its edge, they walked on to what was Mud Crossing, now not muddy at all; and then on down through the orchardless Pip's Orchard, eventually coming up to what had been Sandy Lane, where there used to be cosy houses and little bungalows, but where now there was not even a lane. Seb gasped as they came through the trees to the space where the shops and all the houses and proper roads had been. Nothing – all of them had gone. But there, in the middle, was what the locals called The Hump, a play area for children, with swings and slides and goalposts. The Hump was still there, but every thing else was not. Seb knew that from the top of The Hump he could easily see his house, so, very reluctantly and slowly, he and Hannah walked up to its top, and stood and stared.

Where his house had been, and his garden, and his road and all the neighbour's houses had been, there was just wide open empty space. He stood there motionless, unable to fully believe what he was seeing; but he had to believe his eyes, and his eyes saw nothing familiar. They walked silently down The Hump and to the right, where his road and home had been. It was then that they heard the roaring rumble of the sea, sounding through the clear night air.

He turned to Hannah, who was in a wide-eyed daze, and said, "Just here there was a little cul-de-sac, and at the end you could see over the whole of Glastonbury and all the Levels. Sometimes we would watch the carnival from there, or the fireworks from the Abbey when they had the Extravaganza; but I suppose even the town will have gone now. Come on, Hannah, I don't want to at all, but we've got to go and have a look."

"Alright, yes, yes, we should; but I feel frightened, this is becoming like a nightmare. Seb, may I hold your hand?"

He did not answer, but took her hand in his and squeezed it gently, and began to walk down the gentle slope to where the wall had overlooked the town.

Nothing could have prepared him for what they saw next. Where the low wall had been, the grass ran out to the edge of a high cliff; and in the vast moonlit darkness they could see great white-foamed waves rolling in across a rocky shore, where the town of Glastonbury had been. Staring silently across the surging black water, they saw on the horizon the silhouettes of many tall mountains, with the great bright silver disc of the moon floating high above them. The whole view was awesome, and at the same time awful, and they both felt extremely small and ignorant, helpless and lost.

✡ ✧ ✩

Some time later, as they still looked out over the staggering scene, Hannah at last spoke up,

"What now, Seb, what now?"

He did not answer immediately, but seemed to be deeply involved in his own thoughts, where something new was stirring. In the silence of his heart his growing fear turned now to anger, and in its turn his anger forged a thought within his mind; and in this space a surge of unknown courage overwhelmed him, and steeled him, and urged him, to face whatever was to come.

"Better a hard truth than a soft lie." He said, as if to himself.

"Why do you say that, Seb?"

"My mother said it many times, so often it used to bore me. But I know what she meant now. We are *in* the hard truth for now, and we have to deal with it, and it's better than having to deal with pleasant sounding lies and deceit, and all that stupid stuff from Lemma. Shale was right, we should never have trusted her, but….. "

"I know, I know, but she was so, I don't know, so lovely and attractive and, and….."

"And she spun my head around so that I couldn't think clearly! That's the truth of it; she charmed me and fooled me, and then I stupidly fooled myself."

"And me, Seb; I tried not to trust her, but I couldn't help it. It was like her voice was deep inside me."

"I felt the same, and this is where it's got us. Come on, I need to think hard."

Turning away from the crashing sea, they walked back up to the top of The Hump, and sat down. Not far in the distance was the black shape of the Tor, and the mighty tree that rose above its summit. The night was perfectly still; the air was still, and the whole world they found themselves in seemed still; and they sat within the stillness deep within their own thoughts.

"I think we must go back." Seb said finally.

"But, but back to where?" Hannah asked.

"Back to where this started, back to that door that we couldn't find. It's got to be there somewhere, and maybe when it gets light we can find it."

"And what if we can't?"

"If we can't, then we'll try to find the other door, in that bank by Shadow Stream."

"And then?"

"I'm not sure; all I do know is that everything happened when we went through *her* place, and so we must get back *there* somehow, and get back to what we know."

"But what if….. "

"No ifs please Hannah, not for now. Let's just try to find that door, and we can deal with the ifs in the daylight."

"I suppose it does get light here, doesn't it?"

"We'll soon see, but we know it gets light *there*, and that's where we've got to get to. Come on, let's go, I'm starting to get tired."

As they got up, Hannah stopped and said, "Thanks. Thanks Seb, for being so strong, I was really falling apart back there."

"Well, we agreed to look out for each other, didn't we? So it will probably be your turn again soon."

"I hope not." She answered quietly.

Seb decided to take a different route back to the stream, as, for some reason of his own, he wanted to avoid Little River Pond and all the memories of what had happened there. They dropped down behind the hill where once his home had been, and made their way through a small wood to the south of the next rise in the land. It was dark in the wood; but because the moon was still so high and bright, silver beams punctured through the canopy of leaves and dappled the way in front of them. For any other reason the place would have appeared quite beautiful to them, as the silence was profound, the temperature truly mild, and the landscape they could see was near-perfect and untouched by any human blemish. But in their present situation all that they saw was through their fears.

As they came to the end of the wood, Seb stopped and looked up at the trees. Bending down a branch he examined the leaves of one of them, and they were unlike any leaves that he had ever seen before. They seemed to be multi-layered, with each layer being made up of extremely delicate paper-thin round shapes, some small and some large, but all the layers together being no thicker than the leaves he had always known. Both of them began to touch these leaves, and they seemed almost too thin to feel, with some sort of satin-like quality.

"Amazing!" he said, and pulled at one of the hair-thin layers. He expected it to come off the branch with ease, but it did not; and no matter how hard he tugged at it he could not separate it from the tree.

"I think it's happy where it is." Hannah said, "I think you should leave it alone."

"You're right; but how can something so, I don't know, so delicate be so strong?"

"Are you describing *me*?" Hannah answered with a smile.

"Hah! Maybe so, but let's hope that we don't have to test it."

130

"True; so where to now?"

Seb led them up to the brow of the next hill, where again they could hear the background tumbling of the sea on a multitude of stones and pebbles. To their left they could see what had been Little River Pond not far away, and a few minutes later they came round to the north side of the Tor. As they walked slowly past a few tall bushes, the grass suddenly changed from being shin length to very short, like a perfectly mown lawn. They both bent down to touch it, and it was amazingly smooth and dense and soft, and stretched way out in front of them towards the Tor.

"Can we stop here for a minute? I'm getting a bit tired too." Hannah asked, "But isn't this incredible, I mean the grass, it's so, so gorgeously grassy!"

Seb giggled a little at her description, but he had to agree that it was pretty accurate.

"I know what we've got to face if we can't get back, and it terrifies me." she added, "But if I put all of that, and I'm trying hard to – if I put all of that out of my mind, this place, *here* or *there* or wherever it is, is, and I'm not even sure if I've got a word for it, is immense. Everything here seems so full and, I don't know, just immense."

"It sure is, and, I don't know how to describe it, but it's almost as if what we are sitting on, I mean the planet itself, is immense compared to what we're used to. I mean, sorry, that sounds rubbish."

"I *do* know what you mean, Seb. I've felt it in another way, like we're so very, very small compared to it, like atoms on a giant ball."

"Mmm, and that tree up there, it's huge, I mean really huge, and….. so full of life; even from here I can almost feel it. But, but we've got to go, come on, and I'm sorry for talking like that."

"Don't be sorry; it's all so different, yet, I suppose, so much the same or similar."

"I've heard that somewhere before; but now we're actually seeing it and even *in* it. Heavens, come on, let's find that door."

They got up, turned their backs to the Tor, and walked away. After only a few steps they heard a sound, and stopped dead, and listened. It was coming from all around them, a deep pulsing gentle drone, with a rhythm like a very strong heartbeat.

"What is it?" Hannah whispered.

"I don't know, I don't; but it's getting louder. It's like; it's like some massive didgeridoo."

As the sound grew louder, the pulse within it became more powerful, until the air, the ground, the trees, the sky, and their whole bodies seemed totally full with it. Yet even as its volume increased, it was not painful, or horrible or frightening, and it did not make them want to cover their ears. It was immense, and relentless, and alive.

Seb and Hannah turned instinctively towards the Tor, the huge moon now low behind it, its long and high silhouette completely black; and then they saw it, and gasped in their breaths sharply and together. Standing next to the mighty tree, staring towards the moon, was the incredibly big black silhouette of a great bear. So large was it, that even from their distance they could see that it had its mouth wide open, and that it was from here that the deep pulsing penetrating sound was coming. It closed and opened its huge jaws, and made a beautiful mmmmm-urrrrrr sound, and it was as if the great bear was singing to the moon, and that everything was full of its voice. Slowly it closed its mouth, and its sound became a deep pulsing hum; and slowly it turned and faced Seb and Hannah, and they could feel its mighty presence and the vibrations of its voice moving through their very bones. Then the great bear turned away from them, its voice ceased, and it walked down the far side of the Tor until it was out of sight.

"What the...... " Seb tried to speak, but the words just would not come.

Hannah was totally quiet, staring wide-eyed, her hands cupping her chin and face. Words were useless; silence was the best reaction to what they had just witnessed, and the kind of feelings it had generated deep within themselves.

132

Seb turned away and began to walk, closely followed by Hannah. Fear would be a poor word to describe the effect the vision had on them, complete awe would be much closer to the truth; and as they walked, each individually felt as if some great pressure had been lifted off their hearts, being replaced by a real and certain faith that everything would come right, and that all would be well in the end.

Walking briskly, and without speaking, they made their way down the scarp behind where Paddington Farm and the paddock had been, and fumbled their way through the trees; the moon being now hidden behind the high hillside. They stumbled across the stream, and up to the top of the little rise, close to where the doorway had been. Sitting down, Seb pushed his way down to the thicket screen, felt it, and said at last,

"It's here, Hannah! Be careful, go slowly, come on."

He guided her feet until she was sitting next to him, and they stopped for a few moments to catch their breath.

"I don't know about you, but I'm done for, I've got to sleep, my eyes.... " He could barely finish his sentence through complete exhaustion.

"I feel the same; it's as if all my strength has gone. But where can we sleep?"

Seb pulled back the little thicket, and felt his way down to the grassy mound. Just to its left was a flat space, big enough for both of them to lie down on.

"Pull the thicket across, we can sleep down here." He said.

In the total darkness Hannah edged her way down, and felt the ground until she was next to him, her back against the mound. Without another word they both fell fast asleep, in the hope that the morning, if it came, would surely show them the way.

# Chapter Eleven
# Found to be Lost

Seb awoke first, and he was hot. The sun was high, and filtered through the bushes under which they had slept. His first thought was about the door, and that he had to find it at all cost. As he brushed past Hannah she woke up.

"Sorry, sorry about that; I'm going to find the door." He said.

"I'll help." She replied, moving with him down to the grassy mound, and rubbing the heavy sleep from her tired eyes.

They looked everywhere and all over the mound, with Seb even poking sticks into the grass in case the door had been deliberately hidden beneath it. As he searched, Hannah sat down, perspiring from the heat and what felt like a very short sleep. Her eyes widened as she became aware of some sounds.

"Seb!" she whispered, as she grabbed his leg, "Listen!" But he was too busy searching to stop for a moment; he was desperate to find the door.

She hit him hard on the backside and said, "Seb, it's birds, I can hear birds singing!"

He stopped, and listened, and he too could hear birdsong; and faintly, as if far away, he could also hear voices.

"I've got to keep looking, Hannah – we must get back, we must!"

"Seb, stop, there's nothing there, it's gone. We can't get back that way."

"Damn it!" he shouted, punching at the grassy mound.

"Come on, please, you said if it wasn't there we could try and find the other one. That's all we can do."

"I know, I know, it's just, just, I felt sure we would find it, and sure, somehow, we *would* get back."

"Don't Seb, we've got to be brave and deal with this. We don't have any other options."

"Yes, you're right, Miss *Strong one now,* thanks, let's go and face whatever we have to face, and, heavens, I'm starving! Come on then, take a deep breath. Ready?"

She nodded in reply, trying to force a smile.

"Right, let's go!"

They scrambled up away from the mound, and Seb pushed back the little thicket screen. Sunlight blazed in and dazzled them, as they trotted up to the top of the bank. For a few moments they could barely see at all, as the sunshine seemed so bright after such a long time in the dark.

But then Hannah grabbed Seb's arm, and shouted, "Look!"

"What?"

"Up there, look at the Tor!"

Shielding the sun from their eyes, they looked up towards the Tor.

"What?" Seb exclaimed, "What the……?"

There, on the summit of the Tor, was the old tower; the tower that had stood there for so many hundreds of years; and not only that, there were people in and around it, and dogs playing, and bongo music, and cows grazing on its grassy slopes.

"We're back." Hannah whispered, "We're back, Seb, we're back!"

"Come on, quick!" he said, and ran off down and across the fields for over half a mile, with Hannah sprinting behind him and calling out his name.

They jumped through a little copse, over a steep rise, and then stopped and looked at the view. The paddock was there, the fences, the horse-troughs and the horses – they were all there as they should be; and in the distance, they could just make out the sun drenched tile rooftops of Paddington Farm.

✫　✫　✫

"Twenty past three?" Seb said, looking at his watch.

"Oh no! You mean we've been there all night?" Hannah replied.

"No, no we haven't, it's worse than that, or better I suppose. It's twenty past three p.m., and the date is still the same, still today, look!"

"So, so, what's happened? I must have dozed off and been dreaming."

"About what? What did you dream about?"

"I can't think about this, Seb, I can't; it's just too confusing. I know it wasn't a dream – two different people don't live in the same dream, and look at my arm!"

She showed him the small bruise where he had pinched her. Seb stared at her arm, trying his absolute best to put into words what he thought may have happened to them.

"Look, ok, it's like, this is what we did, oh heavens……. Right, we had a walk; we sat down by the stream, about quarter past two; we met Lemma, and went to her, her *place*; we got out of there, and it was quarter past three, and it was night, and we were…. We were *there*. We spent hours there, came back, fell asleep, woke up, and we were *here* – here! And only about five minutes has passed, and those were the minutes before we realised that we were back *here, back* here. It's got to be a dream, all of it, even Lemma's place!"

As he finished he knew that it was *not* the truth, and tried hard to avoid the thoughts that were rushing into his mind, and which *were* the truth.

"No," Hannah said, "No, none of it was a dream. I don't care about the time, or the day; look at my arm! And I bet you if we went through it all now, we would describe it all exactly the same, exactly, apart from our feelings. People do *not* share, or live in, the same dreams; it's impossible."

"But what else could have happened? We don't have any *proof* that we were in Lemma's place, or *there*; no proof at all!"

For many moments they were silent, each of them wrestling with their thoughts, trying hard to grasp something solid to hold onto amid the tide of flowing confusion.

"Experience, Seb, experience; that is the proof, and that is the bottom line. We did what we did, we saw what we saw, we felt what we felt, we heard it, smelt it, touched it and we *lived* it. We have no doubts, none at all, and that is the proof, and my arm – look! We know, we really know *that* it all happened, and *what* happened; but *how* and *why*…….. but how and why it all happened is totally beyond me. And Seb, and, if it had all been a dream, we would have woken up by the stream, where we were just before we met Lemma, not here! Unless, we were also sleepwalking together."

Seb took in a long deep breath, and sighed. Even though it was completely confusing, he was relieved and reassured to hear Hannah's certain words.

"You're right." He said, "Whatever else we can say, we *did* experience it, and together; and somehow, somehow, we have been *there*, and somehow we got back again. For a moment I was beginning to think that even now we are dreaming, and that *I've* been dreaming all this; and you're just in my dream, and the clay people, the sphere, the visions, the music, all the people, Shale, Lemma, the great bear – all a vast dream, which you and I have been trapped in."

"But if *I* thought like that, Seb, then you and I and everything else is trapped in *my* dream; and that's crazy."

"I know, it is crazy, but, yes, it is. This is nothing like Harry Potter, or Narnia, or Lord of the Rings; and I don't think I want anything else to happen unless I can understand it, or someone can explain it to me. I've just about had enough! And I'm sure it's all happened because of them."

"Who? Who's them?"

"The clay people; nothing has been the same since I made them, or found them, or whatever I did."

Seb took his rucksack off his shoulder and sat down; Hannah sat down next to him. He opened it, and felt inside for the small black velvet bag, and lifted it out. He saw immediately that there was a hole in the side of it, quite a large hole, with threaded and ragged edges. Panicking, he undid the drawstring, and took out one of the clay people, and then the rutilant sphere, and then......... nothing. There was nothing else inside it; the other clay figure had gone.

He turned his rucksack upside down and roughly shook everything out of it, and stared hard at his many bits and pieces. He thrust his hand inside it and felt frantically for anything else; but it was empty. Holding his head as if in great pain, he looked at all his things, at the sphere, and at the single clay figure, and said,

"He's gone, gone, Lynn has gone!"

✫　✧　☆

After a massive silence, Seb stood up and started kicking at the grass in anger.

"I've lost him! After *all that*, I've lost him!"

Hannah did not reply, but she leaned over and picked up the little velvet bag, and examined it closely.

"You didn't *lose* him, Seb, you didn't. He's been stolen."

"What?"

"He's been stolen. Look at the bag, look at the hole; that didn't happen by accident. It's not a tear, or a cut, and it hasn't worn out. Look at the edges, it's as if....... It's as if it's been chewed through, or bitten; my rabbit used to do things like this."

Seb looked carefully at the hole in the bag, turning it inside out, and said slowly, "So did the guinea pig I had years ago. Lemma!"

"What do you mean, Lemma?"

"It's her; it's damn well her! Remember her friends, her *little friends*, those rabbits and weasels and things? It was one of them; they've stolen it, and she's got him now!"

"But how, how did anything get into your bag, you've had it over your shoulder all the time?"

"No, no I haven't." he replied, as he tried to remember his every movement since they sat down by the little stream. "Twice, I put the bag down twice. First, when we were in that.....that place of Lemma's, with the trees and the lake. We

138

sat down, and I put it on the ground next to me. Then she told us where to drink, and, and then, straight away we both felt dizzy. What the hell was in that water, if it was real water? Then I carried it under my arm, until we were underneath that huge rutilant sphere. Do you remember? I felt so incredibly weird that I just couldn't stand up; my legs went, and I'm sure I must have dropped the bag as I fell over. It was dark, anything could have happened."

"But we were only in that room, or whatever it was, for a few minutes. How could something have got into your bag, chewed a hole in the other one, and taken the clay person in so short a time?"

"It was dark, so……..yes, you're right; but hang on, hang on, there's only one way that she could have done it. When we sat down next to that stream that fed the lake, I put the bag down; she went in for a swim, and we talked. One of her, her *creatures*, must have slipped into my bag. Then we went to the next room, and I dropped it. There *was* enough time! I must have carried whatever it was with me in the bag, and the first chance it got it slipped out again, taking Lynn with it."

"But why? Why would she want to steal one of the clay people?"

"Why? God knows why. I don't know why she did anything that she did. I don't even know why she *is* at all. I mean, for heaven's sake, who is she, or, more to the point, *what* is she?"

"I don't know, Seb, I haven't a clue."

"But Shale has; he knows her, or he said he does, and he said that she or he wanted something from us."

"Yes, but he didn't know what it was."

"What else could it have been? I mean, what have we got to offer someone like that? What could she possibly need from us that she couldn't get or make for herself?"

"A clay figure that talks, or at least that did talk?"

"Exactly."

"But why, Seb; what would she want with it?"

"I don't know, but she does."

"Ok, but again, why did she only take one of them? Why didn't she take them both?"

"Maybe she didn't have time, or maybe she doesn't need them both; for the life of me, I don't know. But Shale might."

"What do you mean?"

"If we told him what she has taken, maybe he would know why. Yet I'm not sure if I really care why, I just want him back, and maybe Shale could help us."

"Us?"

"Yes, us."

"Look Seb, I'm sorry, I don't know about you, but what happened with Lemma, and being *there*, and thinking about never being *here* again, and, come to think of it, shadows and storms and everything else, has really scared me. I'm not sure if I want to carry on with this, it's all getting too much out of control. In fact, at this moment, I just want normality; I don't want any more crazy things to happen, and I'm sorry if that sounds weak."

As she said this, Seb smacked his forehead and groaned.

"That's it! That's when it happened!" he said.

"What?"

"In that room, with the sphere; as we went to leave I heard someone shout *help*! It was him, it was Lynn!"

"Ok, I understand, I really do understand how you are feeling, and how much you want to get him back; but, Seb, I feel, I don't know, out of my depth with all this. Every day this week more things have been happening that neither of us understands; and each time it's more, more peculiar, and uncontrollable, and last night *there*, beautiful as a lot of it was, it frightened the life out of me. I was terrified that I had lost everything dear to me; trapped in a world that I never made or expected, and my heart hurt deeply for us both. What else is going to happen? I don't know, you don't know, and I don't think I can carry on. I'm not some young heroine from a fantasy book, I am just an ordinary girl!"

Seb considered deeply her honest confession, and in so many ways he felt the same. Yet he was certain in his heart that he could not leave things as they were.

"I'm sorry, Hannah, really sorry, I didn't know it would get like this. But, but I don't know how to put it, but there is something *real* going on here – scary, weird, but very real. I don't know who or what these clay people are, but I've spoken to them; they were as alive as you and me, and I can't, or won't, leave one of them in the hands of that Lemma. Whatever she wants with them it won't be for anything good, and I know she means to harm him; and that will harm her, Serren, and maybe even me. Heavens, I don't understand any of it; but I am not going to leave him with her, I'm not!"

Hannah touched Seb's arm gently, seeing and feeling the fight he was having inside himself.

"I wish we could talk to someone about all this." She said, "Someone wise and strong, who could explain it all. But no one we know would believe us; and if they did, I'm sure they would stop us seeing each other, and keep us in or send us away, or something like that. We don't have any proof that anyone else would accept, apart from, apart from that rutilant sphere. Why don't we show that to someone?" But Hannah could not think of whom, and neither could Seb.

"Whoever we show it to," he continued, "would want to take it away, and examine it, and measure it and test it, and probably break it or spoil it. That sphere, whatever it is, is part of what is going on, you know that; and it's got something to do with the clay people. We even found it in the exact same place. If that sphere goes, I don't know, I don't know but I'm sure, that if it goes........I can't explain it, but I know I mustn't lose it, not after all that's happened."

"I think you're right, Seb. I don't know what to say, or what to suggest. All I know is that at the moment a lot of this frightens me, and I just want to get back to being me again – silly little me doing my silly little things. I don't think I'm made

141

for all this kind of stuff. I don't mind *reading* it, but I don't want to be *in* it."

"I don't think I do either, and it scares me too; but what choice have I got? I am *not* going to leave him with *her*, but I don't know how to get him back without more stuff happening. But you're right, I think we've had enough for now; and I don't want to think about it any more, I've got brain ache. Leave it with me, Hannah, don't worry, and thanks for being, being such a good friend, and for helping me. I would hate to have gone through all that on my own. Come on, let's go home, and maybe we'll meet up later in the holidays, or back at school next term."

They got up together and headed for home, deep in thoughts and memories. As they walked down the road towards Seb's house, Hannah stopped them, and turned to him, and asked,

"What are you going to do, Seb? What will you do next?"

Her question echoed his own but, frightened and confused as he was, he was certain about the answer.

"I'm going to find Shale." He said quietly.

Without another word, Hannah kissed him on the cheek, and smiled as she looked deep into his eyes. Then they went into his house where their mothers were drinking tea, and tried their best to get back to some kind of normality.

# Chapter Twelve
# Alone, Together

It would be hard to describe fully the range of emotions that Seb went through over the next few difficult days; and the weather seemed to illustrate his feelings. Clouds and rain, followed by brief periods of sunshine; dull mist and winds and unusually cold nights; thunder and lightning and a damp stifling heat – each one of these reflected each of his peculiar moods.

For much of the time he stayed in his room, pretending to read, or listen to music. His healthy appetite waned, and he was difficult to talk to, swinging from prolonged silence to anger, from chatty to argumentative, from happy to sullen, and everything in between. He knew what he wanted to do, but he did not know how to go about it, and he was scared. His fears turned in on him, and made him feel weak and timid, and the word *coward* kept invading his deeply confused thoughts. This hurt him, and seemed to mock at him, and finally began to depress him. He would not look at the one clay person he had, nor at the rutilant sphere; he had hidden them deep under his bed, fearful of what might happen if he handled them.

By day he distracted himself as best he could, and by night he tried hard to sleep; but his dreams were visited by images and sounds that reminded him of all that had happened. So each morning he woke up exhausted, and stumbled his way through the day.

His mother was very aware of his changing moods, and tried to talk to him about it; but he just kept saying that he was ok, or tired, or needed to rest and be quiet. She put it down to Hannah and his feelings for her, and that maybe for the first time, he was in some sort of love; or maybe that they had argued, and he missed her. But every time she suggested that Hannah should come over, he said no. She even telephoned Hannah's mother, and discovered that she had the same concerns about similar behaviour from her daughter, and put it down to the same reason – young love. But they were both wrong; for whatever love may or may not have been between them, it was fear that their children were experiencing; fear and weakness, confusion and wonder, desire for and against carrying on, and the kind of ignorance and depression which makes action so very hard. Alone, was what they really felt.

After four days Seb had had enough. His mother had gone out shopping, and he sat in his bedroom listening to one of the compilation CDs he had made. He stood up and walked to his window, which looked out onto the town and the Levels, and the Channel way beyond; and he remembered the crashing sea and the cliffs, and the gigantic moon, the great bear, and the towering mountains of that night when they had been *there*, and something powerful stirred inside him.

He crawled under his bed and found the little velvet bag, now repaired. He opened it and took out the one clay person, Serren; then he took out the rutilant sphere and placed it next to her on his bed. As he stared at them he became aware of the music that was playing. It was a favourite of his father's, and one that Seb had grown to love – Voodoo Chile, by Jimi Hendrix. As the gently picked wah-wah introduction began, he turned it up loud. He walked over to the bed and picked up Serren, and stared at her. As the main song crashed in with its soaring guitar break, he picked up the sphere and put it in the palm of his right hand. *"Well I'm standing next to a mountain, and I chop it down with the edge of my hand!"* Hendrix boomed out, and the sphere began to turn slowly on its axis. Seb stared at the sphere and at Serren, as Jimi sang out, *"And I pick up all the pieces and make an island, may even raise just a little sand."* Something about the music, something in its atmosphere and words and the sheer guts of it, moved Seb inside; and as it blew through his room he knew exactly what he had to do, and that he was going to do it as soon as possible – find Shale.

144

As the music faded he turned it off, and sat down on his bed, putting the figure and the sphere back into the bag. In the silence of his room he felt nervous, but also excited, deciding in himself that if he had the choice that none of this had ever happened, he would not choose it. However tricky it was, he would rather have experienced it all than not, and hoped seriously that he had the wit and the wisdom to deal with whatever was to come next.

He jerked back with shock as his mobile phone went off, shouting at him that he had just received a text message. It was from Hannah; and over the next few minutes they had an exchange of messages:

Hannah: *Hi Seb, hope you're all right, I keep thinking about everything – what an adventure!*

Seb: *Hello Hannah, yes, sure is, I'm fine. And you?*

Hannah: *ok, keep thinking what a wimp I am, and mum thinks I'm going mad.*

Seb: *I know the feeling, don't worry, you're not a wimp, just being sensible.*

Hannah: *Bored with being sensible, can't get back to normal, whatever that is....*

Seb: *You were never normal! Sorry for everything that's happened*

Hannah: *Ha! Don't be sorry, not your fault, it was amazing and scary*

Seb: *I know, thanks for being there*

Hannah: *My pleasure, so what are you going to do now?*

Seb: *Find Shale, and try to find Lynn, not going to let that Lemma get away with it*

For over five minutes Hannah did not reply, and Seb thought that at the mention of those names she had decided again that enough was enough. But then:

Hannah: *May I come?*

For another five minutes he could not reply as he thought about it all, and whether he wanted to be responsible for Hannah in whatever might come next.

Seb: *are you sure you really want to?*

145

Hannah: *yes!*

Seb: *don't think it's a good idea*

Hannah: *why?*

Seb: *anything could happen – anything!*

Hannah: *I know that!*

Seb: *so why do you want to come?*

Hannah: *coz you shouldn't be alone, you need someone with you – me!*

Seb: *why you?*

Hannah: *coz I'm part of it*

Seb: *how do you know?*

Hannah: *not sure how, but KNOW I am!*

Seb: *???????*

Hannah: *Lynn needs Serren, you need me – sure of that*

Seb: *don't want to put you at risk*

Hannah: *that's my choice – share the risk!*

Seb: *can I stop you?*

Hannah: *no! won't let you go alone.....*

Seb: *sure?*

Hannah: *sure!*

Seb: *I'm going tomorrow*

Hannah: *I'll be round at 9*

Seb: *great, and thanks*

Hannah: *for what?*

Seb: *being so brave!*

Hannah: *not brave, just stupid*

Seb: *makes 2 of us*

Hannah: *I know, c u tomorrow*

Seb: *c u tomorrow, hope the weather's good*

He turned his CD player on again, skipped to an old track called We Used To Know, by Jethro Tull, turned it up loud and lay down on his bed, smiling as the words rang out, *"Each to his own way I'll go mine, best of luck with what you find, but for your own sake remember times, we used to know!"* And the massive guitar solo filled his room, and filled his heart with hope.

# Chapter Thirteen
# Finding Shale

The morning matched their mood – optimistic, excited and full of new energy. The air was warm and clear, moved by a strong southerly breeze; small high clouds drifted swiftly across the near-azure sky, and the sun blazed its light all over the summer landscape. Fear had transformed into resolve, choice into will, and doubt into firm direction.

They had prepared well, hoping that they had packed everything they might need for whatever circumstance may occur. A torch, a knife, scissors, matches, string, binoculars, waterproof jackets, water, food, a camera, a compass and a pen and some paper. Seb thought long and hard about whether to take Star with them or not, but his love for her made him want to protect her, and he left her behind to play safely in the garden. Hannah's mother was picking her up at 6.00pm, so they had a full nine hours to look for, and find, Shale.

Even at this early hour there seemed to be a lot of people about; tourists, dog-walkers, and the usual assortment of hippies, travellers and over-night campers. Seb did his best to avoid the more popular roads and paths, steering them around the west of the Tor to a narrow overgrown lane that plunged down steeply to the east of Maidencroft Farm. All the while they talked about what had happened *there* the week before, trying to remember every detail, and trying even harder to make some sense of it all. They had decided to begin their search by returning to the small hidden pool tucked away behind the orchards; and as they approached it their conversation ceased.

"Right, remember what we agreed." Seb said, starting to feel a little nervous of what may happen next, "If we find him and if it all starts to go wrong, or one of us has had enough, then we pretend we have a call and that we have to go – and that we have to go *together*. Either we both stay, or we both go; *no splitting up.*"

"Definitely not! We've got to stick together, whatever happens, not that I really want anything to happen unless it's good." Hannah replied, certain of this at least.

With as little noise as possible they pushed their way through the bushes and ferns, until they reached the clearing before the small lake. They walked quietly around it, found the bench behind the reeds, and sat down and waited in silence; and waited, for a very long and quiet half-hour.

Seb stared at the bushes, briars and tangled blackthorns on the far bank, and, as with staring at anything natural for a long time, his eyes began to play tricks on him. He saw odd faces and weird shapes that seemed to form into bizarre animals and dreamlike people; large heads and pairs of eyes, with distorted smiles or laughing mouths; hands pointing and legs walking, and strange creatures as big as the bushes.

Hardly noticing them at first, he focussed upon a pair of rainbow coloured twinkling lights, and somehow they seemed familiar to him. Then he could see an almost-hidden delicate nose, and a lovely full mouth that was smiling; he saw a long neck, and bare shoulders, and leaves and little branches that appeared to be in the shape of a slender body, with long and graceful legs. All at once the whole camouflaged form came into shocking focus, and he groaned as he realised who it was – Lemma – and she was laughing at them. He grabbed Hannah's hand, pulled her up and shouted,

"Run Hannah, come on, run, now!"

Without a pause or a question Hannah followed him, as he jumped and sprinted out of the clearing, and along the path that passed to the north of Maidencroft Farm.

Cutting across some large fields, they ran beside a long high hedge and turned uphill, until after about a mile they came to a small wooden fenced copse. Climbing over a high stile, they walked through the long grasses and meadow plants, through a dense patch of evergreen trees, and came to a stop at a broken picnic table almost completely covered by creepers and bindweed. For a couple of minutes they just stood there panting, and trying to catch their breath.

"What are we running from? What happened?" Hannah asked, between puffs and blows.

"Lemma! She was standing there by the pond."

"What? I didn't see her."

"I did, I really did, and she was staring at us, and laughing."

"Where was she? Why didn't *I* see her?"

"Remember her clothes? That room full of clothes, those ones that looked like they were made from leaves and branches and stuff? She must have been wearing one of them. But it was her eyes I saw at first, they were like, like.......I don't know. But except for her eyes she was almost invisible."

"But that means she could be anywhere, and we wouldn't see her." Hannah said, as she looked around at the mess of plants and trees and growth all about them.

"I know, I know, let's think. For heaven's sake, how can someone who looks so........so, like she looks, be so.....uh!"

"I know what you mean. She's like two people in one; not just male and female, but beautiful and, I think, bad."

"That's what I was thinking. But that makes it even trickier; if we can't see her we won't know where she is."

"Unless we stay out in the open, away from anywhere she can hide in."

"You're right; but I don't think Shale is the sort of person that likes to hang about in open spaces, not looking the way he does, and in this heat."

"Who knows? Maybe not; but if we stay out in the open *he* will be able to see *us*, and we might just be able to see him."

"True. Ok, so where can we go?" Seb said, scanning the trees and bushes and thick undergrowth, hoping not to see a pair of bright sparkling eyes.

"There's only one place I can think of." He continued, "The big paddock over there, it's only a mile or so away. It's clear all around, and backs on to the stream which must feed that little pool."

"But what if *she's* there?"

"She could be anywhere. But if we find Shale, I don't think she'll want to mess with us if he's around."

"I hope not."

"Anyway, I think she already has what she wanted. She's taunting us and, and I don't want to think about her. Come on, let's get into the open."

Crawling under a rusty barbed-wire fence, they crossed two large open fields where cows were grazing in the baking sunshine. They picked up a path that took them over a small hill, through a deep coombe, and up the other side to the open meadow beyond. As they walked down the gentle slope they came to the large paddock, which held only two or three horses that day. Climbing over a two-railed fence, they crossed over to the far side, where the space was wide and clear, with not a tree or a bush anywhere near to them. Backing on to another fence were two very large horse-troughs; a very old one made of marbled stone, and another one made out of some kind of metal. They sat down and leaned their backs against the warm stone, and sighed as they took off their bags.

"Keep it close to you this time." Hannah said, "Are they in there?" She asked, meaning the clay figure and the rutilant sphere.

"Yes; and I will. Nothing's going to creep in there, unless it's invisible."

"Good. This is a beautiful place to wait in, such a gorgeous view; it makes me feel so peaceful. I do hope he finds us, or we find him. I think we were very wrong to judge him by his appearance, as we were with......you know who."

"Yes, we were, and I'm so, so sorry."

"There is no need to be sorry." A deep gentle voice spoke out of nowhere.

Seb and Hannah grabbed their bags and jumped up, looking all around them and getting ready to run.

150

"Who are you? Where are you?" Seb asked nervously as he turned about.

"I am Shale." The voice said, as a dark broad figure stood up on the other side of the stone trough. He was smiling, his large bright eyes full of friendship, and his right hand was raised palm towards them, in a gesture that asked them to wait. They were captivated by his big and genuine smile, and a feeling of certain safety waved through them, making them feel relieved, strongly alive, and happy. Without effort or intention they smiled back at him, and it was as if the sun had burned away some heavy and fearful clouds.

"You have been frightened, both of you, and lost. Let it go; you are brave, very brave, and you have come back. I honour you for that." Shale said, bowing before them low to the ground. Rising again he stood up straight, looking much taller than they remembered, and said, "Will you sit down, please, and we will talk."

Neither Hannah nor Seb could speak, or even wanted to, as they sat down still smiling, amazed at the power and radiating strength of the man that sat before them.

"Peace, be at peace, both of you now. I will not let her harm you, by my life I will not. I know where you have been, and some of what you have seen; your eyes carry it with you. Did she hurt you?" Shale asked.

"No, no she didn't." Hannah replied after a few moments.

"What then did she want from you?"

"I don't know, but she stole something from Seb."

"What did she steal from you, Seb?"

Something in Seb made him resist answering the question immediately; not because he did not trust the man that sat so powerfully in front of him, but because he did not know how to express himself in a way that would not sound childish or silly. Apart from Hannah, he had never spoken about this to anyone, and he was not sure how, or even if, to start.

"She stole a small clay figure from me; a little clay person I had made." He answered eventually.

"What did it look like?" Shale asked.

"It looked like, like this." Seb replied, opening his bag, taking out the other clay figure, and holding it up so that Shale could see it clearly.

Shale smiled a broad and long smile, and asked, "Is it exactly the same as this one?"

"No, no it's not, it's.......it's male, and this one is female."

"How do you know that?"

Seb hesitated, being certain that whatever he said next would change everything, and that whatever happened there would be no going back. His answer had to be the truth, or nothing. He looked into Shale's green eyes for what seemed like a long, long moment, and said,

"Because they have talked to me, and I have talked to them."

He placed the clay figure on the grass in front of them, and waited for some response. Shale's smile became even wider, and his eyes appeared to fill with a tear-glaze.

"And you made them?" He asked.

"Yes." Seb replied.

"Just like this one is now?"

"Yes. Well, no, not quite."

"What is the difference?"

"When I made them they just had little round heads with no features; and their hands and feet were small lumps of pinched clay, without fingers or toes."

"And what about the clothes I can see on her?"

"I did not mark them out, or make them either."

"What then caused these changes to happen?"

"I don't know. They have happened gradually over the past few months, and especially last week."

"What was different about last week?"

"I'm not sure what you mean."

"Well, you say that these changes have happened gradually, but that last week they happened more rapidly."

"Yes, yes they did."

"So, what was different about last week, compared to the months before?"

Seb considered the question carefully, and tried to find any sort of answer. Then Hannah sneezed, and he looked at her and said,

"Bless you." And at that moment he realised what the difference was, the only real difference that mattered.

"It was Hannah. She is the difference. Before last week it was just me; but last week I told her about the clay people, and she has been involved in everything that's happened since then."

Shale looked at Hannah, who seemed to be embarrassed by what was being said.

"Have you spoken to these clay people as well?" he asked her.

"No. I wish I had, and I wish I had seen them move; but I haven't." she replied.

"Why is that?"

"Well, it's like......I think it might be better if Seb explains it."

Seb then described to Shale what he thought had happened, and about the icy shadows, and how the clay people had not moved or spoken since then.

"But these changes in their features and their clothes, these have all happened since the passing of the shadows?"

"Yes." Seb replied.

"Then whoever, or whatever these clay people are, they are not dead. Decay is the mark of death; increase is a mark of life, hence, in some manner, they are still alive."

"That's exactly what we've been thinking." Hannah said, "But why aren't they moving now?"

"I do not know." Shale replied, "But it has something to do with Lemma, as you call her. I am certain of that."

Seb was starting to get agitated; their meeting was not going as he thought it would. He had convinced himself that Shale would know what was happening, and that he would have all the answers, not more questions. His heart began to feel heavy again, with the thought gnawing at the back of his mind that he would never understand any of this, and that he was condemned to go on having these ever stranger and more dangerous experiences until, until they stopped, he thought, or until he did – stopped dead. This final thought made him shudder, even in the extreme heat of that glorious day.

"But, but, please, Shale," he stuttered, "I thought you would understand all of this, and tell us what is really happening, and, and help me."

"I *will* help you, both of you, in whatever way I can. But I do not understand all that is happening to you, only some of it, and that I am now involved in it until it is done."

"Until what is done?" Hannah asked.

"All of it, for you and for me; until it is all finished."

"When we first met you," Hannah continued, "you said it was a great relief to have met us. What did you mean by that?"

"You are the first people I have met for a very long time that have seen something of what I see; and, for me, that is a great relief."

"But what *are* we seeing? Lemma called it *there*, I think."

"That is as good a name as any, I suppose."

"But what is *there*, what is it really?"

Shale bowed his head and became very quiet, his breathing now heavy and tired.

"I do not know." He replied at last, "I have forgotten, it is so very long ago."

As he finished his eyes filled with tears, and his face took on the appearance of a big lost child. A huge wave of care and compassion washed through Seb and Hannah, as they sat there in silence, looking at this great man in front of them; and seeing that he was as lost as they were.

"But, Shale, you *did* know where *there* is, didn't you?" Seb asked gently.

"I did." He replied, "It is where I have come from."

"So, please, why don't you go back there, if you want to?" Hannah asked.

"Because I cannot; I do not know how to."

154

"But, but……." It was Hannah's turn to stutter as she tried to find the right questions, "But *why*? How did you get, get *here*?"

"I do not know. I remember only that I was sent here, but it was so long ago now."

"How long ago, Shale?" Hannah asked, preparing herself for whatever answer may come.

"By my reckoning, and it will not be exact, some fifteen hundred years."

"What?" Seb exclaimed, "Fifteen hundred years, you must be joking!"

Shale stared long and hard at Seb, smiling as if in some kind of pain, and said, "Do I look as if I am joking? It is no more a joke than everything that has been happening to you."

"But, but no one can live that long; nowhere near that long!"

"Yet I have, it is the truth; and it is why I look and feel so tired."

"Who sent you here, Shale?" Hannah asked, her question and voice full of genuine sympathy.

"I cannot remember that either."

"Can you remember *why*, why whoever it was sent you here?" she asked, trying her best to be of any help that she could.

"Yes, that is still clear to me."

"So why was it? For what reason were you sent here?"

"To find two…….two," he seemed unsure how to express what he was thinking, "To find two people."

"Is it us?" Seb asked very quietly.

"No, it is not you, I am sure of that now."

"So who is it? Who were you sent here to find?"

"I cannot remember that either."

"But how can you find them if you don't know who they are?"

"I will know them when I see them; of this I have no doubt. I have searched this whole world, many times over, and until now I have not found a trace of them."

"What are you? I mean, what are you that someone *there* would send you *here*?"

"I am.......I am what you might call a soldier, but a soldier who is also a guardian."

"A guardian of what?"

"A guardian of the two people I am looking for."

"But if you were guarding them, how did they end up *here*?"

"They chose to come here, and I was sent to guard them."

"But why? Why did they choose to come here?"

"It is not for me to know *their* reasons. I only know my own and that I was sent here to guard them, and I have failed."

"How have you failed?" Hannah asked.

"Because I have not found them, and therefore cannot guard them."

"But how do you know that they are still here, after all this time?" Seb asked, scratching his head.

"Because I remember following them, *here*, and they would not go back without me."

"Why?"

"Because I cannot get back without them, and they would not leave me here, as I would not leave them."

"Good grief!"

Hannah touched Seb's arm at this point, as if requesting him to stay calm. After a moment or two she asked, "Shale, please, how did *we* get *there*? I mean, we got there somehow didn't we?"

"No, you did not. You were not really there or really here during that time. You were in an image of it."

"But it felt real, and looked real; everything about it seemed real."

"I know, but beautiful as it is, it is but an image, and I am never far from it."

"So how did we see it, or feel it at all?"

"I am not sure, but I believe that it would only happen if you were shown it, or the way to it, by someone from there; someone with the ability to reveal it to you."

156

"Lemma?"

"Yes, I think so, as she is from there, or.."

"But why would she show us all that?" Hannah interrupted.

"To frighten you. To frighten you so much that you would forget about the other clay figure that she stole from you; to frighten you away from her. But she did not succeed, as you have come back."

At this point Seb coughed, stood up, walked about, and then sat down again.

"Shale, you said you thought it was Lemma who showed us *there*; but then you said *or* – what were you going to say, or what?" he asked.

"Or it was these clay people."

"But how could it be them?"

"Did you see any of *there*, or anything like there before you met with Lemma?"

Seb thought back over the past months, and memories and sounds and visions came rushing into him.

"Yes, yes I did; glimpses, just glimpses and sounds and feelings, but I am sure it was *there*."

At this reply, Shale merely nodded, and was silent. The silence grew in intensity, and seemed to block out all the sounds of the countryside, even the wind, the birds and the insects.

After many moments, Seb groaned, holding his head in his hands, wrestling with a multitude of confused thoughts and images. He kept trying to speak but no words would emerge from his mouth, until, he said finally,

"Do you mean that the clay people are from *there*?"

"Not the clay they are made from, but yes, whoever has brought the clay to life is, I believe, from there."

"And.....and you.......you think that they are the two people you are looking for?"

"As I said, not the clay figures, but whoever is making them to come alive – yes, I believe, no, I hope it may be them."

"But, but....." Seb could not express what he was feeling.

157

"But that means we *have to* get the other clay figure back, from Lemma." Hannah said.

"It does." Shale agreed, "Only then will we be sure. But if they do not speak again we may not ever know."

"Wait, wait…." Seb burst in, "Wait! So, right, this is what's happened. The two people you were guarding came here. You followed them, but couldn't find them. Somehow they were buried underground, in the clay. I dug up the clay, made the two figures, breathed on them, and then they came to life, or they came to life anyway. So why? I mean, they could have stayed buried forever; it was only by accident that I went there that day, because I was bored, and started digging; and it was only by accident that I made the figures, and again, it was only because I was bored, and it was easy. If it wasn't for all these accidents and my boredom we wouldn't even be here now!"

"There are no such things as pure accidents, Seb. They are the effects of a series of causes that we do not see, or do not understand; this much I know." Shale said.

"That sounds similar to a definition I was told, a definition of magic."

"It does." Shale agreed.

"It does." Hannah agreed as well.

✫  ✪  ✩

Shale got up and stretched, and tried to wipe the dust off his heavy overcoat.

"I think it would be good to walk a while." He said, "There is much to consider and decide."

Seb and Hannah agreed, though Hannah was still nervous about going too near to trees or bushes, and said so.

"Do not worry; she will not bother us even if we do see her." Shale said.

After they had walked for a few minutes, Seb stopped and asked Shale another question.

"Shale, who is Lemma, or what is she?"

158

"I can only answer once again that I am not sure. She was here before me, and she told me a long time ago that she has been here forever."

"But you said that she had come from *there*."

"In one thing alone I believe she has spoken the truth, when she says that there is here, and here is there; and yes, I am sure that is where she has come from, but I do not know how or why. Either she will not or cannot go back, for some real reason; this is my deepest suspicion."

"So what do we do now?"

"We will find a quiet place and make our decisions." Shale replied.

He led them away to the north of the Tor, and into a very large meadow with a great chestnut tree in its centre. Hannah and Seb were relieved as they sat down beneath the tree; relieved to be far away from any hiding places. They took out their food and drink and offered some to Shale, but he refused politely, saying that he was not hungry. He seemed concerned and worried, and moving within his own thoughts.

As Seb felt inside his shoulder bag, he came across the little velvet bag with the clay figure in it, and then he felt the rutilant sphere. He took it out and placed it in the palm of his right hand, where it began to revolve slowly just above his skin; and then held out his hand to Shale.

"Do you know what this is?" He asked.

Shale looked closely at the sphere for many moments, and he did not appear to be surprised that it was turning.

"Hannah, give me your right hand." Seb urged.

She opened her right hand to him, and he placed the sphere inside it. It rose to a finger's width above her palm and began to turn as before. Shale continued to watch the little sphere, his face expressionless, his whole body still and quiet, even his breathing silent.

"I do not know what it is." He said after a long pause, "I have not seen such a thing before; but it is from where I come from. I can hear it; it is surrounded by music that I *have* heard before. It is music from my home."

Seb put his ear close to the sphere and listened, and Hannah did the same.

"I can't hear anything." They both said at the same time, which made them laugh.

"It is very clear to me." Shale said, "I have heard the music of this sphere many times before, and a long time before I came here. It is.....it is the music and sound of *there*. I am certain of it."

"Do you want to hold it?" Hannah asked him.

"No, I do not. Where did you get it from?"

"We found it, encrusted in a stone, not far from here." She replied.

"Was it where you were digging clay, Seb?"

"Yes," he answered, "it was exactly the same spot, by Little River Pond over there."

"That cannot be by accident, as you might say. They are connected."

"I think you're right." Seb agreed.

"So do I, they must be." Hannah joined in.

"They are, and I am so glad." Shale said, smiling a big warm smile, "But now we have decisions to make."

"And what are they?" Seb asked, beginning to feel excited.

"They are simple," Shale replied, "but not easy. Two things must be done. The other clay person must be returned to you; and the one you have there must speak, somehow, and return to life."

"Lynn and Serren are their names." Seb said.

Shale smiled again, and said, "They are beautiful names. Did you name them so?"

"No, no I didn't. It was them, they told me their names."

"Wonderful....then, as I said, we need to find Lynn and get him back; and Serren needs to speak."

"But how? How can we do it?" Hannah asked.

160

"Simple, as I said. I will find Lynn, and try to bring him back to you. And you, both of you, will be with Serren, and help her back to life."

"Can't we come with you, you might need help?" Seb asked; but Hannah shifted nervously, not agreeing with his request.

"No, you cannot. Lemma is dangerous. She has a violent and cunning nature, and she would enjoy hurting you, physically, mentally and emotionally. It is her way." Shale replied, touching his heart with his large dusty hand.

"But won't she hurt you?" Hannah asked, with worry in her voice.

"She will try, she will try her very hardest to; but I will stop her if I can, and by my life I will succeed. That is *my* way."

"I don't know how to bring Serren back to life." Seb said quietly.

Shale looked at him and smiled, saying, "If any one can you can, both of you, and you will succeed. That is *your* way." He finished with a low gentle laugh.

"How are you going to find her, Lemma?" Hannah asked, "We can't even see her if she doesn't want to be seen."

Again, Shale laughed a little and said, "I have a nose for her, remember, the redolent boy? She cannot change that whatever appearance she may take. I will find her; she will not be far away, and she will know by now that I am coming for her."

"How can she know that?" Hannah asked, peering round the back of the tree.

"She will know, that is enough for me."

"So when do we begin?" Seb asked, feeling the importance of the moment.

"Now," Shale replied, "now is the time, I have been here far too long."

They all got up and looked around them. The day was still beautiful, the sun at its height, the cloudless blue vault of the heavens arching above a sea of various greens. Now, indeed, was the time.

161

"Find somewhere quiet and safe, and there do what you must." Shale said.

"And you, Shale, where will we find you?" Hannah asked.

"You will find me. When you are done, look for me; and when I am done I will find you, I promise you on my life."

"I am worried for you, Shale, I really am. Do you have to do this?" she asked.

"So am I." Seb agreed.

"Your worry will be my care, and I thank you both. Yes, I have to do this, it is the reason I am even here at all. Take care of each other, and I will see you later. Be of brave heart and all will be well." Shale said, as he turned and walked away from them, lifting his coat collar, and raising his right arm in a gesture of farewell.

# Chapter Fourteen
# Finding Lemma

Seb looked at his watch, and saw that it was midday. They were both hot and confused, and unsure of where to go next.

"Do you really think that Lemma is dangerous, like Shale said?" he asked.

"Yes, yes I do. She is, I don't know, she's totally creepy as far as I'm concerned – horrible; and it's even worse because I've never seen anyone as beautiful as her, whether she appears as a boy or a girl. She's just amazingly beautiful, but only on the outside I'm sure; inside, I think she is ugly."

"Yes, yes, I suppose so." He muttered, with just a hint of doubt in his voice.

"Suppose my eye! She *is*, don't be fooled by her."

"I won't, honest, I won't. Right, we've got to find somewhere quiet and safe, and, and try to do what we can."

For many minutes they stood there while Seb considered all the options, and all the places that he knew.

"Well, according to Shale, I don't think she'll be bothering us while he is looking for her, she will be too busy. Do you remember the little wood, that nature reserve behind Paddington Farm, with the picnic table the volunteers made? That's a good spot, and it's quiet, and we can have some more to eat there. Is that ok with you?"

"Sounds fine to me; which way is it?"

"Over there about, well, about a couple of miles I think."

"Seb, do you think we *will* be able to bring Serren back to life?"

"I don't know. I don't think I'm sure of anything any more, except that we have got to try, and try our very best. But, but just sometimes, I wish I had never dug up that clay, and did what I did."

"Do you?"

"Yes. Well, no, I don't suppose I do really; but I had no idea all this was going to happen, and if I had......."

"But you did not, and you did what you did; and it appears to me that none of this has happened by accident, it's more like, like..."

"Magic?" Seb interrupted.

"No, I don't think so; it's more real than that. Magic, if I think about it, is something, something you use or do for a reason. But this, all of this, it is *happening*, it *is*, and no one is doing it or using it. It just is, like, like the lives we know and we have lived so far. It is as real as everything we see all around us, and this world. Although it seems so very different, there is something which is the same or similar, its, its reality I suppose."

Seb looked at Hannah as she struggled to put into words what she was thinking, and said, "Perfect! And without knowing it that is exactly how I have felt about all this. Well done, you really are a.........genius."

"What, for thinking the same as you? Hardly...." She said smiling, "It's just what I think, but genius or not, I'm not sure what we're going to do next."

"Ha! We'll decide that when we get there. Come on, let's go, it's getting hotter."

"Do you think that Shale will be alright?" she asked, as they turned to leave.

"If anyone can handle her, he can. I would hate to tangle with him."

"And I would hate to tangle with her."

"Let's hope we never have to. Right, that way." He said, as they walked down towards the valley and the lush green fields beyond.

They hardly said another word to each other as they ambled on their way, barely noticing the surroundings as each of them was caught up in their own thoughts and concerns. The strong breeze had faded, and then gone; the sun forced its relentless heat upon them and upon all the land around, and walking became difficult, tiring and heavy. Eventually, they arrived at

164

their destination, and trampled their way through weeds and nettles and ferns, desperate to find some shade from the intense heat and light.

"Phew!" Seb puffed, as he sat down at the picnic table. "What a day, I've never known it so hot."

"Nor have I." Hannah agreed, "I wish there was a swimming pool here, I'd jump straight in!"

"Yes, so would I." He said, before taking a large drink of water.

For some while they sat there quietly, looking around, and trying to cool down, with Hannah using a broad fern frond as a fan.

"Well," he said, reaching into his bag, "I suppose we'd better try."

He took out the little clay figure, and placed it gently on the table in front of them. They both looked at it, and without saying anything, they could see that it had changed once again. It now looked complete in every detail, as if made by some master sculptor. The more they looked at her the more detail they could see, from the many hundreds of individual clay hairs, to the delicate and realistic folds of her clothing. Her long and lovely fingers were topped by beautifully manicured nails, as were her toes, and even her eye lashes were visible, formed out of the thinnest clay imaginable. Her mouth and lips looked so very real, and she was smiling as if she had not a care. Even her eyes had the faintest of smile lines around them, and her tiny eyeballs seemed to be looking out into the day, and looking at Seb and Hannah.

"*That* is amazing!" Hannah said, "She really is perfect."

"She is, I know, it's incredible."

"What shall we do? How do we start?" Hannah asked politely, somewhat in awe of the moment and of what may happen next.

"Well, they came to life before after I had breathed on them. I'll start by trying that, but, but don't disturb me, this is important."

165

"I know; I do know how important it is."

"Ok." As he said this he picked up the little clay figure, and cupped it in the middle of his hands. He closed his eyes, and tried to expel everything from his mind, except the deep wish that this would work. Hannah was silent as she watched him, wishing too that the life in his breath would somehow pass into Serren. After one or two long quiet minutes he breathed in slowly through his nose, as deep a breath as he could manage, his lungs completely full of life giving air; and then, with his mouth very near to the clay figure, he began to push his breath out slowly and all around it, until he had no breath left to give. He put her back on the table and whispered, "Now we wait."

Hannah did not respond, she simply waited and watched. For unknown minutes they waited in silence, and watched for some sign of life.

Finally, Seb broke the silence, saying, "I don't think its working; nothing is happening." And his voice expressed his disappointment.

"I don't know what to say, Seb."

"Nor do I, except, except you try. Maybe you can do it, please, Hannah, please try, and breathe on her."

Hannah looked at Seb and knew that she had to try. She picked up the clay figure and, as he had done, she cupped it in her hands and became very quiet. Closing her eyes, she breathed in long and hard, until her whole frame seemed to be full of vital air. After a brief pause, she breathed out and on to Serren, with every fibre of her female nature longing and trying to give life. Placing the figure back on the table, she sat back and sighed, totally moved by the whole experience. Seb was as well; not only moved by what she had done, but by the way in which she had done it, so very full of intense and real desire. It was something he had never seen or felt before.

Again, they waited in silence; and as the minutes passed they watched for any for any signs of life at all. But there were none; none at all that they could see. They sat there for a few more

166

minutes, both of them pondering upon what they should do next; until Hannah broke the silence this time.

"Do you think…….I don't know how to put this. Do you think that she knows what we are doing? I mean, do you think that she can hear us, and even feel our breath, like, like they say that people who are unconscious or in a coma can?"

Seb was stunned by the question, but thought very hard about it.

"Maybe, maybe she can. I don't know but, I suppose, but I hope she can."

"They say it helps to talk to them, I mean, people who are in a coma."

"It probably does, I'm not sure; but I don't think she's in a coma like that. I think she is trapped and, yes, she might even be able to hear us, but that won't help her."

"But it might *comfort* her, to know that we are trying."

"You're amazing! I would *never* have thought of that, being just a blockhead of a boy. It would, you're right, it would. So, if you can hear me Serren, we *are* trying, trying our very best to help you. And thanks, Hannah."

"Yes, we are, our *very* best." Hannah repeated, looking at the little clay figure.

"So, what now?" Seb asked.

"Well, I don't know; but, but we could both try, together at the same time. We could put our breath together and see if that will work. We've got to try something. Shale is out there doing heaven knows what, and this is our part, that's what he told us."

"Yes, it is, it is our part, however futile it is."

"It may appear futile, but at least we are not giving up, not as long as we keep on trying something."

"Ok, let's do it; it might just do the trick."

"Trick?"

"Oh, not trick, but it might work. We can only keep trying, as you said."

"Whose hands are we going to put her in?"

167

"One of each; my left and your right. But I think we're going to have to stand up for this one."

Picking up the clay figure, they stood up, and went to the end of the wooden table, standing as close together as possible. They put his left hand and her right hand next to each other, and Seb managed to place Serren where their two hands joined together.

"Right," he said, "we'll both take in as big a breath as we can, and when I nudge you, we'll put our mouths close to her and slowly breathe out onto her. Ok?

"Yes, ok."

"Now!" he said, and they breathed in for as long and as hard as they could. After a very brief pause Seb nudged Hannah. They put their faces together, cheeks touching and eyes closed, and breathed out slowly as close to the clay figure as they could get.

Seb picked up Serren, and placed her back in the centre of the table. Then they sat down quietly and waited. Neither of them wanted to say anything, or to do anything, as they could not think of what to say or do next anyway. So they waited, and watched, and waited; but there was no apparent change in the little clay figure.

Eventually, Seb sighed and said, "I don't know what to do. It's like having a locked door in front of us and no keys. I am sure she's trapped, whoever she is, trapped in that cold little body!"

He became angry, and stood up, and kicked at the grasses around him. All that had happened to him, all his fears, all his hopes, all his ignorance and impotence and weaknesses exploded inside him, together and all at once; and he sank to his knees, feeling utterly defeated and lost.

"I can't take any more of this, I can't! I'm just a boy; a stupid idiotic ignorant boy, and what do I know of this, any of this? Nothing, nothing at all, not a bloody thing! Damn it, damn it all, this is a nightmare. God it hurts, I feel like I'm falling apart!"

168

"Seb, Seb, don't, don't hurt yourself, please, you're none of those things." Hannah said, as she sat down beside him, and put her arm around his shaking shoulders.

"But I am; I'm all of those things, and more. I've been acting, pretending to be brave, pretending I could handle it – all pretending, when I'm just so full of fear. Why? Why is this happening to me?"

"Seb, dear Seb, you *are* brave, you *are* strong, believe me, I've seen it, I've been with you, I've felt it; and what's the point in being brave if you're not scared? That's not bravery its just stupidity; courage is about overcoming fear and weakness, and without them courage wouldn't exist. Please, come on, this is happening to both of us now; and I need you, I really do, and so does Serren, and Lynn and Shale. *All* of this began with you; Seb, we can't do it without you, and you've got to be there at the end."

"But will it *ever* come to an end?"

"It will, everything does. Come on, be as angry as you like, but stop kicking yourself, please, you could not have done any better, nobody could have."

"Damn it! You're right, I can't stop now; and even if I do, all these things will still keep happening, but I will have even less control over them than I have now. Sorry, Hannah, I'm sorry, and thanks for your, your strength."

"I don't have much of that, but whatever I've got we can share, if you will share yours with me."

"Ha! It's a deal. Maybe between us we've got enough to get us through all this; we've got to have. But, but sometimes I just wish I was a little boy again, playing with toys, safe, and having my safe boyish dreams."

"In my own way I know that feeling, and I wish, I wish for a happy ending, like in all my favourite stories."

"Well, maybe that's down to us, or at least some of it. Come on, we've got to try something else; there must be something we can do."

They got up and returned to the table, both of them looking at the perfectly formed clay figure that lay there, smiling so very realistically.

Seb took two biscuits out of his bag, and after giving one of them to Hannah, said, "I'm not sure what do next, but, but I was just thinking that the clay people came alive together, each time apart from the first, maybe one can't become alive without the other."

"What a romantic thought, and so unlike you, Seb."

"I didn't mean it like, like, um, you know what I mean; but it could be true, couldn't it?"

"I suppose so; yes, it could."

"Not that that helps; we don't want to have to wait until Shale finds Lynn to see if it's true."

"But what if Shale doesn't find him?"

"He will, I know he will."

"You are so very amusing, Seb. You *do* make me laugh, you and all your innocent certainties." An amused female voice said.

Hannah screamed as she jumped up.

"Lemma!" Seb said, grabbing the clay figure and shoving it into his pocket. "Come here, Hannah, quick!"

Hannah moved round quickly and stood next to him, both their hearts thumping wildly as they looked around, trying to find out where Lemma was hiding.

"And you, Hannah, so very wise and comforting; you too make me laugh, especially when you are so full of fear, like you are now." Lemma said.

Though they could not work out where she was, or from which direction her voice was coming, they could smell her, and her scent was very intoxicating.

"Where are you? What do you want?" Seb asked, trying to sound as strong as possible.

"I am here, somewhere near to you; and I believe you know what I want."

170

"No, no I don't! Just go, go away and leave us alone." Seb said, feeling Hannah trembling beside him, and totally unable to speak.

"I will, very soon. I have always found difficult children tiresome. Put it back on the table, and then you may leave."

"Put what back?"

"Now that is *very* immature of you, you know exactly what I mean. Put it back, now, and then leave."

"Why should I? You've already stolen one of them, why do you want the other?"

"I did not *steal* it, Seb, I rescued it; as I wish to do for the one you have there."

"Rescue it from what? We're not going to harm them."

"Listen, both of you, and learn. You do not know what you have, and you do not know what these clay people are, so how can you know what is harmful or bad for them, or even what is good or beneficial for them. You *can not*."

"Do you know what the clay people are?"

"I do. I know what they are, and who they are."

"So, what are they?"

Lemma laughed quietly, and said, "Even the so-called wise men of this world, your pseudo-intellectuals and scientists and thinkers, would find *that* almost beyond their ability to understand, even though they should ever wish to. It is enough to say that while they are with you they are in danger, and they are also dangerous to you."

"Why? They're......they're harmless, and gentle." Seb argued.

"I say again, if you do not know what they are, you cannot know whether they are harmless or gentle, or the opposite, or anything else. You may think that you know what they are, or something about them, but you do not; and your ignorance of your own ignorance is the real danger in this."

"They are from *there*, aren't they?"

"They are."

"And you need them, don't you?"

"I do not need them, I want them."

"But what do you want them *for*?"

"They are trapped here in this place, and I want to help get them back to where they should be. Believe me, Seb, I want only what is good for them."

Lemma's voice changed as she said these words. It became softer and more delightfully feminine, more attractive and convincing.

"But, but.......they came to me, I found them, it is, it's me they really want."

"No, dear Seb, it is not. It is me they want and need; they have been looking for me and want only to be with me." Again her voice increased in its charm and loveliness, and it took on the appearance of a beautiful lover wishing only to be reunited with her long lost beloved.

"But, but all that's happened, all that's happened to me, all.......all of it, it can't be for nothing."

"Everything has its reason, Seb, everything; and you have been caught up in this by accident. They have *used you*, used you to help them find me, and your time with them is now over."

"They haven't used me, they haven't! They spoke to me, they were lovely to me, I..........I feel for them, *deeply*."

"This is their way, dearest Seb. They know what they are doing, and care nothing for who gets hurt while they are doing it. They will break your heart in pieces to get what they really want. I am sorry, Seb, I know how you are feeling, for I can *feel* it."

"But, no, no! You mean everything......"

"Seb! Don't listen to her, she's lying." Hannah said, finally finding the courage to speak, appalled by all that she was hearing and witnessing.

"Not so, Hannah." Lemma said quietly, "I mean what I say, and you are not a part of this."

As she said this, a shadow long and thin drifted across the grasses, and stopped, and covered Hannah. Instantly she became cold, very cold, and she hugged herself trying desperately to keep warm. She tried to speak, but could not; she was too cold, finding only enough energy to breathe, just to breathe. Seb saw none of this, he was too involved in his own heartache and profoundly deep inner sadness.

"You mean, everything, everything was *false*? All this time, all I have felt, all I've........hoped for, false? They've just been playing with me? Just......just *using* me?"

"Yes, dear Seb, that is what they have done to you. I am so very sorry."

Seb's eyes stung from the wash of tears that filled them. He was hurting; hurting in a way that seemed to strain, rip and tear at his very heart and mind, and at all that he had believed himself to have felt and done for the clay people; and finally, at what he had always believed himself to be. A great and uncontrollable misery overwhelmed him, and, like an emotional tidal wave, it washed away all of his certainties.

"I care for you, Seb, I care very much, and I wish only to see you happy." Lemma said, stepping away from the natural background, to stand not far from the table. Seb looked at her and was stunned. He had never seen anyone so beautiful in all his life, and her short covering of leaves and twigs and binding flowers only added to it, and filled his heart with feelings he did not recognize.

"Give me the clay figure, Seb, and all of this will be over. You will still have me, and you will be happy." She said, in a voice so delicate and pure and loving.

Seb reached into his pocket and took out the little clay figure. It did not seem so lovely, and perfect to him now; it seemed to be just what it was – a clay model with all its imperfections, both inside and out. He lifted his head to look at Lemma, and she removed her natural garment. Beneath it she was wearing one of the pieces that looked as if it was made of liquid, and it rippled all over her slender body in slow and long moving waves. It changed from red to gold, from gold to silver, and then from silver to a crystal clear water. She held out her hand, and said,

"*Please*, Seb, please give it to me, and I promise that you will be happy."

He was totally absorbed by the vision in front of him; such a perfect form that energised his every sense and feeling. He stood up, moved away from the table, and went to stand in front of her. Close to, her overpowering beauty and scent almost made him faint; but, with one last look at the clay figure, he placed it in Lemma's open hand.

"Thank you. Seb." She said, "Thank you *so* much; you have done the right thing. We will meet again soon, and I will make you very glad."

She bent down to pick up her leafy clothing, and as she rose again she stopped, and kissed Seb on his forehead. She put her clothing back on, and smiled into his stinging eyes.

"Until another time, Seb. Be strong and happy."

With these words Lemma turned away, and walked off into the trees, slowly becoming invisible as she went.

For a long time there was absolute silence, as Seb stood there feeling numb from his head to his toes, and empty except for pain.

"You idiot!" Hannah shouted, as she stood up shivering, the shadow having now gone. It was as if she had slapped him hard on his face, and he awoke from his numbness into the full light of day.

"You absolute idiot! Why did you give it to her? She was lying, all of it, every single word was a lie!"

"But, what? What have I done? What did I give her?"

"Serren, you gave her Serren!"

He grabbed at his pockets and searched through them; and tipped his bag upside down as he looked frantically for the clay figure. But it was gone.

"Did I........no, I couldn't have given her away. I just shook Lemma's hand!"

"You did not shake her hand. She paraded in front of you like, like she is, and she fooled you, and got you all.........I

174

don't know. But then you gave her the figure; you gave her Serren"

"Oh hell, no! Where is she, where's Lemma? We've got to get Serren back!"

"Lemma has gone; and I bet we won't see her again, now that she's got what she really wanted."

"But I heard her! I remember, she said that the clay people had used me, and didn't care if they hurt me, didn't care about me at all. They just wanted to be with her, and that they were dangerous" Yet even as he said these things, the words sounded hollow and wrong.

"Lies! Everything she said was a lie. She wanted to break you, and hurt you, so that you would do whatever she wanted."

"And I did, I did. I did exactly what she wanted, because I........because, I believed her. She made me feel like........" But he was completely lost for words as his self-belief began to shatter.

"I know how she made you feel; and if I had been you I would have probably felt the same, she was just too much for us."

"But, but why didn't you stop me?"

"I couldn't, Seb, I couldn't. Some.....a shadow came over me and I couldn't move or speak. I saw it all, and felt like screaming, but I was too cold. I just couldn't move or even open my mouth."

"Oh! Damn it all, damn, what the hell have I done?"

"You've been fooled, badly. But listen, listen to me; for all her looks and charm and scent and......whatever, she is a liar and a cheat. None of what she said was true, none of it! You *did* find the clay people, but *not* to give them to her. Everything she said about them was a lie too. Don't believe her, don't believe any of it; don't hurt yourself, it's what she wants you to do. All your feelings about them were right; *believe them*, believe them all, and forget everything Lemma said and seemed to offer you."

"God, I am pathetic."

"No, no you're not. You're just a boy with boys' feelings, and she preyed on them like a vulture."

"That's what it feels like."

"I bet it does; and, as I said, if I had been you I would have probably done and felt the same."

"Would you?"

"Yes, I believe I would. She was so......so, well, so, I'm sure you know what I mean." Hannah said, trying to hide her blushing.

"I do."

"I know how you were feeling, I do. Well, there's only one thing to do now."

"Which is?"

"Find Lemma, and get the clay people back!"

"How?"

"You tell me, Seb, you tell me."

"I know, you're right, and somehow we've got to do it. I am so sorry, Hannah, I'm just a ......"

"Normal boy with normal feelings, and an abnormal sense of guilt. I felt what she was doing to you, and you didn't stand a chance. You did your best, Seb, so forget it all, all of it, and think about how we can get them back."

"Thanks, Hannah, I really mean it."

# Chapter Fifteen
# Thunder within the Earth

Heavy grey clouds began to rush across the sky from the west, and a chilly breeze ruffled through the treetop leaves around them, as Seb and Hannah sat in silence eating the last of their food. Seb's embarrassment, shame and sadness had changed gradually into a kind of focussed anger, and he thought as hard and as well as he could about how to get the clay people back; and tried to decide whether he had the courage even to attempt it.

He looked at his watch and said, "Two o' clock. We've only got a few hours left, and the weather seems to be changing fast. Do you really want to try and get them back?"

"We've got to; or just forget about it all, all of it."

"I meant do *you* want to help me try. I know I've got to, it's all my fault. But if you want, we can go back home and wait for your mother, and I'll come back tomorrow and……..and do whatever."

"I'm not sure if I do *want* to, as you put it, but, but like it or not I *am* a part of this now, and I can't leave you to do it on your own, I can't and I won't."

"What, in case Lemma charms me, and fools me again?"

"Well," Hannah smiled, "there is that; not that I think you would let her this time. No, it's, it's like we agreed; either we both go on or we both stay. We've got to stick together in this, and either do it together or forget about it."

"I can't, I can't forget any of it. All this scares me, but I'm even more scared of doing nothing, for all concerned. And we mustn't forget Shale; he's out there somewhere, looking for Lemma, and maybe we can help him or he can help us."

"Well, I hope he finds her before we do, and gets the clay people back. That would solve everything."

"And that's probably what will happen. But, but I think we've got to try, otherwise I'll never forgive myself."

"I know, but don't be too hard on yourself, Seb, nobody passes every test first time. And I agree, we've got to give it a go. But how?"

"That's what I've been wondering. Somehow we've got to find her, and hopefully we'll bump into Shale on the way."

"But what will we do if we *do* find her?"

"Get the clay people back."

"Easy."

"Piece of cake."

"But, seriously, if we do find her, how will we get them away from her?"

"I don't know."

"I think she might hurt us."

"I don't think so, she could have done that already. For some reason I don't think she wants to hurt us physically, just confuse us and scare us."

"She's done *that* already."

"I know, I know, but second is more certain, and we'll be ready for her, her…….charms, or whatever they are. Well, I will be at least."

"So, maestro, what are we going to do?"

"There's only one thing I can think of. She could be anywhere, but we do know one of her *places*, where we were the other day."

"What? Go back there?"

"I can't think of anywhere else to look, can you?"

"No, I can't, but…."

"I know what you are feeling, and I feel the same, but, listen, you don't have to come with me, you really don't."

"But I do, Seb, I do, I am sure of that now."

"Right, come on then, let's make a move, the weather's starting to look a bit ugly."

"But we couldn't find the door, Seb, behind that thicket thing."

"So we'll try to find the other one, the one just by the stream. And if we can't, maybe that's all we can do for today."

"Ok then, let's go."

They packed their bags, threw them over their shoulders, and made their way down through the copse and over two broken stiles. As they entered a large flat field, Seb could see a dark shape on the horizon where another hill was rising. He got out his binoculars and looked through them.

"It's Shale!" He said, "Way over there, walking fast. And, and, no, he's gone now, over the brow of that hill."

"And who is that?" Hannah asked, pointing to a far away rise just to the north of the Tor.

Seb turned and focussed on three figures walking along the ridge of the hill.

"My god! I don't believe it." He shouted, giving Hannah the binoculars.

"Lemma, its Lemma! And who's that with her, they look sort of familiar?"

"They are." Seb replied, "That's that…..Ade, and the other one is Mr. Baines. Heavens, they know Lemma!"

"That might explain a lot."

"It might, but I can't work it out at the moment. Right, that's it, sod them all! Shale's making for her *place*, I'm sure he is, and she may well be too. That is where we are going. Are you up for this?" He asked, as if all of his fears were evaporating away.

"Yes. I really think I am."

"Good. We'll go this way." He said, pointing towards the broad fields behind the hamlet of Wick.

They walked off into the west, and within a couple of minutes it began to rain. It was not heavy at first, but hard enough to wet their summer clothes, as they rummaged in their bags for their waterproof jackets. Passing through the cow pastures beyond Maidencroft Farm, they made their way in silence, heads down against the increasing wind. Even though they aware of them, they ignored the occasional deep shadows that seemed to be trying to distract them, or scare them, or deter

179

them from their path. Feeling their chill, they passed on through them, and their combined determination robbed the shadows of most of their power.

"Don't let them bother you." Seb said.

"I won't, I'm fed up with them, and they can't make me any colder than I am."

"Ha! That's the spirit! Are you ok?"

"Fine, just a bit cold and wet. Is it far to go?"

"About another mile or so. We're coming at it from a different direction this time, so I hope I can remember where it was."

"We'll find it, if it's there."

No sooner had Hannah said this, than the wind increased ten-fold in strength, and almost blew them off their feet.

"Come on!" Seb shouted, "Down there, make for the trees!"

"Ok, I'm coming; quick!"

They ran as fast as they could over the remaining fields, until they found the shelter of the many streamside trees. Taking off their hoods, they found a dry area within some large beech roots and sat down, puffing. All around them the trees were creaking and squeaking, groaning and bending as they were whipped by the fast swirling winds.

"Do you know where we are?" Hannah asked.

"I think so. But the stream is a lot deeper and faster than it was, and not how I remember it. I think we need to go upstream about half a mile or so, and then cross it and search the other bank. And it's getting very dark."

"I know, I was trying to ignore that. Do you think this weather has got anything to do with *her*?"

"Could well be, nothing would surprise me where she's concerned. I bet it's sunny in Glastonbury, and that this lot is just here, now, just where we are"

"Weather made for two, eh?"

"Ha! I'd rather have cups of tea for two, and a couple of rounds of toast."

"Mmm, so would I, we'll make sure that we have that later."

"Deal! I think it might be better to try and stay under the trees, and make our way close to the stream, in case we miss that little bay where the door was. It's going to be tricky, especially if it gets any darker; and we're going to get very wet."

"I'm already wet, and I don't care. I just want to get the clay people back, and be done with *her* for ever."

"Same here. Right, come on then, and watch where you're walking or you'll end up in there." He said, pointing to the deep rushing stream.

It did get darker, and very quickly, and they found that sticking close by the stream was a great deal harder than they had imagined. The wind kept flicking branches into their faces, as they bent and struggled and sometimes crawled their way through the mass of tangled creepers, sharp and pointed thick briar tendrils, weeds, nettles, grasses and hidden tree roots. They came upon a patch of undergrowth so thick and so broad that at first there seemed to be no way forwards. It also barred the way to their right away from the stream, and to its left was the ever deeper and faster torrent of water.

"I'm going to have to try to cut a way through." Seb said, "Shame we didn't bring any gloves, these thorns are really nasty."

He opened his shoulder bag and searched inside it for the knife he had thought to bring along. Pulling it out, he saw that the little black velvet bag was stuck to its blade. It took a lot of effort to pull them apart, and he realised unconsciously that the rutilant sphere inside the bag must be magnetic. This did not surprise him, and he hardly even registered the thought, so keen was he to try to cut their way through the densely tangled barrier.

Within a couple of minutes Seb had to stop. His hands and arms, face and head were bleeding from the scratches and punctures inflicted by the sharp thorns. His little knife was all but useless for hacking at the thick mass in front of him, and he

181

sat down, breathing hard, his face stinging from the sweat in his wounds.

"I can't do this!" He called out to Hannah, as he backed his way out of the small clearing he had managed to make. "It could take forever to cut through these with this, and I can't take any more of those spikes and things, they're hideous!"

"Heavens, Seb! Come here, come on, wash your face in the stream, it's covered with blood. Forget that way, it's not worth it."

He did as he was told, and tried to dry his hands and face on his wet t-shirt.

"I don't recognize this place." He said, "I've not been this way before, probably because of this lot. If we go back on the path I don't know if we'll spot the door. I think it's the water for us! At least it's a sort of path, and we can see where we're going."

"I hate to say it, but you're probably right. Do you think its far now?"

"No, it shouldn't be. I think we're very close. We can cross here and wade our way along by the other bank. Ready?"

"Ready." She replied, sliding into the rush of cold water.

Although the stream was not very deep its speed, combined with the slimy stones and weeds and submerged tree roots, made it impossible to walk without holding on to branches and overhanging plants. After about ten minutes, and with great difficulty, they managed their way around a long sharp bend, and then they saw the little shingly bay open up straight in front of them. Somehow, the running water did not fill it, and as they walked up to the steep bank they found that the shingle and stones were completely dry, untouched by the stream flowing just a short distance away.

After catching their breath and trying to warm up their chilled wet feet, they walked up to the bank and examined it. At first it looked just like any other earthy bank, with its broad arch bordered with thin tree and plant roots, and a few pretty riverside flowers. Seb scraped at it with his knife, and to their

182

relief, the outline of a door started to appear. Hannah helped him with her fingers, until the whole shape of it became clear. She banged on it with her fist, trying to work out what it was made from, and it made a thick dull but hollow sound.

"Don't, don't Hannah. If she's in there we don't want her waiting to welcome us."

"Sorry, but it's so weird, it doesn't look like it's made of anything, wood or stone, it just looks like part of the bank."

"I'm sure that's how she wants it to look; you would never know that it was here. But I can't see any handle or latch, or a lock, or anything to open it."

"When we were here before, how did *she* open it? Did she have a key or something?"

"No, I don't think she did. She just sort of pushed it open."

"So maybe it isn't locked, try it."

Seb put both his hands on the door and pushed, but nothing happened. He tried again, this time pushing harder and using his shoulder; but the door did not move at all.

"Come on, we'll both try." He said, turning to Hannah.

They both put their shoulders to the door and pushed with all their strength, but again, it stood hard and fast closed.

"Wait, "Hannah said, "let's think about this. When we came here last time you were in front of me, and I couldn't see the door. What did she do, exactly, can you remember?"

"Well, she just walked up to the door and pushed it open."

"That's not very exact. We are doing that and nothing's happening. Try to remember *exactly* what she did, and how she did it."

He thought for a few moments, and then said, "She stood there, for just a second, then put her hand to door and pushed."

"Where? Where did she put her hand, *precisely* where?"

"Well, just here, I think." He replied, putting his hand on the door.

"Try it then, push."

Seb did push, but once again without any visible effect.

"And that's all she did? She didn't whisper a magic spell or something?" Hannah asked.

He smiled at what she had said, and replied, "None that I heard. I don't think she's into speaking spells. But, but hang on, now I think of it, I think she used *both* of her hands. One here, and one about here, or here." As he said this he pushed gently against the door with his hands, and it began to open slowly without a sound.

The door opened fully into darkness, and a delicate scent drifted out of the space within. Seb took one step inside and was immediately surrounded by a heavy and complete silence. The darkness was total, and it too seemed to bear down on him like an invisible weight, pushing him backwards as if in warning.

He turned to Hannah and said, "It's creepy in there. I can't see a thing; but I can smell her. She's in there, somewhere. It's decision time, Hannah."

"We've made our decision. Do you really want to walk away and leave the clay people in *her* hands, to do......to do whatever she wants to them?"

"No, no I don't, and I hope she hasn't already. But I'm not sure if I want to walk *that* way either; into the dark, and into heaven knows what."

"I don't think what we *want* has anything to do with all this now, it's what we *need* that counts, and we've already decided that."

"I know, I know......thanks, I've never been keen on the dark but, you're right, they need us and, and what the hell, I couldn't live with myself if I turned away now. Right, I've got the torch, and help me with that big rock, we'll keep the door ajar with it."

They shuffled the rock into place so that the door could not close, and then stood within the quiet dark space. Seb turned on his torch and they walked forward a couple of steps. There was no sign of light anywhere, and as they went to walk down the steep stairs in front of them they heard a slow crunching grinding sound, and then a loud metallic click. Turning quickly they knew, and then they saw, that the door had broken the heavy rock, and that it had closed itself behind them. They walked back to door and looked at it carefully, searching for a bolt or a handle or a lock, but there was none. It was seamless and smooth, with not even enough space around its edges for fingers to gain a grip. The way back was shut, locked, barred and blocked, and whether by choice or from need there was only one direction open to them – forwards.

"Mmm, that's that then. Right, let's get this over with, Hannah. I don't think we should talk unless we have to, and try to walk quietly, we might just surprise her."

"Let's hope so, I don't want her to surprise us. I wish I had brought a torch too."

"We can take it turns holding it but, just to be on the safe side, I'll tie this string around my waist and you do the same with the other end. At least we shouldn't get separated that way."

Joined together by a thin white string they made their way down the stairs, and along a high arched tunnel that had many openings on either side. It was so dark, and the beam of light was so thin as it pointed straight ahead of them, that they felt as if they were floating, with their feet hidden from them as they walked. Eventually they came into a wider space and they could see that it was a room; but it was a big empty room, with three closed doors at its far end.

"Well, which one?" Seb whispered.

"Does it matter?" Hannah replied.

"Of course it does."

"Why?"

"*Why?* Because, I don't know, because, it's like those stories – three doors, but only one of them leads to safety."

"I don't think any of them lead to safety. Maybe we should open each one of them and see what's behind."

"Good thinking, good. Ok, you open the left one first."

"*Me?*"

185

"Yes, you said it didn't matter which one."

"Oh, alright, *great*, but stand close to me."

She turned the door handle very, very slowly and then pulled; but the door would not open. She tried pushing it, but still it stayed closed.

"It's locked." She whispered.

"Right, I'll try this one." Seb said, as he too very slowly tried the middle door's handle. The result was the same – locked.

"One left, or we're trapped, and I really don't fancy that." He whispered.

This time he just turned the door handle as he would normally, and it worked; the door opened quietly towards them. Stepping through, they found themselves in the room of many clothes and, from somewhere, there was just enough light for them to see by. In that dim light all the clothes looked like they had faded to grey, though some of them sparkled a little or reflected what meagre light there was. As they approached the far end of the room they heard voices coming from the passage in front of them. Seb turned off the torch, and they stood still, and listened.

"That's Shale! That's Shale's voice." Hannah whispered excitedly.

"I know, and the other one is Lemma's. They're talking; you don't think…"

"Don't think what?"

"You don't think, no, they couldn't be surely?"

"What, couldn't be what, Seb?"

"Well, in this together, friends or something like that?"

"Never! For heaven's sake, Seb, pull yourself together."

"Sorry, sorry, I'm just…."

"Scared? Frightened?"

"Yes, both!"

"So am I. Come on, get a grip, please, please, for both our sakes!"

"Ok, sorry, I am. Right, if we crawl along here to the end of this passage we should be closer to them, and be able to hear what they're saying."

"Alright, you first."

They lay down, and very slowly and quietly edged their way to where the passage opened up into the same vast underground scene of trees and lawns and the long silent pool where they had been before. Here too the light was hardly bright, but it was enough to enable them to see everything clearly, even the colours of the bushes and flowers, leaves and grasses. They could also see Shale and Lemma, standing beneath a large tree on the wide smooth lawn that ran down to the middle of the lake. Hiding behind a tuft of marsh reeds, Seb and Hannah watched and listened, and hoped that they would have to do nothing more than that.

"Now I know what a silly, foolish man you are. You would be wise to leave here while you can, and forget what you cannot possibly change." The soft voice of Lemma seemed to float through the air.

"Give them to me and I will go." The deep voice of Shale replied.

"I will not, and you shall not have them. I have waited many long years for this time, and I will be free of them." She said, holding up the clay people in her right hand.

"You will never be free of them, whatever you do now; you know this to be true."

"Not so. *You* know this, I know it to be different. They will never find each other again, never, and I will break them to dust."

"Then you seal your own fate, and it will be permanent."

"I care nothing for fate. Fate is for men, and the likes of you."

"Whether you care for it or not hardly matters, without them your prison is complete."

"Do not talk to me of prisons, and fate, and *them*. This world is enough for me."

187

"No world is enough for you and your kind. You are holding in your hand the only chance of something better."

"Then I will break that chance now, as your better is my worse."

"You cannot break them, you know this too."

"I do *not* know this, old man. *I*, not you, know what I can do; so beware of what you do not understand."

"I am aware of what you can do. I have seen the ruin you leave behind you many times over. Give them to me, and you have a chance of freedom."

"What do you know of freedom? You, a soldier-brute, bound to the whims of your masters."

"The bond is one of mutual love, not one made from force."

"Love, you say, love, the universal binder! Ha!"

"You should not quote what you do not understand; it makes you sound childlike and foolish. For the final time I ask you, give them to me."

Lemma bent down, and from under the roots of the tree she drew out a long sharp broad shining sword. She pointed it at Shale and smiled.

"You have seen what I can do with this. Leave now, I have no wish to hurt you."

"I will not leave without them."

"Then you will not leave at all, it is nothing to me. You are free to enjoy this place for ever. Farewell, old man."

Shale took three steps towards Lemma, and stood just beyond the point of her gleaming sword. He held out his hand and stared at her, urging her wordlessly to give him the clay people.

"You are a fool, and always have been. You have no weapon that can harm me." She said.

Shale said nothing in reply as he breathed in deeply. They stared at each other for many long moments, and tension filled the silent air with a charge like a lightning shaft.

"Leave." Lemma said.

But Shale did not speak, as his shoulders seemed to broaden immensely.

"Enough!" Lemma exclaimed, and with blinding speed she drew back the sword with both hands, and made to cut Shale down.

A roaring shout of "No!", so loud and deep and full of power burst out of Shale's open mouth that it knocked Lemma off her feet, sending her crashing and rolling backwards. Seb and Hannah covered their ears in shock, but it felt like the ground they were lying upon was shaking from the sheer force of Shale's gigantic bellow, which rumbled around the open space, vibrating through the rocks the trees and water. The sword tumbled out of Lemma's hand, and disappeared into the lake. The clay people were bounced out of her other hand as she crashed into the knotted roots of a great oak tree. Finally, Shale's violent roar ebbed into silence as he walked up to Lemma, and looked upon her beautiful but broken body.

"I am sorry." He said, "I did not want any of this, or to harm you."

He picked up the clay people and walked away from her, exhausted by the whole experience.

As Seb and Hannah were about to stand up, they saw Lemma roll over and get to her feet, and she was smiling. Once again, her short clothing of all things natural fell away from her, and beneath it she was lined with the transparent garment of clear water.

"Wait," she said pleadingly, "please wait. I was so wrong to have doubted you."

Her voice was like the voice of a forgiving mother, so very sweet and loving, sincere and of the heart. "Please, forgive me; let me comfort your weary soul. Come into my arms and find peace and safe rest."

Shale turned and looked at her, and was spellbound by her beauty. Seb started to move, but Hannah grabbed his arm and whispered, "No!" terrified by both of the people in the clearing in front of her.

"Dear, dear man, forgive me. We have seen so much, and now it is our time to share and to be together. Please, mighty warrior, I love you."

As Lemma said these words, Shale was unable to move; he was totally charmed by the power of her form and her sincerity. He smiled; a smile of relief and relaxation, and from a deep sensation of safety at last. In the blink of an eye Lemma reached into her hair, pulled out a long thin sparkling steel needle, and forced it deep into Shale's beating body and heart. Hannah screamed, and Seb shouted, and they both leapt up to their feet.

"Away, children, this is not for you!" Lemma ordered, and they both froze in their tracks.

As Shale staggered backwards, his eyes now full of the truth, he stumbled, and fell, and the clay people bounced far away from him. Lemma walked slowly over to where Shale was lying on his back, and she still held the deadly needle in her right hand. She stood astride of his barrel-like chest and looked down at him, and smiled. He was still breathing, and he stared back at her, and he too was smiling.

"Good bye, old man, our many meetings are over; enjoy your well earned final rest." She said, her voice full of triumph and sarcasm.

Shale's only reaction was a deep and crackling gentle laugh.

Behind the reeds Seb could not contain himself. He felt like his head and heart would explode if he did not do something to stop the horrific scene he was witnessing. His first experience of real adult violence filled him with revulsion and anger, fear and disbelief, and he panicked as he tried to decide what he should do. He felt in his bag and put his hand on the knife. Then he felt his remaining apple, and his binoculars, his torch and compass, finally closing his hand around the little rutilant sphere.

Lemma bent over from the waist and looked closely into Shale's bright eyes, while at the same time placing the needle above his weakening heart. She kissed her left hand and put it gently onto Shale's forehead, as if in a gesture of fond farewell. At that moment, Seb jumped out from behind the reeds, pulling

Hannah out with the string. He stretched his arm back as far as he could, and with all his years of intense cricket practice pumping through his fit young body, he threw the rutilant sphere at Lemma with every bit of strength that he possessed. It struck her leg with massive force in the space behind her knee, and she screamed, and clutched at her leg, and fell over sideways in raging agony and anger. Pulling herself up onto one leg, she turned and stared at Seb and Hannah, her big wide open eyes sparkling like flaming diamonds.

"That was your final mistake, and I will deal with you in one moment. Stay there!"

As she shouted her command, Seb and Hannah froze with fear, and could not find the will or the strength to move in any direction. They were rooted where they stood, and could only await what she would choose to do next.

Lemma stood up and limped towards where the clay people lay on the grass. A low rumbling thundery sound came from within the earth, and the ground began to tremble and shake. She tried to walk on, but as she approached the clay people there was an enormous bang and blast, and the very air itself exploded with the deafening noise of thunder. With irresistible speed and power the ground split open beneath her, with a tearing splitting awesome *boom*. She fell, twisted, thrust out her hands and grabbed on to the edge of the increasing crack in the earth. Hannah and Seb fell over as they watched the ground rip open, until it reached the side of the lake. Water began to gush into the crack, and in the middle of the lake a great wave formed and surged towards the bank. With a mighty heaving roar like the sea it crashed over the bank, and bore down with its enormous weight and power on top of Lemma's head. She disappeared beneath the wave as it bubbled and frothed and battered its way into the darkness of the deepening crack. Then, for just a second, there was absolute silence. But it was swiftly followed by another unbearable blast of thunder, as the split in the earth closed and the water rolled back into the lake.

Seb tried to get up, but his knees were shaking and weak. He looked at Hannah, but she was lying on her front, hands over her ears, and she was trembling and sobbing uncontrollably. He managed finally to stand up, and he could see Shale on his hands and knees crawling across the green lawn. Seb bent down and put his hand on Hannah's back.

"Are you ok? Please, Hannah, please, can you hear me? Are you alright?"

"I, I think so." she replied between sharp sobbing breaths, "Oh god, what has happened?"

"It's over, I think it's over, but......but Shale is hurt, hurt badly. We've got to go and help him if we can."

Hannah got to her knees, still sucking in sharp breaths, "Where, where is he?" she said.

"Over there, he's crawling......no, no he's not, he's fallen and he's stopped moving!"

As Hannah stood up she saw Shale lying in the distance, and her face crumpled up into tears once again.

"Please, Hannah, please, you've got to help. We're ok, she's gone, she's.......gone!"

Seb grabbed her hand, and gently but urgently he led her along the lakeside, and up onto the lawn where the great bulk of Shale was lying on his back. They knelt down on either side of him, and a huge surge of uselessness overcame them.

"Shale, Shale, what can we do?" Seb asked gently, his eyes filling up with stinging painful tears.

"Enough...." Shale replied quietly, "You have done enough for this time, both of you. You are safe now, be happy."

"But, but what about you?" Hannah asked between deep sobs.

"Enough for me as well, Hannah. I feel I have done enough too."

"Shale, for heaven's sake, what can we do to help you?" Seb asked, dreading the forthcoming answer.

"You can take them, take them with you, and release them from their prisons." Shale replied, as he opened his large right hand to reveal the clay people lying in his palm, undamaged,

192

complete and perfectly formed. "They did it. They did all that to save you both from Lemma." He said, his voice becoming soft like a delicate whisper.

"But what can we do? How do we release them?" Seb asked.

"*You will find the way*, I know you will." Shale replied.

"Shale, don't, please don't………we can help you, please, please!" Hannah said as she cried.

"*Until another time*, Hannah, and you too, Seb. Take them, and help them, both of you. And take this too." As Shale said this he opened his left hand, where the rutilant sphere turned slowly above his palm.

"But……but, I don't know what to do, I don't….oh, Shale, why is all this happening?" Seb groaned through his tears.

The reply from Shale was silence. His eyes were closed, and his body was completely still, and his life appeared to have left him. No breath came from his mouth or nose, and he was silent – totally and peacefully silent.

"He's dead, Seb, he's……oh god, he's dead!"

"I know, I know, damn it all I know. Come on, up! We've got to think." As he said this, he took the clay people and the rutilant sphere from Shale's unmoving hands, and stood up.

"But, god, what do we do, what do we do Seb, we can't leave him like this? Do we, oh no, do we have to bury him?"

Seb took Hannah's hand and stepped back from Shale. He put the sphere and the clay people into his bag and closed it tightly over them. Hannah began to cry again, the appearance of death overwhelming her.

"Listen, listen Hannah, we've got to….."

But before he could finish his sentence an astonishing change happened to Shale. Very slowly his body appeared to be sinking into the ground, as grasses and flowers penetrated through him, and surrounded him in a flowery form. Before they could even gasp he was gone, the new grasses and flowers marking out where his body had been lying; and a delicate white butterfly landed upon where his heart had been.

Many minutes passed before either of them could form a clear thought or word. The light in the sylvan scene where they stood had become much brighter; but still they stared at the brilliant grasses and flowers in the exact shape of Shale's fallen body.

"Look, Hannah," Seb began, "look, too much has happened. I don't know what to say. He's gone, gone.........and I don't know where or how; and so has she, somehow, she has gone as well, and it's all to do with the clay people. He said that we have to help them, and we will, we, I don't know how but we will. But I think we should get out of here as quickly as we can. Do you agree?"

"Yes, yes, I suppose I do." Hannah replied quietly, her mind in a whirlpool of thoughts and images and feelings.

"Come on, Hannah, please, be strong, we've got to do something."

"I know, I know, Seb."

"Look, if you've had enough, I understand, I do. We'll get out of here and go home, and that's it, you don't have to do anything else."

"But I do, Seb, I do. He said that we have both got to help them, and, and after what we've just seen I can't just do nothing. He said they had saved us, and I believe him, I really believe him; he was.......he was telling the truth, and he asked us as he........as he went. Do you think the worst is over?"

"I don't know but, but I think it could be. She has gone and can't harm us now; and he has gone and cannot help us now. So it's just us, you and me, and the clay people, just like it was before. Maybe a happy ending is in sight."

"Maybe it is, at least for us; I *do* hope that it is. What an incredible time this is. I don't know why but I feel like laughing."

"So do I, so do I, what a crazy amazing adventure!"

And they laughed from their hearts, as much from relief as from happiness, and their spirits lifted and lightened as they looked at the wonderful scene all around them.

194

"Ok, we've got to get out of here, but which way?" Seb asked as if to himself.

"I don't want to go back *that* way." Hannah replied, pointing back to the way they had come. "And I don't want to see her clothes again, or anything else to do with her."

"I can understand that, and I doubt very much that we would be able to open that door from the inside. So, I think, we'll have to go *that* way, and find the other exit."

"But, but Seb, what if, what if it leads us to *there* again?"

"I was thinking the same, but I think it was her doing, she somehow led us *there*, or to an image of *there*; and she's gone now. I think it is our best bet if we want to get out of here at all."

"Yes, you're right. I'll be so glad to get back into the sunlight and fresh air."

"Or rain and wind!"

"Either will do, I'm not fussy."

"You've changed then."

"Mm, watch it; you know what I mean."

"I do."

As Seb said this, he opened his bag, took out the apple and polished it on his t-shirt. He went over to Shale's flowery form, and placed it where his right hand had been. Hannah took out an orange and did the same, placing it where Shale's left hand had been. They smiled, and turned, and without another word they walked away to the end of the scene, and into the long tunnel beneath the trees.

It became very dark very quickly, and Seb had to get out his torch once again.

"Last time we were here there was a red light from that giant rutilant sphere, or model or whatever it was." he said.

"I know, and I'm glad it's not here now. I don't want any reminders of *her* for a while, a long while."

"Nor do I, come on, this is the room where it was."

The room was empty now and quiet like a forgotten cave, and as Seb shone his torch around they could see the heavy wooden door on the far side. It was not locked or bolted, and he opened it with ease as he turned the thick round handle. After walking in the dark for a few steps they came to the other door, and it was not locked either.

As he turned the little wooden handle, Seb looked at Hannah and said, "No surprises; I just hope that there's no more surprises."

She smiled back at him and nodded her head, holding her breath in readiness.

Seb opened the door and they passed through, and went up to the small thicket screen at the top of the steps. The door closed firmly and finally behind them, with a loud metallic *click*.

"Well, here goes." He said, and pushed the screen up and out. Hot and bright sunlight blinded them for a few seconds; but then they looked around, and up to the distant Tor, and saw on its vivid green summit the old sunbathed tower of Saint Michael, surrounded by people and pets.

# Chapter Sixteen
# The Clay People

By mutual agreement, Seb and Hannah decided not to see each other for a few days. They were tired, confused, relieved and hurt from their recent experiences, and neither of them wanted anything else to happen until they were ready for it. Seb was going to keep the clay people with him, and see if there was anything he could do to bring them back to life. He asked Hannah if she would look after the rutilant sphere, as it now had memories for him that he would rather forget, at least for a day or two. Hannah agreed, and said she would see if the sphere did anything different or new, and that she would let him know if it did.

As the days passed they were not sad or depressed, and they kept in touch frequently by telephone and text; but they were quiet and thoughtful, knowing that sometime soon something would have to be done to try and bring the whole series of happenings to a conclusion or to an end of some kind.

Their families noticed little change in them, and they both had good days out, away from all that had been going on. By coincidence, they were both due to go away at the end of the following week; so they knew that there were only nine days left for everything to come together, before holidays and then the new school term would most certainly get in the way.

Seb tried everything he could think of to help bring the clay people back to life again, but without any visible success. There were no further changes in their appearance of any kind, and it was as if they were complete in themselves – complete but lifeless – and he had the beginnings of a nagging doubt in his mind that they would ever move or talk again. But each time the thought arose he pushed it away, and tried hard to think about something else.

Whenever she could, Hannah examined the little rutilant sphere; but, apart from its movement above her hand it did nothing else unusual. She even tried to heal a small cut on her finger with it, but without success, and the wound had to heal in its own good time. In the back of her mind was a growing certainty that it had something very real to with the clay people, but what it was she could not tell. So every time the feeling arose she tried her best to ignore it, and busied herself by doing and thinking something else.

By night Seb was having wild and realistic dreams, full with images of *there*, the clay people, Shale, tunnels, cliffs, huge trees and birds, the great bear, and always somewhere in the background, Lemma. They were not nightmares, but they were difficult and tense; yet within them all he kept hearing music – beautiful, happy and familiar music.

Hannah had similar dreams, though hers were also about seas and thunder, lakes, incredible clothes, islands, horses, wooden ships, shadows, and again the great bear, with the scent of Lemma somewhere just behind them all. She too kept hearing music in her dreams – beautiful, happy and familiar music.

As time went on, each of them separately began to realise that something had to be done, and soon. The adventure, as they called it, had to have some sort of an ending, or they must put it behind them and get on with their lives. They were agreed on this, and they arranged to meet again on the fourth day after they had left *her* place.

The night before the meeting was full of turmoil and uncertainty for both of them. How can they ever bring the clay people to life? What do they do with the rutilant sphere? How can they repay Shale, and the clay people, for saving them, and for getting them through such danger? Will it all ever end whatever they do, and however hard they try to get on with their lives? What did it all mean? Was it all over? Why? Why them? These and other questions troubled their waking and sleeping hours, and none of the answers they thought of seemed to offer the promise of peace.

✫  ✩  ✩

They met at 8.30am, in the little lay-by at the foot of the Tor which, to their relief, was empty of cars and vans. Already the day was very warm and a high mist floated above the landscape, hiding the tops of the tallest trees and the dew-covered summit of the Tor. They took a wide arc to the north, deliberately avoiding the Shadow Stream and the doorways to and from the place where so much had happened the previous week.

As they ambled along they talked at length about their memories and experiences, and even though there was much that they were concerned about, they found that there was also a lot to be happy about. They laughed at each other's version of the various events, and how they felt about them, and the little things that one or other of them had remembered or forgotten. The subject of what they were going to do next was not mentioned, even though they both knew that it had to be decided upon, and that today was the day for decisions.

"Where are we heading for?" Hannah asked.

"Oh, I'm not sure; maybe around the back of Wick, and up the sheep paths over there." Seb replied, pointing into the distance. But he did know where they were heading for, he had made up his mind early that morning, and he was taking a roundabout route to get there. He had decided that they should go back to the Little River Pond, and to the bank of clay where everything had begun, so long ago, as it now seemed to him. To go back there was the only thing that he was certain about, and he trusted that what was best to do next would become obvious when they arrived there.

As the day became hotter the mist lifted and disappeared, and they took off their light jackets and talked and walked. They cut across the fields away from Gog and Magog, and took the steep sheep-path up to the top of the scarp that looked over

Paddington Farm, with Wells in the distance, and the green back of the Mendip Hills lining the horizon. The view was breathtaking and big, overarched by a cloudless azure sky, alive with birds and insects and the growing heat of the day. As they climbed over the stile which led onto the old track towards Maidencroft Farm, Hannah began to realise where they were approaching.

"Are we going back to that pond, Little River Pond?" She asked.

"Yes." Seb replied with a smile.

"Why, why do you want to go there again?"

"I'm not sure, yet; but that is where it all started, and hopefully it might finish there as well. Have you got a better suggestion?"

"No, no, not at the moment, I'm not really sure about anything either, but we have to do something. I've been thinking about it all and, and I'm not sure how to put it, but it's........I mean, what I really want is to understand all of this, or try to forget it. Some of it is incredible and beautiful, and some of it is not, but either way I feel I've had enough of acting in the dark. I just want to know what's going on, or leave it all alone until I do."

"I feel the same. All these things seem to be happening *to* us, not *by* us. It's as if we don't have any choice about it, and I am tired of that. Whatever we decide, I think even a bad decision is better than no decision at all; otherwise anything could happen, and I'm fed up with being a pawn in someone else's game, especially as I don't know the rules."

"So am I; you've put it very well."

"Thanks, about time I did."

At the sharp bend in the lane they crossed over a stile, and walked the short distance up to the clay bank that overlooked the pond. It was almost empty of water now, save for a small black pool in one corner, and the mud was crazed and cracked from the heat of the previous few days. They sat down, took out some food, and ate in silence as they pondered.

Seb remembered back to the wet Sunday morning of air, mist and songs, when he had first dug up the clay; and the peculiar thought entered his mind that he seemed to be only a little boy back then, but that now, after so many strange and difficult experiences, he felt different. He did not feel like a man, but definitely like a young man – stronger, wiser and more capable. He wished almost that he could turn the clock back and do it all again, knowing what he knew now; but that, for all of us, is hardly possible.

"Well?" Hannah said, interrupting his private memories.

"Well what?" He asked in reply.

"You know; what now?"

"Well, ok, um, do you have any ideas?"

"Sort of, I think, but you go first, you must have thought of something."

"I have, but I don't like it; yet I don't know what else we can do, apart from nothing, and I'm tired of doing that."

"So, please, what is it?" She asked gently.

"Put them back, Hannah. Put them back where they came from." Seb replied with a heavy heart.

"What do you mean?"

"Here, back here, back into the clay where I found them."

"You mean, do you mean, bury them?"

"Yes, I do, I can't think of anything else. I can't bring them back to life, and maybe nothing can. Maybe it's all over, maybe there is nothing more, for all I know this could be it. Maybe what we've done is enough, and we're not needed any more; we just got caught up in something we don't understand, did our bit, and now it's time to walk away and leave the stage. Maybe it's for someone else to do whatever, if anything, needs doing; because I feel I have played my part, and maybe that's all I needed to do."

"That's an awful lot of maybes, Seb."

"I know, I know, but what about you? What do you think we should do? If you don't want to put them back, do you want them? Do you want to look after them until whatever else may happen?"

"No, no I don't. I have had the same thoughts but I would never have suggested it, knowing how you feel about them. I know what Shale said, I know what he wanted, but there's too much we *don't* know. He said that we would find a way, but I'm doubting that very much. We may never know what or who they really are, or what this little sphere is, and like you, I don't want any more things happening *to* us, unless we have chosen them, and know what we're doing."

"And if we put them back maybe they will find their own way, or find somebody else to help them, if they need any help. I don't want to wait however many years it might take for the truth of all this to become clear, and maybe it never will. I know, too many maybes again, but that's all we've got to go on, maybes. If there is any thing real in them, and I am sure that there is, then they'll find their own way no matter what; and if they need us, they know where we are. But for now, I think, enough is enough."

"It's hard to say, Seb, but I do agree with you. I can't think of anything else we can do for them, and we can't just wait forever. So, what do we do?"

"I feel sick; sick that I'm even thinking of doing this. It busts me up, and it's awful! After all that's happened that it comes to this, and I am sorry. Sorry to you, and sorry to them, and sorry to Shale that I'm so pathetically ignorant."

"So am I. I don't know what else to say, but I think we have done all we can, and we can't go on like this any more."

"I know, I know, heavens, what a horrible sad moment this is."

As Seb said this, he opened his shoulder bag and carefully lifted out the clay people. They both looked at the lovely figures and at their handsome smiling faces, and their beautiful delicate hair and hands and clothing; and it was indeed an extremely sad moment.

Knowing that it would probably come to this, Seb had brought with him a trowel, a chisel, and a hammer; and he took them out of his bag and laid them on the ground next to the clay people. Hannah took the little rutilant sphere out of her bag, and carefully placed it next to them as well. Then they sat there in silence for many painful minutes.

"But I'm *not* just going to bury them." Seb said, trying to lift their spirits a little. "I'm not going to dig a hole and dump them in it, and cover them up with more clay. I'm going to make them a cave, and you can help me, please."

"Of course I will, I'll help, that's a lovely idea." Hannah replied, smiling.

Seb got to work immediately, and banged the chisel into the hard dry clay at the exact spot where he had been digging all those months before. Hannah piled up the clay as it broke off from the bank, and they worked together with purpose and in silence. The entrance to the cave was taking the shape of a semi-circle, with a wide flat floor, and a broad arch that narrowed as they dug further into the bank. Both of them perspired as the heat of the work and the day began to affect them; but they seemed determined to complete it as soon as possible, and they encouraged each other quietly with suggestions and thoughts. Before too long they had finished the main part of the digging, and they took turns now at rubbing water into the arch and the floor, trying their very best to make the interior of the cave as smooth and symmetrical as possible. It went back into the bank for the length of Seb's arm, and he strained to make sure that no part of it was left rough or ugly or breakable.

When they could improve it no more, Seb took out a square flat piece of plywood from his bag, and placed it on the floor of the cave. It fitted and sat well, and they were pleased at how strong and cosy and dignified it looked inside. Hannah gathered a few daisies, vetch and cowslips and placed them all around the entrance. Finally, they sat back, and agreed to let the cave dry out before doing any finishing touches, They ate some more of their food, and then sat quietly, listening to the summer sounds and looking frequently at the little clay people.

After some minutes, Seb said, "I really don't want to do this. I hate myself for it, and for being so weak and stupid. Ohh, this is awful. But I can't do anything more for them. Maybe in a few weeks, if I feel better or stronger about it, I'll come back and get them out of there."

"You're not weak or stupid, Seb. It's been dangerous, and you have been strong, and we're not adults. And even if we were, I don't think we could have dealt with all of this any better than we have. I will never forget any of this, *never*; and if you do choose to come back here let me know, and I'll come back with you – but don't make it *too* soon."

"I won't, unless I am totally sure about what needs to be done. Otherwise, I will let it all go and, as you said, never ever forget it. I might even write a book about it one day, but only if I can think of a better ending."

"Do you think this *is* the end, or the final chapter?"

"I suppose I do, and it reads something like – and they all lived totally confused ever after!"

Hannah began to giggle, and replied, "Better confused than bored, and what a time we've had. Thanks, Seb, for letting me be a part of it."

"Do you mean that?"

"Yes, I do, really."

"Thanks, but I don't think I could have come through it all without you, so......thank you Hannah."

"Do you mean that, Seb?" She giggled.

"Yes, I really do. Now, come on, let's finish this off. I'm not going to just pile clay in front of them; behind that fence there are lots of stones, and we can make a wall out of them, and then block off the cave with clay."

After a number of trips backwards and forwards carrying stones of various sizes, they stood still for a few moments, looking at the small cave, and knew that they were very nearly done.

Seb bent down and picked up the clay people, and Hannah picked up the rutilant sphere, which still shone with a brilliant lustre as if unaffected by everything that had been happening. They lay down on their fronts next to the cave, and Seb, very slowly and carefully, placed the clay people half way inside it and among the flowers. Standing upright and looking at each other, they were still smiling and still as utterly charming as ever. When he had finished, Hannah gently placed the reddy-gold sphere in the gap between them and withdrew her arm. The space inside glowed with a deep red warmth.

"Good bye." She said, "Good bye; and as Shale said, *until another time.*"

Seb turned for a second, and pulled out of his pocket a shiny gold-coloured medal, with a red and green striped ribbon attached to it. It was one of his prized possessions, won at school for running, and it had his name inscribed on the back of it. He placed it in the cave in front of the clay people and the sphere, and arranged it as neatly as he could.

"There." He said, "You deserve this more than me, my amazing little champions. Good bye, and thank you, for everything."

Without a pause, they began to build a small dry-stone wall in front of the clay people, and within fifteen minutes it was finished. The only thing still visible behind it was the warm red light of the rutilant sphere, shining through the tiny cracks and gaps in between the well placed stones.

Then came the tricky part, as they replaced the lumps and clods of clay in front of the wall, trying their very best to make it as invisible as possible, as if the bank had never been touched by human hand. Seb finished it off by placing a few twigs and pebbles and grasses on it, and even drew a hoof print with his finger, to make it look as if a cow had walked down to the pond to drink. They stood up and looked at what they had done; and they were pleased and saddened by all of their efforts.

"Well, that's that." Seb said.

"Yes, it is." Hannah agreed, "Come on, let's sit up the top and finish our picnic."

205

She touched him gently on his shoulder, and without another word they moved up to the top of the bank and sat down, and sighed deeply and long from their hearts.

☆　☆　☆

Twenty minutes later, with the heat and light of the afternoon sun still shining upon them, they began to pack up their bits and pieces, and got ready to move on.

"It's going to be strange, very strange, trying to get back to normal life again, whatever *that* is." Seb said.

"Isn't it just," Hannah replied, "and I've only been involved for a short time. But my only regret, if that's what it is, is that I didn't get the chance to see the clay people move, and hear their voices, and talk with them. Apart from that it's been awesome; and, I suppose, all's well that ends well."

"Yes, I suppose so, we're safe and sort of fine; but to me it's a disappointing end, really disappointing."

As Seb finished speaking they became aware of two men climbing over the stile to the right of Little River Pond. It was Steven Ade, and Mr. Baines.

"Here comes trouble, Hannah. Come on, get up, and if I say run, run like hell over towards the Tor, there's lots of people over there."

They stood up and watched as the two tall men walked towards them, fearing that danger was approaching.

"Good morning, Seb, and you, Hannah. What a fine day it is." Ade said, in his patronising whining tone.

"Yes, morning all." Mr. Baines added.

Seb and Hannah greeted them as politely as they could, and hoped that the weather was going to be the only topic of conversation.

"I think you know why we are here, Seb." Ade said, without a glimmer of a smile upon his face.

"No, no I don't. We're just off. We've had our picnic and we've got to get home." Seb answered nervously.

"All in good time." Mr. Baines said, "Give them to us and you can go; and then you can forget *all* about it." His voice was stern and very teacher-like.

"Sir, I don't know what you mean. We've got nothing to give you."

"Ever the fool eh, Seb? You're just the same at school." Mr. Baines added.

"As your master said, give them to us, Seb, and nothing more need be said of all this." Ade ordered, his tone now serious and menacing.

"What do you want? What is *them*? I don't know what you are talking about." Seb replied, starting to get angry.

"Seb, come on, let's go; we don't have to listen to this." Hannah said, as she began to get annoyed with the two bullying men standing in front of them.

"Those clay people, lad, the clay people. Hand them over now!" Mr. Baines demanded.

"She's dead you know, dead! So that is an end to it, and leave us alone." Seb replied.

"Who is dead?"

"Lemma; that girl, or boy, or whatever she is, is dead. Now we've got to go, please."

"She is definitely a girl, son, but maybe you're too young to appreciate that fact; and that is impossible. Now, for the last time, give them to me!"

"No. They've gone, and so has she. It's all over."

"Ha! Right, boy, that's enough!" As Ade said this he lunged at Seb, who turned away quickly and shouted, "Run!"

Hannah turned to run but fell over immediately, as Ade grabbed Seb by his shoulder bag. Seb fell over too as he struggled to hold on to his bag. The two men towered over them, and their faces were all distorted by anger, or desire, or both.

"Run, Hannah, run!" Seb shouted again.

But Hannah did not run. She got up and screamed at the men to leave her friend alone, with a surging courage overcoming her fear. Ade ripped the bag violently from Seb's shoulder, turned it upside down, and shook out all its contents, which bounced and tinkled on the hard ground.

"Where are they, boy?" Ade roared, and went to attack Seb. But then he stopped, and turned to Baines in surprise. "Why?" he asked, "Why the hell do you say that?"

"Say what? Come on, get on with it." Baines replied.

Ade grabbed Seb by his shirt and pulled him up to his feet, and shook him hard, demanding to know where the clay people were. He pulled back his fist to punch Seb in the face, but then stopped again.

"What did you say?" He asked Baines.

"What's up with you, Steve? Give me your bag, Hannah!" Baines said, now getting very angry. As he went to steal Hannah's bag, both he and Ade stopped, and looked at each other, their eyes opening wider and wider.

"What?" Ade said, putting his hands over his ears.

"I, I.....why?" Baines said, and dropped to his knees. Ade did the same, and looked confused, shocked, startled and hypnotized; and they both shook their heads, and went silent.

Seb and Hannah stared at them, not knowing whether to run, or to watch these men who were in total turmoil.

"She's gone!" Ade said, "And she tricked us, fooled us, and made us into her dogs."

"Oh my god! What have we done? Whose voice was that?" Baines said in utter confusion.

"It was in my head! What the hell's happened? Oh no, Seb, I'm sorry, please, I am sorry."

"Get up, Steve, get up! We've got to go. Seb, Hannah, we're sorry, we were, we were.......I don't know what to say. *She* did this to us, and we let her. No. we wanted her to, no.......Come on, I'm going, and I'll never mention this again, *ever*!" Baines said, pulling Ade to his feet.

With one long, sad, pathetic, humble and humiliated look from them both, they turned and walked away as quickly as they could. After a few moments Seb and Hannah looked at each other, and raised their eyebrows in mock surprise.

"Well, that was easy." Seb said.

"Piece of cake!" Hannah replied with a smile.

"What happened there?"

"I don't know; I haven't a clue."

"They seemed to, I'm not sure, it's like they woke up or something, or came out of a dream."

"Or a spell."

"What do you mean a spell?"

"I think Lemma charmed them, as she did to us, and somehow the charm was broken."

"But how? They seemed to be hearing voices."

"They did, but I don't know whose."

"Come on, I need a drink; and then I'll pack my bag again and we can get away from here. I want to go to the top of the Tor on the way home. I need to see some people, *normal* people."

"I know what you mean; all that was really horrible."

They sat down on the top of the clay bank, and drank warm but refreshing water from their bottles. Neither of them knew what to say as they were very shaken by what had just happened. As Hannah was about to get up, she looked down at the dry clay in front of them, and thought she saw tiny sparkles of light. Seb put his things back into his bag.

"Well, *that* really is that!" He said, turning to Hannah.

But Hannah did not reply; she just sat there staring, her head to one side.

"Hannah? Hannah, what's up?"

She remained silent, transfixed by what she was seeing and hearing. Seb looked down the clay bank, and then he too saw the little twinkling lights emerging from the ground, like micro stars bursting out of the clay.

"It's them!" He shouted, and tumbled down to where they had been digging. "It's them, Hannah, come on!"

209

She slid down quickly and stopped next to Seb. The lights seemed to be dancing around and above the clay, and they could hear soft, familiar and happy music.

"Heaven's above, it's them!" He said for the third time, and began scraping away at the ground in front of them. When he came to the small wall of stones, they removed them carefully one by one. As they got to half way down they could see the little rutilant sphere glowing in mid-air, and turning gently on its axis. When the last stones were removed they saw them, the clay people, standing beneath the little sphere hand in hand, smiling and bowing in welcome.

After a few seconds, the clay people walked to the front of the little cave and, still holding hands, they bowed once again, and each held up one hand.

"Hello Seb, and hello Hannah." Serren said, her voice delightfully happy.

"Hello to you both. What a joy it is to see you again." Lynn said, and his voice was as happy and as sincere as Serren's.

Hannah let out a little scream, and then covered her mouth quickly as she stared at the clay people in absolute astonishment.

"You're back! By all that's incredible you're back. Oh, hello. Hello again, I'm, I'm *so* pleased to see you again. Hannah, Hannah this is Serren, and this is Lynn. At last you've met them, the, the clay people."

"Is that what you call us?" Serren said, with a little laugh.

"I suppose that is what we are, for now, and it is a good name." Lynn said, and he laughed as well.

"H, hello, hello, I don't believe this, sorry, I do, I do. Hello Serren, hello Lynn. I am very pleased to meet you after, after......." Hannah finished, not knowing what to say next, and still overcome with surprise.

"I thought you were dead!" Seb blurted out, "I really did, and that's why I put you in there. I, I didn't know what else to do. I just wanted to protect you."

210

"And you did well, Seb, extremely well. We are both very, very grateful to you, and to you Hannah, for all that you have done and suffered on our behalf. Please, both of you, accept our deepest thanks and praise." As Serren said this, she put her tiny hands to her lips, kissed them, and offered them to Seb and Hannah, bowing low and gracefully to the ground. Lynn did the same, and it was all that Hannah and Seb could do to hold back their tears, which were a mixture of pure joy and relief.

"We have remembered nearly everything now, Seb, and soon it will be time for us to talk." Serren said.

"I thought it was all over." He said, "I thought, I thought you had gone forever. Please, please, what are you? Where have you really come from? What has been happening to me, to both of us?"

"It may well be all over, Seb and Hannah. We do not know yet, and it will be for you to decide." Lynn said quietly, "But, for now, you should rest, and save your questions, your very good questions, until another day, when we shall be ready for them and ready to answer them."

"Lynn is right, Seb; rest and refresh yourselves, as we will too. There will be time for this soon, and we owe you more than you can possibly imagine, and for so long. When we are all recovered we will talk, and we will answer."

"When, Serren, when? I feel like I'm about to burst." Seb asked urgently.

"In two days, brave Seb, in two days, if you both will agree to meet with us." Serren replied.

"Meet with you? Aren't you, aren't I……aren't you coming back with me?"

"No, not this time, Seb; will you meet with us?"

"Yes, yes of course I will."

"And you, Hannah, is this what you want?"

"Yes, it is." Hannah replied after a long pause. "I would love to talk with you both, and find out what's been happening."

"That is not easy to understand, Hannah, but in time it will all become clear."

211

"Where will we meet you, and when?" Hannah asked.

"In two days, when the sun is up, come to the door by the stream, and it will be open for you."

"There?" Hannah said, "You mean *her* place?"

"It is not, and never was her place. It is our place, and it is your place if you wish to accept it."

"Accept it?" Seb questioned.

"Yes. Will you still come?" Serren finished.

"I will." He answered.

"And so will I." Hannah agreed.

"What a happy time!" Serren said with a beaming smile, "This is all so very good. We will see you in two days and, until then, be glad and full of cheer."

"But, how will you get there?" Seb asked.

"We will get there, Seb; you made us fine legs, remember?" Lynn said, and they all began to laugh.

"But it would help us if you would bring this with you." Serren said, still laughing and pointing at the rutilant sphere.

"Of course we will; and Hannah will look after it until then, if that's ok with you?" Seb asked.

"Yes, that's fine." Hannah replied.

"It is all fine then, especially our legs." Lynn said, still smiling, "But, if you do change your minds, the door will be open until midday; and we will know that you are not coming if you are not there by then."

"I'll be there!" Seb and Hannah said in unison, which made them all laugh once again.

"Good, good, and so will we." Said Serren, "You are extraordinary, both of you, and we know now why. You have had so many things happening to you, and you have persisted against your fears. So put away those fears for now; what may happen next will be by your own choice, so be happy and of good heart. We honour you."

""And please, Seb," Lynn said, "when we go back into your cave, pile the clay loosely in front of us and move those stones away."

"I will." Seb replied.

"Two days then, by your own choice." Serren said, "And until then goodbye, and stay bright."

"Goodbye." Hannah and Seb said in reply.

Serren and Lynn turned around and walked back to the middle of the cave. Hannah took out the rutilant sphere, and then wrapped it inside her bag. Seb closed up the front of the cave, moved the stones, picked up his bag, and started to walk away.

"Come on, " He said, turning to Hannah, "let's go and sit on top of the Tor."

"Ok," Hannah replied, "I feel like doing some sunbathing."

"So do I, and I want to relax, just relax and float downstream."

"Ha! I know what you mean. What a beautiful day! I feel like dancing and running."

"Go on then, why not?"

And Hannah did dance and run, to the music she still heard in her mind; and Seb smiled and jumped about too, and their dancing was a delight to behold.

# Chapter Seventeen
# Ambrosia and Nectar

After they had sunbathed on the Tor, Seb and Hannah walked home slowly, feeling more relaxed and happy than they had done for many days. Most of their talk was about the clay people, and they were full of questions and observations, thoughts and pleasant memories, and the bright day seemed very good. It was Hannah that first put into words what they had in the backs of their minds.

"Serren said, do you remember, that what will happen next will be by our own choice? I don't know what that means, but, but do you think that there is more to come, and that it's not all over?"

"I remember, but, to be fair, she actually said that what *may* happen next will be by our choice. I think there is a difference between those two little words *will* and *may*."

"Yes, I suppose there is, *Mr. Bright*. Nothing definite then?"

"No, nothing definite; but what I think she meant was that there *is* more to come, and that it is *not* all over, but only if we choose it and want it. In other words, or at least how it appears to me, that it's up to us, up to us whether we want to carry on, with them I suppose, or we stop it all now and walk away, and remember it all for the rest of our lives."

"Mm, I think you're right, Seb. So we know, I suppose, that walking away will or should or may bring an end to it; but we don't know yet what the other option is or involves, and what we are really choosing. Maybe, no definitely, that's what they want to talk to us about. What do you feel about it?"

"I'm not sure. For me it all depends on what that other choice actually is, and what it might mean. I'm really happy that they're alive and safe again after all that.......all that stuff that happened and, and I'm not sure that I really want it to be over. Honestly, there's something about them, and their voices, and the music, and…..so many other little things that I don't want to lose or forget. I feel, I feel……….I'm not even sure how to put it, but I feel they need me, or even us; but for what, I really, really don't know."

"Us?"

"Yes, I think so, *us*. Lynn said it very clearly, something like, it might all be over, *Seb and Hannah*, and it will be for you to decide. That's us, isn't it?"

"It is, yes, I'm sure you're right. And now that I've seen them and heard them, and, sort of felt them, I mean their atmosphere, I do know what you mean. They may need us, I don't know why, and I can't even imagine why, but I think that they do *want* us; want us to do something for them, or with them, or maybe even both."

"Good grief! All this from a plastic bag full of clay; its unbelievable!"

"No, Seb, I think it is very believable. If this was just some sort of magic and stuff *that* would be unbelievable. But there's something real going on here, I can feel it, really, I can feel it right here." She said, touching above her stomach with her right hand.

"Are you sure?"

"Aren't you?"

"Yes, yes I am."

"And so am I. It's as real as anything else we see and do, but we just don't understand it…….yet."

"Wow! What a blast!" Seb said, as he laughed and shook his head.

Later that day they went to their separate homes, having agreed to meet at nine o' clock on Thursday in the lay-by beneath the Tor; and they silently prayed that the weather would be good.

☆ ☆ ☆

The hours that followed seemed to go on and on forever. In their own ways they tried to appear as normal as possible; but inside, as each hour went by, they were feeling a growing excitement.

Seb spent a lot of his time playing music and pretending to read, and sitting in his flower-decked garden. He was deeply convinced that a moment was approaching that could change his entire life, *if*, and it was a big if, he chose it. He was certain that the clay people were more than they appeared to be, very much more, and that he trusted them, and fully believed that they would not do anything to harm him or Hannah. He also became sure in his heart that unless they proposed something that terrified him, he would carry on, and see the adventure through to its end. Yet, hard as he tried, he could not even begin to imagine what the clay people may say or do next; and it felt like a hundred birthdays and Christmas days were being rolled into one, and were only hours away, and he had no idea of the present that was awaiting him.

Hannah busied herself with her sister, and little jobs that her mother was asking her to do. Yet she too, as often as she could, kept finding time and space for herself, either in her room or on frequent dog walks, to ponder upon everything, and especially upon what may happen next. Many times she asked herself if all this was for her. Did she want it, or need it, and would she carry on? The quiet answer was always yes, unless the choice she was offered was too frightening. She kept trying to find a word that best defined her feelings about it all, and returned again and again to real, wonderful, and awesome. She imagined that she would have the same feelings if she came across a unicorn, or an angel, or a band of flying fairies, and she was happy that she felt this way. Though there was an element of fear in her heart, it was the healthy fear of something powerful and good but as yet unknown, and not of something ugly or bad. She felt ready to make her choice, and hoped that Seb now felt the same.

At the appointed time on Thursday morning Hannah's mother dropped her off in the lay-by, where Seb was waiting as patiently as he could. After hellos and goodbyes they were finally left alone, and stood there nervously, hardly looking at each other, and waiting for each other to say something.

"Well, are you ready for this?" Seb asked, as he turned towards her and nodded.

"Are you?"

"No, but yes, yes I am, as ready as I can be; and you?"

"The same, and I'm, heavens Seb, I am *so* excited. I'm so happy to be here. Just think, if my mum hadn't had to go out that day, I wouldn't be here now, and I wouldn't even know what you were doing."

"Another *accident* I suppose."

"Mm, I don't believe in accidents any more, well, not like I did at least. Do you think that they are going to be there?"

"Yes, I'm sure of that, and I wonder what they are thinking now."

"They're probably thinking about what *we* are thinking about, or something else like that."

"Maybe, but I think they know what they are going to do next, unlike us I'm afraid."

"But we do, don't we?"

"And what is that?"

"We're going to go and meet them, aren't we? Or else we should turn away now."

"Do you want to turn away, because you can you know?"

"No, definitely not, not at all."

"And neither do I, so come on then, let's go and do it. I can't wait any longer."

Hannah laughed, and so did Seb as they walked away from the Tor.

The weather could not have been better. It was warm, bright and clear, with little pure white clouds slowly drifting across the pale blue sky. Butterflies and bees and numerous birds and insects were flitting about doing whatever they do on such a very fine day, and the grasses and meadow flowers leaned with the breezes, and joined in with the dance of summer life.

Seb and Hannah crossed the road and made their way down to Little River Pond. They stopped for a few moments to look at where they had made the cave, but there was not a trace of it in the clay bank. It looked as natural as it should, as if nothing but nature had touched or disturbed it. They did not talk very much, and when they did it was usually to ask each other if they were alright, and ok, and other friendly and caring questions like that. Coming down through a broad copse, they crossed a large field of tall grass and climbed over the fence that bordered the paddock. The horses that were there were fresh and lively and trotted about playing games, and enjoying the pleasure of running in the sunshine. When they got to the wooden bridge over the Shadow Stream they turned right, and walked along its bank for about a mile. Seb recognized where they were and stopped.

"Well, it's over there, just on that bend beneath the willows. Are you ok? Are you sure you want to go on?" He said, as if talking to himself as well.

"Yes, and yes, but I think I need a drink first, my body is so full of adrenalin."

"So do I, I feel the same. Have you got the little sphere with you?"

"Yes, it's in here, I wrapped it up in silk."

"Good, that's good." he said, and they both took a long drink of water, trying to look as casual as possible. But inside, they were thrilling with excitement, as Seb's shaking hand revealed.

They could not put off the moment any longer and so, with a smile and a nod to each other, they pushed their way through the last few coppiced alders and jumped down into the shingly bay at the bend in the Shadow Stream. This time the door was obvious, as it was open just a few inches and their arrival had been expected.

"Ok, well, here goes." Seb said with a sigh.

"Seb?" Hannah replied, "Are we going to stick together? I mean, either go on together, or not?"

"I hope so; it's what I would like. But it all depends upon what happens next."

"I know, but it's what I'd like as well, and I think we feel the same about it all."

"Ok then, let's find out."

As he said this he turned and walked up to the earthy door, pushed it gently, and entered, closely followed by Hannah. A few steps brought them to the top of the stairs, and they heard the door close quietly but firmly behind them. The little round mirrors in the walls and ceiling glowed brightly, and they walked down into the arched tunnel and through to what had been the room full of clothes. To their amazement every piece of clothing had gone, and they could see now that the source of the light within it was from stars, hundreds and hundreds of twinkling stars set into a deep cobalt night sky. In the centre of the domed ceiling was a bright silver disc in the shape of a clear full moon, and the whole scene took their breath away, and made them laugh. They did not need to speak as their astonishment was obvious to each other, and, shaking his head, Seb whispered to Hannah to move on from the starlit room.

Passing through another illuminated passage, they came into the open space where Shale and Lemma had fought and fallen. At first the sylvan scene looked just as it had done before, but as their eyes adjusted to the light in the place they could see that the lawns and grasses were full of the most beautifully coloured flowers, many many thousands of them stretching away into the distance. Birds and butterflies flew all around, and the silent pool was dappling and rippling from the many risings of fish, and the insects that skimmed its glassy calm surface. Everything here looked so very clear and clean, and the colours were so vivid and vibrant that they seemed to be alive, and attracted the eye to them by their natural radiance. Hannah and Seb were speechless, overcome by the mood of the place, a mood of light and loveliness and life.

"Look!" Hannah said eventually, "Look, there's a table over there by the trees, with four chairs around it. Come on Seb, it's for all of us."

And what a table it was. As they approached it they saw that it was made from some kind of light golden wood, but it seemed to be of a growing wood, still alive, with little leaves and blossoms on its twisting legs and table top edges. On its round flat surface there were foods and fruits and drinks of such kinds that they had never seen before; and, at its centre, under a small canopy of flowers, there stood the clay people and they were smiling with their right arms raised, in a friendly gesture of welcome.

"Hello Serren, hello Lynn, it's *so* good to see you again." Seb said, his face full of smiles and happiness.

Their reply was one of silence, as they stood there still, motionless, with their little arms raised in the air.

"Hello, are you ok? What is the matter?" He said, his voice tinted now with concern.

"Seb, what's wrong with them? What's happening?" Hannah asked, and this was not even the last thing she had imagined might happen.

"I, I don't know, I don't know. Serren? Lynn? Please, what's......." As he finished, Seb picked up the clay people and looked at them, and felt them. They were cold.

"Oh no!" He said in horror, "No, not her again, please!"

"Who, Seb, who?"

"*Lemma*! Lemma, she must have done this, or one of her blasted shadows!"

"You mean, no, no, are they dead?"

"I don't know, damn, and I don't know what to do now. But I think that they have gone."

"I would not go without saying goodbye to both of you, Seb and Hannah." A gentle female voice said from behind them.

They span around and nearly fell over with shock, as they saw standing tall and upright in front of them a most incredibly

220

beautiful female, and next to her, a male of the same height whose handsome features and form almost overwhelmed them.

"Who, wh, who are you?"

"I am Serren, and this is Lynn, the clay people as you called us."

Hannah gasped and held her head, her eyes as wide as they could be. Not only was their beauty quite staggering, but their clothing was equally fabulous, making them appear so attractive as to be the most lovely people that Seb and Hannah had ever seen, or had even imagined to be possible.

"Hello Seb, and welcome Hannah, this is for us a great joy." Lynn said, and both he and Serren bowed low and to the ground, their arms stretched out straight behind them, in a gesture overflowing with grace.

"But, but, is it really you?" Seb asked, looking at them and at the little clay figures in his hands.

"It is, Seb, it is; believe me it is really us." Serren replied.

"Yes, this is how we are." Lynn added, "What you have in your hands is how we appeared to be, and for that we will always be grateful to you both."

"Come please, Seb and Hannah, come and sit down with us, and we will eat and drink and talk. It has been so very long." Serren invited, and led the speechless friends to the table.

Lynn poured them each a golden drink from a jug which seemed also to be made from a living wood, and offered up a heartfelt toast.

"This is to you, both of you; with our deepest, deepest thanks for all that you have done for us." He said as he stood up.

"Yes, yes, we honour you both; you have achieved so much more than you know." Serren added, and she too stood up, and lifted her cup in a toast to Seb and Hannah, who just sat there in silence hardly able to breathe or move.

The taste of the drink was indescribable, unlike anything they had ever tasted before; but they could tell that it was natural and pure, and full of the flavours of fruit and life. The food was delicious as well, with breads and cakes and fruits, the likes of which they had never seen before. It was a table replete with natural delights, and as they ate and drank they felt the energy of it infusing into their bodies.

"Please, Serren, *who* are you?" Seb asked his first burning question.

"Well, we have told you our names, and that is who we are." She replied.

"I think he means, and I don't want to sound rude or anything like that, but I think he means *what* are you? I mean, what are you both, and where do you come from? You are obviously not made out of clay. Please, I'm sorry, but I don't know how else to put it." Hannah asked as politely as she could.

"I understand and please, do not be nervous, either of you. You may ask us these things and we will answer you, as well as we possibly can at this moment." Serren replied with a beaming and contagious smile.

"Yes, we will." Lynn agreed, "But you do not have a word here for what we really are; and the word we use you would not understand, at least for the present time."

"But there must be something, some word or other that could tell us about what you are." Seb said, struggling hard with his thoughts.

"I have considered this carefully." Serren replied, "And it is difficult; but in this place there are many words in many lands, and over many long years which point at what we are, but none of them defines us or will give you the full truth."

"But, please, try, we need to know, don't we Hannah?" Seb asked, and Hannah nodded in agreement.

"Then I will use words that you know; but you should be very careful of everything you have heard concerning them, little of which is very accurate or true."

"We'll do our best." Hannah said for them both.

"In that case then, we are, both of us, Rulers, and what you may know as Elves; or put another way, we are Ruling Elves." Serren said, as both she and Lynn bowed their heads.

"What! Elves?" Seb blurted out, "Elves! You mean like in the Lord of the Rings?"

"Seb!" Hannah said, grabbing him by his arm.

"Sorry." He said in embarrassment.

"Do not be sorry, Seb." Serren replied, "We know of that fine story, and of the type of elves it describes. We know many that are like them."

"You mean, sorry but, you mean you *know* elves like that?" Hannah asked.

"We do. That tale has much of truth in it."

"What do you mean? It's just a story, someone just imagined it all."

"*Just* imagined, Hannah? That hardly does it justice. There is nothing that can be imagined which does not have *any* reality. What imagination sees must already be there in *some* form, and time and place."

"What?" Hannah said, the implications of Serren's words erupting into her mind. "You mean that, that, some of that is true? About elves and orcs, and rings and dark lords?"

"Yes, some of it *is* true, or to be more accurate, partially true. We have seen it, and know of these types of characters and peoples and their rings."

"But, how? I mean where? Hang on, please, Serren, are you saying that anything people imagine is actually real, somewhere, sometime or some place?"

"And in *some way*, Hannah. Yes, that is indeed what I am saying."

"Good grief!" Seb exclaimed, "Who would believe it!"

"Very few, Seb, very few, if any at all at the present time." Lynn said.

"But, but, what about those other things, I mean all those other stories like Harry Potter, and Narnia, and the Northern Lights, and, heavens, all those others – you mean that they are true in some form, or happening somewhere in some way?" Hannah asked, bursting with too many thoughts simultaneously.

"Yes, Hannah, that is what I mean; as I have seen them as they are in reality, and know of them, though not as they are described in those tales. But yes, they are happening or have happened in some form, somewhere, and this is *some* of what people have seen in, what you call, their imagination."

"Are they *there*? I mean, are they there where you come from?"

"Very many of them are but not, as I said, in the same manner as they appear in those stories, and not in the same place at one time."

""So, please, where is it? Where do you both come from?" Seb asked, trying his best to understand what was being said.

"Again, Seb, there is no word here to name it; but we will tell what *we* know it as when we have finished our time in this place."

"*She* called it *there*, but she also said that it was *here*, and that they are the same."

"That is only partly true. *There* is *here*, but they are similar and not the same."

"But how can that be? How can there be two different places in the same place? I don't understand, and I'm sorry."

"Do not apologise, Seb. To most people here what I am saying would seem ludicrous and impossible; but that is simply because they have not thought about it, or considered it, with the depth it really requires. *Here* is made of matter, or the stuff everything here is made from; *there* is made of matter as well, but it is denser and faster and holds its form for longer than that which is found *here*, and this is why it is rarely visible in this place. *Here*, the time is always seen as the present; but *there* the parts of time are *all* alive – the past, the present and the future. This is why, young Seb, there is here and here is there, because of matter and form, speed and motion, and because of time."

"I sort of understand, but I'm not sure I do really. It's.....it's vast."

"I'm not sure that I do either, but it sounds, it sounds sort of lovely and real." Hannah joined in.

"It is." Lynn replied.

"But, but it must be very small, *there* I mean, if it is here as well." Hannah asked, as she stumbled to find the right questions.

"Do we look small? We appeared so in our clay bodies, and even then they were deceptive. No, Hannah, *there* is not small, not when compared to here. Do you have the little sphere with you?"

"Yes, it's in my bag." As Hannah said this, she pulled out of her bag a piece of brilliant red silk, in which the rutilant sphere was wrapped. Taking it from the silk she held it out to Lynn.

"Does this sphere appear large to you, Hannah, or to you, Seb, when compared to the size of this world?" Lynn asked.

"No." They replied at the same time.

"But the size of *this* world is like that of the sphere, when compared to the place you call *there*." Lynn finished, and smiled. Serren smiled too; and Seb and Hannah began to laugh, so staggered were they by the wonder of it all.

"But *there* is like here, isn't it? We've seen it, or we've seen an image of it, as Shale told us before he....before." Seb asked, still smiling, and deeply enjoying the moment.

"It would be more true to say that here is similar to parts of there; and the man you call Shale said well, and did well. What you both saw and felt was an image, void of life, except for the sea." Serren said, as she looked at rutilant sphere.

"But, but it wasn't void of life, was it Seb?" Hannah asked.

"Well, I'm not sure, I don't remember seeing any..........yes, yes I do! The bear, the great bear singing to the moon!" Seb answered.

"It was alive! I know it was, we heard it and saw it move, and, and I think it saw us." Hannah said excitedly.

Serren closed her eyes, and did not say anything in response to what Hannah and Seb had just said. Lynn became quiet as well, and looked at his hands as if deep in thought.

225

"Have I, have I said or done anything wrong?" Hannah asked, unsure of the reason for the silence, or of what kind of silence it was. Seb touched her arm in a way that asked her to be patient and quiet. The living silence continued for many long moments, until Serren opened her azure eyes and smiled.

"That is wonderful." She said, "Then you were indeed there; not completely or fully, but you were there. I am so very pleased to hear that."

"Yes, that is very good." Lynn agreed, "It confirms what we already believed, but needed to be totally certain about."

"Wh, what do you mean? What did you believe?" Seb asked, his question, like an arrow, speeding towards the bull's-eye.

"It confirms that you have been there before." Serren answered, "Before you found us buried in the clay. We knew this to be true of both of you, and what you have just told us seals the circle. This is *such* a happy moment." As she finished, Serren stood up and put her hands to her beautiful face and laughed; and its sound was as lovely as her form as it flowed through the space of that place, and thrilled everything with its deep inner joy.

Lynn stood up, and bowed his head to Hannah and Seb, and said, "Yes, you have indeed been there before, both of you and together; and it has all been worthwhile because of the end. This is a wonderful time."

"How? I mean, when? I don't remember ever going to that place before, I really don't." Seb said, becoming even more confused.

"And neither do I. We've only known each other for a couple of years, and not very well at that, at least not until a few weeks ago." Hannah agreed.

"Do you really not remember, either of you?" Serren asked, her voice at once gentle and firm.

Seb and Hannah looked at each other, unsure of what to say or do next. Serren sat down on the grass next to them and crossed her legs, and looked up to them, as if searching into their very souls.

"Have you not had common dreams, which have come and gone many times throughout each of your lives? Recurring dreams, as you may know them."

Again, Seb and Hannah were speechless, as each of them searched deep within their memories.

"Yes, yes I have." Seb answered eventually.

"And what is that dream, Seb? What is it that you see and feel?"

"Well, it's, it's difficult to describe, and I have never talked about it before, but it's something like – I find myself walking up a green grassy bank, and the sun is shining and it's warm; and I come to a flat open space, and there is a building there, a huge old ruined building, with large blocks of stone all around it. But I can still see the broken arched windows and doorways. And I feel, I feel…..safe, absolutely safe, and relieved because I am back there, and happy, and it feels more like home, or sort of home, than anything I have ever known, even my own home over there. It, it makes me feel that I am exactly where I should be, and that I want to stay there forever."

"We know that place, Seb, and so do you; it is a place very close to your heart, as it is close to ours as well." Lynn said, his tone both understanding and strong. "That is not what you call a dream, it is a memory."

"And what of you, Hannah, is there a dream that has run through your life?" Serren asked, as gently and kindly as she could.

Hannah could not stop the tears that were welling up inside her eyes, and she touched her mouth, and remembered.

"Yes, there is, and it's………I've never told anyone about it, but, but it is always so beautiful. I am sitting on a hillside and it's summer, and warm, and someone is sitting next to me. I don't know who it is, but it…….it just feels right that that someone is there. I am looking down onto a wide open plain, which stretches down to the sea. There are mountains in the distance, and a great rocky island far out to sea. And there are horses, hundreds or thousands of horses running free across the

227

plain, and I am laughing, and happier........happier, I think, than I have ever been, and.....and just like Seb said, it feels like I am exactly where I should be, and want to be, and I just want to stay there forever. There is more but....." As she finished, Hannah bowed her head and cried. Once again Seb touched her arm, and Serren stood up and put her hand on Hannah's shoulder.

"Dear Hannah," she said, "we know that place as well, and it is, as you say, so very beautiful. Believe me, that is a memory, of a place you have known and loved; and if I am not wrong, I believe the person sitting next to you there is the young man sitting next to you here."

"Seb?" Hannah said looking up.

"Me?" Seb said looking at Serren.

"Yes Hannah, it is Seb. Does that not feel very true?"

Hannah looked long and hard at Seb, and stared deeply into his young eyes, and said, "Yes, yes it does; I would never have known, but it is."

Seb blushed with embarrassment by what was being said, but he could not deny that everything he was hearing sounded real, more real than he could ever have expected. He looked at Hannah and somehow, somewhere, deep inside his memory, he heard the sound of many horses running totally free and wild.

"Then, then these are memories, not dreams, memories of *there*?" He asked.

"Yes, they are, you have my word Seb that they are." Serren replied.

"So......what does it mean?" Hannah asked, "We've been there before, somehow, and, and at some time. But what does that mean for us now?"

As she said these last few words, Seb stood up and put his hands around his face, and he knew then what the answer would be.

"It means, Hannah, and you, Seb, that the time is right for your return. You may go back there now, if this is what you so choose. The decision, as always, is yours." Serren answered, as she sat down again on the grass. Lynn walked around the table and sat down next to her, and smiled.

Hannah stood up and turned towards Seb with a look of amazement in her eyes. Seb looked back at her, his mouth half open, and tried to slow down his thoughts.

"What's happening? Seb, what's happening? Is this real?" She asked, as a smile beamed across her young face.

Seb took in a deep breath and tightened his lips, and squinted as if in bright sunshine.

"It's real, Hannah, it's real; this is what it has all been about. This is what I've been missing for all of the life I can remember, though I didn't know it or even think about it. I feel, I feel, I feel it's what I want, and what I need. It feels……..right, and I feel……different. I just can't put it better than that."

"You mean, you mean we can go *there*, and to where the horses are?"

"I think we can, if we want to."

"But, but what about *here*?" Hannah asked, turning to Serren and Lynn. "We'll be missed, our parents will worry, they'll go crazy, and school and…..everything!"

Serren stood up and looked long at Hannah, and at Seb.

"The time *there* will take care of that and your worries. You will not be missed, I assure you. *Years there are hours here*, and you are free to return here whenever you choose. That is my deep promise to you both, and I would never wish to distress those closest to you."

"Do you……" Seb stuttered, "Do you…, I mean, please, do you *need* us to go back there?"

"Yes, Seb, we do, but only if you choose to freely." Lynn said, as he stood up and looked at them both.

"But, but why? Why do you need us?" Seb asked.

"We need you both to finish what you started, as only you two can; but I cannot say more than that. If you go back there you may understand, nothing I could say at present would be of any real help, it would only serve to confuse you. The choice is yours, Seb, and yours also, Hannah; do you wish to return there with us?"

"Do you want us to?" Hannah asked, looking now at Serren.

"I do, Hannah, yes." Serren replied.

"Will it be dangerous?"

"It may be; but you are both stronger than you know."

"But, what, I mean, what if we get hurt there, or even die there – what will happen to here?"

"Be at peace about that, you will be safe, it would be very difficult to explain how and why while we are here. Life will run its course whether you are there or you are here, and, as I promised, you are free to return here whenever you choose, and for whatever reasons you may have."

"How? How can we do that?"

"You can, Hannah, you can. The little sphere you hold in your hand is the rightful key to that."

Hannah opened her hand and looked at the rutilant sphere, and wondered at what it all meant.

"Hannah, what do you want to do?" Seb asked, as gently and calmly as he could.

"I want to do whatever you want to do; I don't want to stay or go on alone." She replied.

"Are you sure? I won't make this decision for you, I won't, it would not be fair on either of us." he said, as Serren and Lynn walked away from them.

Seb and Hannah talked for a long while, as they walked to and fro from the lakeside, each of them expressing their hopes and fears, yet both of them knowing in their hearts what they truly wanted to do.

"I know, I know. And I *do* know what I want to do." Hannah said, as they sat down again at the table.

"And that is?"

"You first."

"Typical. No, Hannah, ladies first."

"No, Seb, age before beauty."

"You are a pain, I've always thought so. No, sorry, I didn't mean that, but sometimes you're too clever for me."

"Only sometimes?"

"Ha! Right, on the count of three, then we'll say *I want*, and then either *to go* or *to stay*. Deal?"

"Deal."

"Right, let's do it! One, two, three...."

And they both said, "I want to......" and for a second there was a momentous silence; "*to go!*" they said at exactly the same time, and they laughed, and felt so full of excitement.

"We're coming with you!" Hannah called out to Lynn and Serren.

"Yes, we really are, if that's ok with you?" Seb said as they approached.

"That is more than ok, Seb, that is wonderful. It will be *our* pleasure to take you back with us; and, by our lives, we will look after you." Serren said, and kissed Seb on both cheeks, and then turned to Hannah and did the same. Lynn kissed them both as well, and he laughed, as did Serren and Hannah and Seb.

"But, but when are we going to go?" Seb asked, almost bursting with the thought of it all.

"Are you ready and happy to go now?" Serren replied.

"Now!" Seb and Hannah said at the same time.

"Yes, there is little reason to wait any longer."

"Phew, well, I'm ready." Seb said.

"And I think I am ready too. Will it take long to get there?" Hannah asked.

"No, Hannah, just a few minutes. Remember it is also *here*."

"Though I did not know what you would decide, you will need these for where you are going." Lynn said, and called out a word that neither Hannah nor Seb understood.

From out of the trees walked a pair of beautiful horses, both strong and handsome and friendly. They were very dark blue-brown, with white tails and manes, and they were almost identical except that one had a white star on its forehead, and the other a golden brown one. They walked up to the table and stood still, and gently lifted their heads.

"They are called Ambrosia, and Nectar." Serren said in greeting to them. "Ambrosia, with the gold star, will be with you, Seb; and Nectar, with the white star, will be with you, Hannah. You can trust them always, and they will learn to trust you."

Seb and Hannah could hardly believe what they were seeing, such magnificent animals with such lovely intelligent faces.

"Are they really for us?" Hannah asked.

"They are not *for* you, Hannah, they will be with you, and it is their choice to do this as well." Lynn replied.

"Heavens, they are so beautiful." Seb said, almost lost for words.

"So, Seb and Hannah, are you ready to go with us now?" Serren asked.

"Yes, yes I am." replied Hannah with a laugh.

"Yes, I am too, definitely." Seb answered, "But, please, I've got one more question, and it will be my last, at least for now, honest. You said that you would tell us what you know *there* as, what you call it, when you have finished your time in this place; is that now, I mean, have you finished?"

"Yes, I believe we have, until another time." Serren answered.

"So what do *you* call it, what name do you use for *there*?"

"We call it the *Plane of Mʋrr*,[1] and its symbol is written like this."

Serren drew her finger across the table, and this symbol appeared in white upon its surface:

$\mathcal{CM}$

"Good grief!" Seb exclaimed, "That's what it is! It's the symbol on the card!"

"Yes, Seb, that is what it is." Serren said, touching him on his shoulder.

---

[1] pronounced Murr

"Heavens above, the Plane of Mvrr!" He burst out, with a massive smile and a shake of his head.

But as he was about to leave the table he caught sight of his two little clay people, and his heart missed a couple of beats. He bent down and picked them up and placed them carefully into his bag. They were just too precious to leave behind after all that they had been through together. Hannah saw what Seb had done, and she was glad, and smiled, and she was happy.

Without another word, they all turned to the east, together with the two wonderful horses, and walked down to the end of the silent pool, under the trees that swayed as they passed.

The End of Book One, and the story concerning
*The Clay People*.

To be continued in Book Two.

# Postscript

The conversation between Seb and Hannah, and Serren and Lynn, went on for a great deal longer than is related here. It touched even more upon the types of matter (or the *stuff* that things are made from), and time, motion and relative speed and size. They also discussed the fate of Shale, and of Lemma, and what may have happened to them during the thunder within the earth.

Seb and Hannah also discussed their profound choice at much greater length than is written here; finally deciding that as they were not expected home for another seven hours, which in the other place would be seven years, they would return there with Serren and Lynn, and come back whenever they felt it was too much for either of them. They also decided that they would return *here* during the first hour of their being *there*, in order to be absolutely sure that, and how, they could do it. They would stick together, no matter what, and would not stay or return without each other.